LOSING SHEPHERD

LOSING SHEPHERD

A NOVEL

PAUL HEADRICK

Cover design by Doowah Design.
Photo of Paul Headrick by Jim Friesen.

This book was printed on Ancient Forest Friendly paper.
Printed and bound in Canada by Hignell Book Printing Inc.

Acknowledgments
Many talented people gave me valuable advice as I wrote Losing Shepherd. My thanks to Jerry Cayford, Mark Cochrane, Jim Friesen, Katherine Headrick, David Jones, Shaena Lambert, Mary Novik, Ros Oberlin, George Potvin, and the Sea of Cortez Writing Group. I'm grateful to Karen Haughian of Signature Editions for her incisive editing. Heather Burt read and commented on countless drafts, and I'm deeply indebted to her for her wisdom and continuing support.

We acknowledge the support of the Canada Council for the Arts and the Manitoba Arts Council for our publishing program.

Library and Archives Canada Cataloguing in Publication

Title: Losing Shepherd / Paul Headrick.
Names: Headrick, Paul, 1957- author.
Identifiers: Canadiana (print) 20210327545 |
Canadiana (ebook) 20210327553 |
ISBN 9781773240961 (softcover) |
ISBN 9781773240978 (EPUB)
Classification: LCC PS8615.E245 L68 2021 |
DDC C813/.6—dc23

Signature Editions
P.O. Box 206, RPO Corydon, Winnipeg, Manitoba, R3M 3S7
www.signature-editions.com

For Jerry

I

MARCEL'S WAY

1

"Here's the traitor Gordon Bridge buckling his youngest son into his car seat."

"Here's the hypocrite Gordon Bridge taking his parents to the symphony."

"Here's the bastard Gordon Bridge making love with his wife."

For months this contemptuous inner voice accused me. Over time the volume diminished, then the program grew silent for stretches, but the commentary would reassert itself unpredictably, start me moaning, head in hands. What must other parents have thought, standing beside me while waiting for the end-of-day bell, or Leo and Gavin themselves, looking up from their play?

I'd made a mistake. I reviewed *The Stendhal Effect*, Taylor's new book. Because our relationship itself was famous—the two young novelists, literary stars, friends since childhood—and because I criticized, I got plenty of attention. You remember. The review splashed the *Globe* book section, blasted around the internet, and for months dominated discussion in our nation's snug, sensation-hungry literary world.

I had kept it a secret from him, to surprise him, and he was surprised.

"What were you thinking?"

Indeed. I knew, the moment after he asked the question, or I felt the weight of the knowledge—like the weight of a big meal that still needed digesting. It didn't take long after I'd hung up the phone to know exactly—just an hour or so of moving around my study, looking in on the boys and then going back to the study, picking up the book, putting it down. Finally, I flipped through the pages, reading a bit. It was better than *Heart City*, which was very fine, but still a first novel. Also a step further from *An Earlier Encounter* (and no, I haven't forgotten that *Encounter* won the Giller and made the Booker short list).

I had panned a masterpiece.

Such self-deception. I had manufactured flaws that didn't exist, I'd invented subtle literary, even moral, failings, and I'd been so stupidly enthused by my project that I hadn't acknowledged to myself what I was doing.

I held the book in my hands. Stared at it.

I'd been showing off our friendship. Look, everybody. Observe how I can discern the subtle problems to which others will be blind. Behold, oh behold, the strength of our connection, the power of our love, and our respect for literature: enough strength, power, and respect for one to assimilate from the other such cold, public scrutiny. Readers would know that Taylor expected nothing less from me and that my analysis formed the hard stuff of real friendship.

For several days it satisfied me to be ashamed of my attention-seeking. Then, I dropped a glass. I tripped. I tugged harder than necessary at Leo's jammed jacket zipper and saw fear in him. The realization I'd been trying to refuse emerged through these ugly little signs: the shameful truth so quickly settled on appealed to me because I could face it more easily than another, deeper truth, much more painful. My story that I'd merely been grandstanding amounted to still another self-serving lie.

The Stendhal Effect didn't die, my review didn't kill it, but of course I established a context that influenced other reviewers. Sales stalled. Face it, that result was predictable, and I'd ignored it. I'd tried to damage Taylor. I'd always recognized the competitiveness between us, but what accounted for this urge to wound? For how long had this sickening aggression been building in me?

2

"There's simply no way to avoid it. Look at any story you've enjoyed. You'll see. Stories have conflicts. They must."

Taylor and I sat at the back of our grade nine English class, opposite corners. A guest author, Pamela Henderson, provided a holiday from our painful, laboured study of *Romeo and Juliet* with a pitch for a student short story contest.

"Those conflicts raise questions. That's why a story makes you want to keep reading. You want to answer those questions."

She'd published a collection and a novel, but we'd never heard of her and she didn't impress, at first. Then, unexpectedly, her wheedling tone had dropped down, deepened into authority. She wrapped up her presentation with suggestions—commands.

"Those questions better lead to answers. They just have to, or you haven't got a story at all. It can be a surprise. It can be simple or complicated. But it's *got* to have answers."

I knew the formula already, yet, put so starkly: a revelation. I heard a buzzing in my ears, felt an unsettling energy, a rippling in me. I looked across the room at Taylor. He'd turned away from me to face the window. He was rapping his pen on his notebook.

I couldn't finish my dinner that night. What had happened to my adolescent boy's appetite? I still remember my puzzlement, gravy poured over the second helping of roast and potatoes, as always, but my hunger gone.

I managed one bite, another, and stopped. "I'm sorry, I shouldn't have taken any more. I'm actually not that hungry."

"Gordon?"

"Are you feeling okay?"

"Sorry. Yes. I'm fine."

"You can have it later."

As he took a sip of wine Dad gave me a look of concern. Mum covered my plate in plastic wrap, not looking down at the task, not at me. Gaze nowhere, an evident bit of frustration wrestled with a will to tolerate, and she put the plate in the fridge. I retreated upstairs to my bedroom desk.

MY FIRST ATTEMPT IS A BANK ROBBERY. I CAN RECOVER A LOT but not the impulse behind this initial entry in the juvenilia. You can see the conflict, though. The robber wants the bank's money; the bank doesn't want him to have it. And the questions. Will he get the cash? Will the bank stop him? Well. There's certainly a story here. Blue ballpoint, yellow lined pad—story to write.

The initial pages set out the bank's architecture, the position of the reception desk, style of windows, the robber, his size, posture, clothing. A few hours, much crossing out—I'm pleased with my seriousness and care. I'm pleased with my certain knowledge that Taylor, my best friend now for an entire year, is intent over his own manuscript. My friend, writing.

Compose a sentence. Read it. Look up, out at the backyard: it's not Paris, New York, not even Toronto, just my Vancouver, green lawn, beyond it the community centre and the sprawled playing fields of Douglas Park. Resist self-consciousness, nothing to be embarrassed about—I'm a writer. At last: arrival and entrance. I think about my next word as the wind stirs the dark leaves of the apple tree. Taylor and I are writers.

That literary feeling, entirely justified, most so on the second read-through: recognize my failure, that's okay, don't crumple the paper, please not that cliché. Just fold once and slip into the basket for recycling, a nod of approval for Taylor, undoubtedly rigorous, self-critical, just like me.

I close my bedroom door. No disturbance threatens, and even when Mum and Dad come upstairs after watching *The National*, if they glance my way they'll just walk on, say good night in passing. They'll think I'm doing my homework late. But I want the door closed.

The robber passes the teller a note. There, you see? Begin with the conflict. "I have a gun." The reader can fill in: is the bank sleek and modern, is it old stone dignity? Who cares? Nobody. Not with a loaded gun pointing at the second paragraph.

I know I've made better, keep my head down, a little light-headed, and push on.

Then, mouth dry, cold, I shift in my chair, and the robber waits, nervousness intensifying, second by second. Ass sore, hard chair, never bothered me before. Taylor? Are you suffering this way?

Ignore my discomfort and write on. The teller is moving too slowly. He's pressed a silent alarm button somewhere, must have.

Now it's my skin, it's papery dry, ready to tear, and I take the pages in my hands and stand. I'll read out loud, proclaim to the window view, Douglas Park out there beyond the fence, but my body shakes. I'm weak, spinning and fevered.

ON TIME, DAD, KNOCKED, DRAWN AS HE PASSED BY THE unprecedented closed door.

"Gordon? Are you okay?"

"I'm sick."

Dad brought me aspirin and a glass of water. Mum said, "I should've realized when you wouldn't finish your food. I'm sorry."

"That's okay."

She glanced down, the beginning pages of my story on the desk, then she turned to me, and something lit up for a moment, a shimmer of possibility. But she turned back, put out the light, and left.

I closed my eyes and drifted, an image persisting: Mum's face as she reached for the light switch, serious about something—furrowed brow, drawn-in lips.

I felt fine in the morning, even better than fine, refreshed and cool, a bizarre recovery. At breakfast, when Mum offered that I could stay home from school, I declined. Again with her lips—I hadn't seen her take that expression before, couldn't read it.

"Twelve-hour flu," said Dad.

I felt my discipline, pulling my bike out of the basement and riding down the lane. Staying home to write would've been cheating. On arrival in homeroom I nodded at Taylor and took my seat beside him. He nodded back. We understood, and nothing needed to be said. Carry on as normal, POWs planning a break; don't let on.

That night I finished a draft, and the next night I polished and tinkered, grew bored, a bad sign. A dead story.

Such failure. Who was I, after all? What could I become? An entire future, an identity, first offered and now denied to me. The illness of the night before was nothing to this ... this judgment passed.

The next morning, Taylor came into homeroom a few minutes late, red-eyed, panic-stricken; he too had failed, and he was looking to me for assurance.

I knew right away, just seeing him so obviously confessing his struggle, that I could try again; I wasn't beaten. After he'd slumped into his desk, he glanced over, and I nodded at him. I rested my forearms on my desk and clenched my fists, and he did the same, a two-fisted kid's vow to go on.

The promise fulfilled that night: a woman plans to leave her dull and selfish husband. Will she?

Taylor and I avoided each other, just the homeroom nod in the morning.

She does, she leaves him. It's an adult story. I like it but it's not right in my kid's handwriting.

I asked for a typewriter, but Dad brought home a discarded IBM XT and a printer from his office. "One of us is going to have to figure out how to use these things. Typewriters are doomed."

A few days along, I'd grasped enough word processing to produce a document, and with the adult story finally in my hands, the next step was clear: no cover, no staple, just the loose pages. I walked down the hall to Mum's study, home to her labours as a literary reviewer.

I have buried a memory, probably, of an original transgression. Toddler me trotted into the study and drew a response, sharp and clear—do not interrupt. I can imagine but I can't remember. But I had to have learned, early on, that if I needed her attention, I stopped in the doorway and waited. I wouldn't wait long, but sometimes she'd remain still, hands on the keys, mid-sentence, I presumed, and then she'd type, perhaps as much as a paragraph, before turning to me, confident that what she'd hear would be important.

Mum was a statue. I realized that from my room I'd heard her typing and that she'd stopped as I eased down the hallway.

Only her desk lamp was on. She sat with her hands in her lap, gaze still focused on the paper in the Selectric. Her desk faced the wall to my right, and the lamp cast her shadow large on the wall behind her, to my left. Directly across from me the window looked out on the house next door, and, though night had come, Mum had not drawn the curtains; I could see the darkness and my own reflection.

The light from the lamp on my mother's face, the darkness behind her, her stillness, her gaze resting on the paper in front of her, and her beauty: I hadn't noticed before that my mother was beautiful. Other people must respond to the fall of her thick, dark blonde hair to her shoulders, her composure, the confidence she projected, tall and slim. Her profile was sharp but also graceful, and her skin glowed in the reading light. For the first time I could bring to consciousness a quality of admiration in glances from classmates' parents when I was younger, when she would pick me up after school.

It wasn't disturbing to see her this way, just distancing. I looked down at my story and back at her. Still she hadn't moved.

It *was* important. She would be glad. She'd want to read it.

I could hear her breathing. Her shoulders rose and fell.

She straightened in her seat but didn't turn, and she placed her hands on the keys, and then she removed them.

I understood. Something in the long curve of her back finally told it: Gordon, my son, your story simply isn't good enough.

A woman leaves her husband. It could be fine in all sorts of ways, but I was fourteen years old, and it wouldn't be fine in the way it needed to be. The obvious imitation of my then great love, F. Scott Fitzgerald, would be charming and precocious. Horrible.

Okay. The deadline remained months away. Write another one.

I had no doubt, trying to fall asleep after her silent refusal, that I could create better. Inspiration would visit me and I'd think of a new idea while easing into my dreams. When inspiration didn't come I tossed and turned, I thrashed about and tried to call it the creative process. How unhappy I was. How impatient to be older, smarter, and a real writer.

I know now about the other feelings I couldn't name and acknowledge. My resentment. Hers too. Mine, that the story needed to be good enough to warrant an interruption, a claim on her. Couldn't it just be … I'm your son; be interested? Hers, a bit trickier, not so easy to get at, or not without making her look very bad, because isn't it rather bad, for a mother to resent her son for suggesting, just by the particular sound of his feet on the hall runner, the rustle of a few pages, the obvious writing going on for days and the serious child's engagement, purpose—isn't it very bad to resent him for suggesting that something other than simple, clear honesty could be called for?

Encouragement. What would be so hard about a little encouragement, Mum? Why resent your child's desire?

Sleep came, but only after an effort of will, a turning of my mind and a decision, or recognition: the encouragement I'd need would come from Taylor.

3

Soon, Taylor and I grew less self-conscious with each other and returned to our usual ways. I didn't ask him and he didn't ask me, but we knew. It was good for our writing to become part of normal life. I put off the next step, with the deadline distant still, sensing that some calm should develop before I tried again. I assumed that Taylor, too, had flamed out and then taken time to gather himself, though I never did confirm.

My third effort: a boy in high school yearns to ask a girl out, makes elaborate plans to do so, and finds a way to forgive himself when he chickens out. Fitzgerald is still in there, but now it's right. The story should aspire in just the way its young protagonist does.

Once or twice in my childhood I made a decision that, so many years later, I still applaud myself for. I decided to act as though surface and reality were one, as though the disturbing depths hid nothing of importance, disturbed not at all, didn't exist. Me at dinner: "There's a big short story contest at school. Actually, the whole province. I've written a story for it. Would you like to read it?"

"Love to!" said Dad.

"Certainly," said Mum.

Dad dropped by my room later that night. In the instant before he spoke I looked at him as I had at my mother those nights some weeks before, seeing him for the first time as others would. Of course, I knew that he was bald. I could have told you he had a dark beard that he tugged on when he was tense and that his forehead glowed a bit when he grew cheerful with a couple of glasses of wine, as it glowed right then. He wasn't homely, certainly. Approachable. His shoulders were sloped. If I wanted a character in a story who looked friendly, unintimidating but not insecure, I could describe him.

"What a great story!"

"Thanks, Dad."

"What's first prize?"

"Books, I think."

"Well, make room on your shelves. What a great story! But I bet she'd have said yes if he'd asked."

Which was the point.

For two days Mum made no comment. My determination to ignore the fraught depths didn't reach so far as my launching out with, "Hey Mum, how'd you like my story?"

"I'm going to be working late tomorrow night," Dad said at dinner.

"Wherefore?" said Mum.

"'Wherefore'?" said Dad.

"Yes. Wherefore are you working late?"

"Wherefore."

"It means 'for what reason.'"

"Yes. Yes, of course."

"It occurs famously in *Romeo and Juliet*. 'Wherefore art thou Romeo?' Some people think it means 'where.' It does not."

Dad, glum, shoved a piece of meatloaf with his fork. Then he gave his beard a pull. "Is it also in *Hamlet*? 'I have of late—but wherefore I know not—lost all my mirth.' Or something like that."

"You're exactly right. It's also in *Hamlet*." Mum was maybe not entirely happy with Dad's bright contribution.

"It's just that report I told you about. Deadline's coming up."

"Oh, yes, that report."

And there you have it, Mum's review.

I'd used the word in my story: "wherefore." Very cleverly slipped in. Sophistication.

I reread my romantic tale, back at my bedroom desk. "Wherefore" grabbed the centre of the story, occupied it, and the entire narrative pivoted around it. The story seemed written for the word. It was an excuse for the word.

I reprinted the page, "why" substituted. I began reading yet again, and I saw that while before I'd been anticipating from the beginning, waiting for my self-admiration at "wherefore," now I was attending the unpretentious improvement.

Wise fourteen-year-old, I put off further editing for a week, after which my fresh take found pretension everywhere. With a will I dug in to the revision, cutting and simplifying, till the characters liberated themselves from my need to impress.

The next afternoon, when Taylor and I walked home from school together, we didn't talk. Could it be? No. Too much of a coincidence, to have finished our stories on the same day. Still, silence, till we came to his house. Surprise in his eyes, mine too, I suppose, as we looked at each other.

"Well," I said, brave move to break the ice.

"Yeah," he said.

"Well."

Why couldn't I speak? Why couldn't Taylor?

He was waiting for me. He felt that I should speak without his guidance. What right did he have to assume that authority, so smug, thinking of himself as the mature one? Or was I being unfair? He was only embarrassed. Or we were both deciding, wisely, with so much still ahead of us, that we should move independently? He'd probably submitted his story weeks before. Maybe he was still working on it.

"See you tomorrow."

"See you."

Home, walking quickly, running, into the house and crashing out again, to mail off my edited story now, now, now.

Late in the spring our English teacher announced the contest result and distributed the winning entry.

After school, sitting in Taylor's bedroom, I at his desk and he cross-legged on the floor, released and relaxed by our defeats:

"Here." Taylor holds out his story.

I take his and pass mine to him, without comment.

"This is going to be good," says Taylor. He's holding up my manuscript and he waves it at me. But he's not referring to my story. He's talking about us. Reading each other.

"It is. Nothing but good." I'm facing him, and I swivel to the desk, put his story down so as to begin, but then turn back to him. He's still looking at me, something fiery-intense in him.

"Okay," he says, and he begins to read.

Taylor's was set in a medieval European court. A gripping marvel. The court astronomer believed, like everyone else, that Earth was flat, and into his world came an extraordinary young man of science who knew that it was round. The young man was arrogant, angry, and domineering, while the much older official astronomer was the opposite: patient, understanding, sensitive, enlightened, nobility itself. Slowly he crumbled.

My story was better than the winner. Taylor's was better than mine. We didn't care that we hadn't won because we knew that we'd started. Together, that spring afternoon, with our mutual regard we initiated ourselves.

"How was Taylor's story?" said Mum when I told her about the outcome of the contest, a highly interesting question, as I hadn't mentioned Taylor in connection with it.

"Great. It should've won."

"Hmm," said Mum, which was exactly what I'd been saying to myself while thinking about Taylor's story, and, sure, noticing my jealousy, but also noticing how much stronger my pride in him was.

Years afterward, Taylor and I composed a panel of two at a writers' festival, and I spotted Pamela Henderson in the audience. She must have been in her late fifties when she spoke to our class. Now she was an old woman, grey and reduced. I nudged Taylor, whispered to him and managed to point her out. We both had read her work by then, of course. She wasn't great, but she was good. Craft marked every one of her stories, each a hard-earned victory over a lack of deep talent and so an homage to literature.

At the end of the discussion the first to the mic asked the predictable question about influences, key moments, etc. Not a bad question, really, but usually answered poorly. Taylor, even more eloquent than usual, spoke about Pamela, the gift she had given us, how grateful we both remained, and when he asked if I had anything to add I said that she deserved to be read. I urged that she be read. I considered pointing her out in the audience, but she had her head down and I thought it possible she wept.

Her work was out of print by then, but one month later I read in *Quill and Quire* that the Henderson corpus would be reissued. Such is the power of my words as a celebrity novelist.

THE DAY AFTER TAYLOR READ THE REVIEW AND CALLED ME, I wrote a letter to him. I offered nothing in mitigation, asked only for guidance. I proposed a long letter to *The Globe*, immediately, if he thought best, but I knew that he would see the problem. It would be read as abandonment of judgment on behalf of friendship and would only make things worse. He didn't reply to the letter, nor to the others, mailed roughly once a month for close to a year.

Then Yvonne sent a note. "You have no idea. None. How can you be so stupid? Stop it! Just stop. Stop." She underlined the final "stop." Tore the paper doing so. I might have thought that a bit histrionic, but Yvonne was never one for unnecessary drama.

Ultimate-stakes intensity carved in ball point. I had no idea, and I stopped.

Stupid and contagious, I'd murdered our friendship; I'd celebrated the narrowest conception of myself and killed the best of me, and I didn't know what I'd done to Taylor.

My capacity for guilt and self-punishment did prove to have limits. I couldn't stop being a father, son and husband, day after day. I took Gavin to daycare and saw Leo to school, and I spoke to a gym teacher who needed to be reminded of a shy child's feelings. I walked with the boys up the narrow, leafy streets off Commercial Drive to Trout Lake, on the lookout for adventures. I checked on my parents and saw that they got to their concerts, and I made sure that they didn't drive at night. Again I discovered that Jess could be shocked, angry, and exhaustively critical, but after all couldn't be anything but on my side and couldn't stop needing me.

Father, son, and husband, but not writer: I stopped writing. I didn't *decide* not to write anymore. My writer-self had stepped away, leaving behind something else that I continued to call "me" out of convenience. Sometimes I'd hear a sound, and I'd look up from whatever I was doing, or I'd turn a corner in the house and catch maybe a glimpse of something, novelist Gordon Bridge, spectral, lurking, unreachable.

Royalties would eventually diminish, but no matter. Jessica made partner, and financially we were at ease. But other consequences followed the literary paralysis brought on by my betrayal of Taylor, a man I loved—my friend, fellow initiate, whom I loved. Consequences, ramifications—shudder along with me.

4

I wiped Gavin's nose, then I held the tissue in place and asked him to blow. A glob of yellow snot had bubbled out of one nostril when he exhaled, but had then retreated.

"Try again, Gavin. You'll get it. Blow one more time."

Jessica hadn't yet left for work. She emerged from the kitchen, mug of coffee in her hand, and she looked at me as I crouched over Gavin by the front door, Leo patient beside.

Gavin tried to do as I'd asked, but he produced instead a grand inhalation and then choked and coughed. He looked at me for approval. I looked at Jess to confirm that I wasn't wasting everyone's time, and gently she said "Gordon" to let me know that I was.

Gavin was a chubby kid. But even though I'm notoriously skinny, he took after me with his perpetual colds. I knew this truth because my mother had reminded me of it for years. "You were a snot-nosed kid," she'd say, and also "you're a snot-nosed kid"—the present tense applied when she employed the phrase to finish one of our political arguments.

An important example of such an argument took place after a family dinner, Taylor as guest—important because of what it led to. But let's pause before this conversation, just to glance at the distracting literary issue of remembered dialogue, that preposterous memoirist who recalls all the conversations from years past, word-for-word.

What's worst is not the falsification. No, what's worst is exactly the same as the problem with such dialogue in novels: bad dialogue. We know that the memoir is untrue, because nobody talks that way, and so everything is undermined, authority gone, trust asked for but not earned. But I promise you, the brief exchanges you've read already, the longer ones to come—they're truthful. That's the way they spoke—Jessica, Taylor, Mum, everybody.

And, so, family dinner …

"Your first provincial election and you're throwing your vote away."

"It's not a throwaway, Mum. It's a statement."

"It's a rather unintelligent statement, voting for a party that can't win. If enough of your friends do the same, you young people will elect the Liberals again. You won't get your green agenda from the Liberals."

"Now, dear, Gordon," my father said, nodding at each of us in turn, "this is an important discussion, as it always is, I think it's fair to say, but you must admit it's kind of repetitive, and I'm sure that Young Taylor here would enjoy the last of his broccoli soufflé more—"

"Timbale."

"Pardon?"

"It's not a soufflé. Timbale."

"What about the NDP, Mum? You question the intelligence of my vote, but you apply no intelligence whatsoever to your own choice. What happens when the NDP has to decide between the environment and union jobs? It's a choice they'd have to make, y'know, probably right away, with that coal mine up the coast."

My father, having made his effort and failed as always, reached for the port on the sideboard.

"So now you're sneering at union jobs," said Mum. "You sound like you've been reading *The Economist*. Next you'll be quoting Ayn Rand."

"Oh, sure. There's your intelligent statement. Why don't I respond with Stalin's environmental record? We can trade straw-man arguments all night. What fun."

"A glass of Taylor-Fladgate, young Taylor?" said my father, proceeding without waiting for an answer, but Taylor responded mid-pour anyway.

"Surely, Mister B."

"Do you want two-tier health care? Do you? I simply don't see how you can reconcile yourself … how you can contribute to more of that politics of greed and resentment."

"I consider it by thinking of the long term. I think of the planet," I said.

"You're naïve."

"You're knee-jerk."

"You're a snot-nosed kid."

"Port, dear?"

Taylor and my father had an ironic, almost intimately mocking connection. He was "Young Taylor." My father was "Mr. B." or "*The* Mr. Bridge." They'd agreed awfully quickly to collaborate on these fictionalized selves. Something about it had always pissed me off, but I'd never said or asked anything about it. I guess that I hadn't wanted to concede that it got to me at all.

Taylor and I strolled out after that dinner, and, my irritation with my mother cresting, annoyed by everything, finally I asked. "What's that 'Mr. B' business, anyway? 'Mr. B.' 'Young Taylor.' What is that?"

Taylor, now a very tall young man, looked down at me as we walked the woodchip running trail of Douglas Park. "I've wondered if you'd ever say anything."

"So, what's up? You've always done that, even back when we were kids. '*The* Mr. Bridge.' What is that?"

"It's that thing you've got going on with your mum."

"We've got a thing going on?"

"In some relationships the couple derive energy from their exclusivity. They may not have much to say to each other when alone, but with others it becomes important that only they engage."

"You think of me and my mum as a couple? Fuck, Taylor. You—"

He stopped. "You want to hear this or not? Are you and your mother like that when you're alone? Do you have arguments like that, where nobody else can get a word in?"

I didn't have to answer or note that when alone there was little chance of anyone else getting a word in, as the point was clear. We walked on.

"We're co-operating with you, you and your mum. Your father does that ineffectual thing. I do the stupid bright young man thing."

"And Mum and I have our thing."

"Your dad is being kind to your mum. To both of you, but especially to your mum."

"How so?"

"What can he do? If he insisted on politeness from the two of you, you'd both sulk. You're such terrific sulkers."

"Lovely. We're a couple and we sulk."

"So, he does you the favour of not intruding, except as 'Mr. B.' He doesn't intrude a genuine self. You'd have to consider the claims that such a self makes. Maybe you'd finally notice how rude you are for ignoring him. He's ineffectual 'Mr. B.,' and I'm 'Young Taylor,' a cheerful nonentity. We're such thin creations that we can slip into the same room as you and your mother without bothering you."

"It's all a favour to us," I said, and I admit I made a mental note of that "thin creations" line for possible future use.

"Well, you should allow us a bit of humour about the whole thing. Anyway, that's part of the favour too. If we were silent, that would risk something, wouldn't it? It could be pointed. You might think we minded.

"It takes some confidence, you know, to be generous in that way. For your father to be."

Taylor stopped there, giving me some time to reflect on this news about my dad. I tried not to sulk as we walked on, my head down, watching the wood chips under my feet.

YEARS EARLIER, WHEN I WAS THIRTEEN, MY FATHER ASKED ME to play chess with him in the den one night after dinner. It was an odd request, as it had been some time since we were evenly matched.

Dad opened with Ruy Lopez but screwed up after eight moves. When I castled he got up. He took an old cigar box down from the top of the bookshelves. In it were photos, and he pulled one out.

The man in the old photograph looked at the camera, grim, even fierce—impressive eyebrows and an outsize moustache. He rested one hand on a large globe that stood on the table beside him. I own the world, the gesture tried to say. He was short. Unless it was a strangely tall end table, he was diminutive.

"It's my great uncle Avram. I never met him. That part of the family had moved on to England from Romania, and in another generation, to Canada. But Avram never left England."

"How tall was he?"

"It's hard to be sure. Probably around five-two."

"I've got his chin."

"Yup."

My voice had not begun to change, in contrast with the croaky, erratic comedy my male classmates were producing, Taylor included. I awaited the growth spurt everyone had long promised, extrapolating logically enough from the evidence: father six feet tall, mother five-eight, all the uncles and aunts, all the grandparents, not huge but certainly not short.

My father showed me another photo. Avram's littleness was even clearer, because beside him stood a woman, much taller.

"That's Rachel. Avram's wife."

She had her hair in a bun. It was either grey or blonde, impossible to tell from the black and white photo. Avram looked in his fifties, Rachel far younger, thirties at most, and she smiled vivaciously for the camera.

"Wow," I said.

"The family stunner," said my dad. Fair description. She had high cheekbones and perfect little teeth. The forbidding dark dress buttoned up to her neck and the hair pulled back failed to dull the eroticism of her starry gaze, hand lightly resting on Avram's shoulder.

"You'll probably have this growth spurt everyone talks about," said Dad. "But it might not happen so much. It's possible it won't. I don't want you to worry about it. You'll find, y'know, you'll find ..."

He was uncomfortable but determined to proceed, and for once I was wise and kept my mouth shut.

"You'll see that you have other advantages. You'll get to an age, y'know, when being the smartest man in the room, effortlessly the wittiest, will give you a crucial edge. It did for Avram." He looked at the photo again. "He was a journalist. Famous for his conversation."

I appreciated our talk, but at the time I didn't let on to myself how much. What my father said even remained consciously unimportant to me when the growth spurt indeed proved brief and undramatic, so his helpful caution had its effect without his getting the credit. No, not till that night, circling the park with Taylor, when I recalled that episode with the photos and began revising my tale of my and my parents' life. What emerged in the new version was my father's strength.

"THEN THERE'S YOUR MOTHER AND ME," SAID TAYLOR, breaking the silence as we completed our first lap of the park.

"Yes?"

"Your father saw that she was jealous for you, so he needed to make a connection to protect your friendship with me."

I was going to ask what he meant, but before I could frame the question, I knew: "She's afraid you'll be better than me."

"She is."

"The snot-nosed kid is going to be a literary star, and nobody is going to stop him."

This quality of my nose to which my mother gave so much attention is borne out by independent evidence. The photos of me as toddler show it quite clearly, if one looks carefully. In the posed shots, after a quick wipe, only a trace of shiny dampness remains, reflecting the flash; candid, definitely snot-nosed.

I was indifferent then to any sensations of sticky dripping, as Gavin was later in his turn.

GAVIN WAS INDIFFERENT, IN FACT, AT THE SCENE OF MY TIME wasting, gathered with the boys at the front door, pointlessly trying to get snot out of my youngest before heading off to daycare and then school. Nudged by Jessica's gaze to be on my way.

A surprise on my return. A shock, it's fair to say. Jess still hadn't left for work. She stood at the top of the stairway, tall, blonde, acutely professional in one of her tailored, dark lawyer outfits, looking down at me, the snot-nosed kid-dad, as I came in the front door.

"I made fresh coffee," she said.

She had never done this. Wisely enough, she'd determined early in her career that being a good lawyer would be insufficient. If she were to advance and receive the recognition she deserved, she would need never to mess up, and she didn't, never arrived late or missed a meeting, or dealt with intramural conflict in any way other than professionally. No colleague, client or judge ever had grounds for complaint. Now she would be late for work.

I got my coffee. We sat across from each other in the breakfast nook off the kitchen, the friendliest family space in the house.

"This has to stop."

"Searching for snot?"

She looked at me over the rim of her mug.

"All right, Jessica. How do I stop it?"

"You just do. You're a writer. You start writing. You have to."

I'd thought she hadn't noticed. Why would she? I'd never talked about my works-in-progress before; there was no observable difference now in our lives, nothing to reveal my block. Her exhausting career demanded so much; how would she have the energy to be sensitive, pick up on the signals?

But she had noticed, and she'd given no hint, provided no warning or gradual escalation to this point.

"You have to."

She'd delivered a threat. The force of my gratitude stunned me.

5

I forced out a few sentences then deleted them. I flailed around, with posture, gestures, any stupid trick at all to untie the strands of instinct and habit I imagined knotted up somewhere deep in my medulla. But the old voice returned, sneering: "Here he is, Bridge the reprobate, chasing unearned redemption."

The voice retreated when I just continued to do what I'd been doing. When Mum and Dad didn't need me, the boys were at daycare and school, Jessica was at work, and dinner was prepared, that amounted to little. I listened to the CBC a lot. But, turn on my computer, open a document? Sneer.

I handwrote a new letter to Taylor, rambling and pleading, a departure from all the earlier crafted efforts, embarrassing, and I didn't send it. I'd kept Yvonne's note, her carved warning, and it reminded me. No matter the content, a letter from me would have a dark potential.

Jessica continued to be patient. I came to see that she had indeed provided hints of concern about me, but I'd failed to read them. She'd begin talking about her work or ask the boys about their day at school before we'd even sat down to dinner: no danger of meaningful silences. She mustered enthusiasm when I suggested something social on a weekend, ignoring her law-fatigue. These efforts, considerate gestures, all saying "I know, Gordon," and "I'm not going to rush you."

No rush, but still ... as a favour to me she'd issued an ultimatum, and it gave me permission that I couldn't do without, but it wouldn't be a favour if it weren't real. We both knew it, and nothing more needed saying. A month passed, and I didn't know how long she would wait, another few days, another year.

I CONFESS, MY GRATITUDE FOR THE STEP SHE'D TAKEN stewed into bitterness. Did she have to be so extreme, to bring everything to bear, risk so much? When I think back I can picture Jessica, and I see a shift in her, too, something stiff, movements deliberate, as though she encountered a new resistance in the air as she moved, the field of her resentment for what I had forced her to. Or maybe I'm imagining, an ex-post facto imposition.

I woke early one morning and rose to the quiet house. I'd had a dream whose contents had vanished on waking, dangerous stuff maybe, slipping out of consciousness into some deep psychic chamber where I wouldn't have to face it, vanished, except that I remembered it had been about Barbara Frum.

In my study I woke my laptop and opened a document. "Last night I dreamed of Barbara Frum." Then, "Last night I dreamed of Barbara Frum again." I added the final word only because the sentence needed it to complete the pentameter, but I liked the way it suggested something persistent and significant.

And my accusing voice? Silent! Confused by the poetry, perhaps, but who cared? I was writing—hands fairly tingling on the keyboard.

The dream fragment and the sentence didn't mean much. I had no reason to expect my anima to enter my fantasies in the form of a famous, deceased broadcaster-journalist and not much interest in pursuing the question; I had an interest in writing.

I had nothing else. It had to work. Look, Jessica! I'm writing.

I managed the family breakfast, saw Jessica off, delivered the boys to daycare, school, and then I continued, and by the time I needed to pick up Gavin and Leo, I'd completed my first sonnet.

> Last night I dreamed of Barbara Frum again.
> How did I feel? (It is the key question.
> The emotional content of the dream —
> that's important, not the figuration
> of objects and people: tunnels, mothers.
> Embarrassment, and not the nakedness
> before the crowd, is what really matters.
> And yes it's true of all experience,
> as Barbara Frum clearly knew, and told us.)
> I can't remember what else she asked me,
> what I said, or wore. I was frivolous,
> as it happens, though not wanting to be.
> I felt nervous, a little too left wing
> for her, and unwise, and woke with longing.

When Jessica got home and asked what was for dinner I snapped at her. Her eyes opened wide, and a few minutes later, when I burned my thumb taking the casserole from the oven and shouted "fuck," she returned to the kitchen.

"We've got some cava somewhere, left over from the office party," she said. "I'll dig it out for the celebration." Then she pulled me to her and kissed me, just sweetly on the lips at first, then more slowly, then harder when I responded, and she gently grabbed my crotch and squeezed.

When I had dinner on the table, Jess entered with the cava on ice. She'd changed into her fantastical gold lamé pantsuit, and my heart danced. A sexy smile my way—she knew exactly what she was up to, stirring dull roots with spring rain.

Gold lamé, my God, that so much time can pass and still I can just imagine the kitschy-but-beautiful fabric itself, nothing else at all, see it shimmer, feel it. A wave of desire. Regret.

I WENT TO A PARTY AT A FRIEND OF A FRIEND'S, A BUNCH OF law students and their pals, days only after my first novel publication. Who was that woman? I never saw a goddess go, but lord, her confidence, the way she moved—tall, relaxed, the star of the *passeggiata* just crossing the room. A guy introduced us. "Jessica, this is Gordon. He's a famous novelist. Ha ha ha."

The joke was on him. She asked about *Monica Documented* and I asked about UBC law, and a couple of hours later I found her when she was getting ready to leave. "Yes," she said, "I'd like it if you called. Have you got a pen?"

Would I have had the nerve to ask for her number without the weight of my first publication steadying me?

Matters rushed along, stalled, reversed, sailed ahead, a confusing, jittery business for us both. I couldn't quite believe, though my literary breaking through took on a blonde luminosity that I can still squint and see.

I suggested a drink at Cloud 9, the rotating restaurant on top of The Landmark, a hotel tower on fashionable Robson Street. Hokey tourist destination. Weird idea. "Sure," she said.

Touristy or not, nothing can be said against the view, which went well with a couple of Manhattans. We got silly, laughed together that night more than we had in weeks altogether, something about the drinks and the Rat-Pack vibe. A few rotations onward, not getting tired of the glittery city lights but time for serious law student and novelist to be wrapping things up, I told her.

"I've been nominated for a prize."

"For *Monica Documented*?"

"It's not huge. It's the Ethel Wilson Prize—the BC Book Prize for fiction."

"Congratulations!"

Clink of glasses.

"What great news!"

"It is. Thanks. It's not ... there's not much money involved, not much in sales, either. But yeah, I'm kind of pleased."

"Gordon, this is great."

"Thanks."

"You don't seem quite happy about it."

"The, uh, the prizes. They're given out at a dinner. You know. An awards dinner. This isn't exactly the most exciting evening. But I was wondering if you'd go with me."

"Oh. Well, yes. Of course. Wow! Congratulations!"

Clink of glasses again.

"Wow."

"Yes."

"So."

"Yeah."

That was it for the evening's laughter, not what I'd intended, but clear enough in retrospect. My asking her to join me and her accepting, after an important second to work up to it, demonstrated seriousness: the event promised to be long and unexciting but at the same time important for me, maybe—first published novel, chance at a prize. So, I was asking her to do me a favour by coming along, and I'd invited her to share in something, and she'd agreed. And I hadn't asked Taylor, the friend she'd heard all about, literary comrade, essential to my success.

By the time I arrived to pick her up I was nervous again, not about the awards, but what we were embarking on. Jessica opened her door, stood tall and golden before me ... I burst out laughing.

She smiled and waited, but the laughter surged on—not my usual laugh, conventional and hearty, but something ridiculous, "eesh, eesh, eesh." I came close to controlling myself, looked at her smiling patiently, started in again. "Eesh, eesh." Tears came. It hurt, laughing that hard. Even in the moment, I knew that my hysteria had to do with more than the immediate cause. A deep old well of high-pressure anxiety, now tapped, now gushing.

When I'd finally exhausted myself into sobriety, Jessica brought me a glass of water. I drank it sitting on her couch, while she stood above me, still indulgent, but we both knew there'd have to be an explanation.

"You look incredible. You're fabulous. I wouldn't have thought a woman remained in the world who could pull off a gold lamé pantsuit. Certainly there isn't another who would stand there in her golden gorgeousness with a kind smile on her face waiting for her idiot date to stop spewing."

"So, the humour?"

"That you're going out with me."

She grabbed me by the lapels, yarded me off the couch and pulled my face to hers. "There's nothing funny in that at all, buster." Then she shoved me away, and while she called a cab I had a moment to appreciate her diction, to celebrate being called "buster."

I won the Ethel Wilson, and I wasn't stupid or arrogant enough not to be grateful and not to know that I was lucky, but still—an anti-climax. Afterward, a toast: here's to you, Avram, honoured great-great uncle.

6

I listened, wanting to be optimistic, but afraid. Days passed, and still, nothing. I even offered, speaking out loud: "Here he is writing sonnets, Gordon Bridge ... the ..."

No whispered insult completed the sentence. The vice began to loosen—exquisite relief, but it worried me. Why, now, should I be freed?

Contemplating, poetic, I'd gaze out the window of my upstairs study, and so I witnessed a woman move into the Victorian wood-frame directly across from us on Kitchener Street. Our new neighbour wore a skirt and heels, even when she took her reluctant old French bulldog for his walk. Together, every afternoon that spring, they made their way with care down the broad porch steps and proceeded in the shade of a grand maple to the end of their walkway. There, always, the dog stopped.

"*Viens*, Marcel," the woman said, accent Parisian. Marcel *ne venait jamais*, at least not without a lot of coaxing. She pleaded with him, bending down to convey her Gallic concern. "*Viens*, Marcel. *Viens*." Marcel looked up in jowly perplexity.

"And?" said Jessica when I described the scene to her.

"And?" I replied.

She put her hands on her hips.

"Okay, you're right. I think of it as a metaphor. I'm asking the damn thing to come along, and I'm a bit impatient, but I'm worried that it's old, and the effort is too great, and although a walk is good for it, maybe I should just let it sleep."

"'The damn thing' being the sonnet, an old kind of poem that needs exercise to maintain its quality of life."

"Yes. Very well put," I said.

"Is nobody else writing sonnets?"

"I don't know. I suppose. I'm not on top of that world so much."

"You're single-handedly keeping the sonnet alive." She laughed, but there wasn't much mirth in it.

"I'm not entirely serious, Jess."

"Well, what do I know about it, anyway?"

So, it was grandiose, thinking, even half-seriously, that I was the one to take the old form for its constitutional. And maybe Jessica's humourless laugh signalled that my engagement with the project hadn't entirely satisfied her injunction: "you have to." Who needs an accusing inner voice with that kind of support?

English is naturally iambic, but my lines refused to do what should have come naturally. I heaved at phrases that wanted to jump around from spondees to trochees to anapests, anything but five lousy unstressed, stressed feet. I sweated. Grumbled. I hadn't expected an outpouring of quatrains ad couplets, but neither this … incompetence. Would it have been a relief to have been silenced by my old accusing enemy? No, of course not. Surely not.

I started off a new effort, "She says I love *Ideas* more than her." Hacked away, looked out the window, turned to "Rescue" and read a few lines. Hacked some more. Listened. Appreciated the silence. Deep breath.

Then, suffering with another uncooperative line, I understood. Humbling myself while trying to make that metre thing work, I was atoning. I was penitential. That's why I wasn't being accused anymore.

I laughed out loud. Laughter—so complicated, sometimes. Thinking about what I was doing. Making connections. Recalling an old joke, all it contained and portended, so intricately tied up with Mum and Dad and, yes, the birth of my friendship with Taylor.

7

"What should we do for spring break?" said Dad.

I didn't know. I was eight years old, hadn't much sense of what we'd done before or even what spring break was.

"Let's go to Disneyland," said Mum.

Dad set his knife and fork down, placed his hands on the edge of the table and pushed himself back in his chair as if to rise, but he remained seated.

"You object to Disneyland, Michael?" said Mum.

"No! It's a great idea. Don't you think so, Gordon?"

I looked at Mum and then Dad. Was Mum kidding?

"Gordon, wouldn't you like to go to Disneyland?" said Mum.

"Yes. That'd be great."

ON THE FIRST DAY'S DRIVE SOUTH WE STOPPED AT A MINING museum. After the tour, we wandered in the gift shop.

"You can get a souvenir if you like," said Dad.

"Just one," said Mum.

This was the familiar structure, Dad with the offer, Mum with the restriction, and it settled me a bit, after the disruption of Mum's startling proposal of the holiday.

I chose a pennant. It seemed sporty. Celebratory.

That night, installed in our room in a highway-side motel, after a pizza dinner, Dad asked if I'd like to learn to play chess. He'd brought his board along.

He explained the game, and we played. He reminded me about how different pieces moved, and it was difficult, but I enjoyed the challenge.

Would I win? Up to that point when we'd played cards or board games I won my share. I even had my triumphs at checkers. When very young I fell for it, of course, but we'd kept pretending, as I grew, that I didn't know that he let me win some of the time. Maybe I'd beat him at chess right off, and it would be great, showing how smart I was.

He mated quickly. Deep breath. It's okay. Next time.

"Want to go for a swim?" said Mum after we put the game away.

"What? It's freezing out."

"The pool's heated," said Dad. "You change here, put your robe on and run down to the pool, leap in, and you're good."

"Will you come with me?"

"Nah, motel pools are for kids."

I floated around. I swam a few lengths, practising my crawl. I stood in the shallow end, only my head above the warm water. Chlorine mist rose off the pool and evaporated in the chill sky. It was really something, having the entire pool to myself. I turned and looked up at our room, the silhouettes of Mum and Dad walking about.

I moved my arms back and forth in the water, playing with the resistance, and I knew, at once, a fact I'd had no inkling of till then: my parents talked about me. They had serious conversations about me. They'd discussed the trip. Why don't we stop at this museum? Would you like to buy a souvenir? Just one. Would you like to play chess? Would you like to go for a swim? All had been considered and planned. Mum proposed Disneyland. Dad shoved his chair back. He'd been taken by surprise, and then everything had been worked out.

It made me feel good that they were doing it and even better that I understood.

Mid-afternoon the next day we stopped in a beach town and strolled the pier, ate fish and chips, and then to the gift shop, where I bought another pennant. Then another few hours on the road, the next motel, dinner. And the game.

So much more was at stake. This wasn't Crazy Eights. Not Clue. I'd never been nervous before, playing a game. My hand shook as I reached for a pawn to make my first move. But Dad would know, and he'd let me.

He explained the knight again. He let me take a move back. And another. He took a pawn. He took another pawn. One of my bishops. I was trying not to cry.

"Checkmate," said Dad.

"Why don't you go for another swim, dear?" said Mum, looking up from her reading.

"I'll put the game away," said Dad.

I turned my back to them as I dug my suit out of my bag and quickly changed.

In the moonlight again, the warm water, cool air, the drone of cars passing on the highway. I held my breath underwater, squatting in the shallow end, staring at one of the below-surface lights that illuminated the blue pool. I was trying to prove something. That was stupid. I leaped up and down, smashed my hands on the water. If I could go back in time I'd congratulate little Gordon on finding these ways to release his pain and anger. Mum's proposal of the holiday, that was an innovation, sure, but this? From Dad? I'd thought we had an agreement, a private partnership in joy and relaxation to offset all that seriousness in our world.

Night three. Now I'd win. And on into the game, no pieces taken yet, Dad moved a pawn and exposed his knight to my queen.

He'd done it deliberately and there would be more blunders leading to my victory, and I didn't care that I knew, grinned up at him and then reached for my queen, almost touched it.

"Check," he said.

"What?"

"Look."

By moving his pawn he'd opened up the diagonal from his bishop to my king. I never got the chance to take the knight, because he mated three moves later.

I held it till I got to the pool, and thrashing back and forth I could tell myself I wasn't crying because the water took my tears. I stayed out a long time. He'd be sorry. He'd wonder why I hadn't come back. But nobody came out to see if I'd drowned, and I knew it was another losing game I was playing.

I'd planned one of my sulks on my return, but Dad wouldn't let me. "Hey, Gordon, let me show you something." He hadn't put away the board.

I flopped down, passive-aggressive limpness. He'd moved the pieces back into the position they'd been in before he tricked me.

"It's called 'discovered check,'" he said. He explained it, showed me a few other examples, and then moved on to pins and forks.

"Discovered check is my favourite. It's cruel, isn't it? Your opponent thinks something harmless is happening, and then, wham!"

The next day, I remained silent during the morning drive, and also through our tour of a small-town historical museum. "I don't want anything," I said at the gift shop.

I planned to turn down the offer of the chess game, but I didn't. It would have showed too obviously that I cared. I sulked, though, and I lost again. "You're getting better," said Dad. "Chess takes a long time." He explained some of the principles of position. I told myself I wouldn't pay attention, but I did.

In the pool again, I imagined my losses stretching into the future. I'd show him. I'd get better and one day I'd beat him. I'd say, "Why don't you go for a swim, Dad?" That'd be clever. He'd remember and he'd be sorry that he'd been so mean. But I eased around the pool, no energy for thrashing, no interest in holding my breath, and I peered down that chess-game timeline at one defeat after another, seeing myself grow. My urge for vengeance ebbed. For the first time an adult version of me came into view.

I looked up again, and again the silhouettes, and I knew this too, the business of my losing at chess, was being discussed. I wept once more. Why was I crying this time? I didn't know. I wanted to rush back to them immediately, but it was better to wait, just a few more minutes, and then, not to burst in upon them, but just be normal, like nothing had happened.

"Did you have a good swim?"

"Lovely." That was a mature thing to say. I felt it, that step forward. Was there a wrenching, a feeling of loss at the same time? I guess there must have been.

I think my parents located a cheerful irony in the whole operation as we continued south. I picked up on their happiness. I enjoyed going for ice, trying to figure out the noisy air conditioners, and running back and forth on the rickety walkways that clung to the motel sides. Disneyland knocked me out, at first, but I resisted, and finally it was only another amusement park, grander than Vancouver's Playland, certainly, far bigger, fireworks, everything. But I felt defensive on behalf of my home and of my new maturity, so I refused to be impressed.

The spring break road trip became tradition, and I decorated my bedroom with the cheap heraldry of tourist traps from Seattle to San Diego to Palm Springs. Mum went along with this enthusiasm because she saw it as inoculation against popular culture, a bit of kitsch then to guard against a dangerous philistine infection later. Or maybe she simply thought it fun? Sometimes I wonder if

I'm unjust, if I've always assigned to her too pure a version of an identity that she really wished would be recognized as false. After all, she did set Disneyland as our first destination, enjoying, I think, the shock it gave Dad.

AT THE BEGINNING OF GRADE EIGHT, SCIENCE GEOLOGY unit, Taylor and I were made lab partners. Setting up our first lab, he told me he collected rocks.

"Wow. Really? That's very cool."

I'd blown it—too admiring, awkward—God, too needy. Where had this weakness come from? I needed a sarcastic tag, a note of ironic grade-eight cool.

A trace of a smile appeared on Taylor's lips.

I'd been fooling myself. I was needy. I was sickened by it beyond reason. What was going on?

"Do you collect anything?" Taylor asked.

"Pennants," I said, preparing to snicker before he could get there ahead of me. I'd outgrown them, but they still made a cheery circle of my bedroom walls. I'd planned to take them down at the beginning of the school year, and when the first day came and went I told myself I'd get around to it later.

Taylor didn't snicker. "Really?"

"Yes."

"Are they yours?"

"Yeah, sure, they're mine."

"I'd like to see that. I mean, if you'd be willing …"

"Oh, sure. No problem."

There was something weird here, such a serious interest in a collection of pennants. A bit of weirdness was okay, though. That just-recognized neediness was threatening to burst out all over. I wanted to shout my plea: Be my friend!

"You're sure."

"Of course. Today, if you like. Come on over after school."

"THAT'S THEM. I COLLECTED THEM WHEN I WAS A KID."

"Oh, shit," Taylor said. He smiled, the first time I remember seeing his big, warm grin, so friendly. I thought right away of Gatsby, pleased with myself for being so literary.

"I'm such an idiot. I'm such an idiot," he said. He laughed and repeated his charge of idiocy. Then he explained.

"I thought you said 'penance."

"Yeah. 'Pennants.'"

He laughed again. "P-e-n-a-n-c-e. Penance. I thought … I don't know what I thought. The priest gives me prayers, or sometimes work to do. I couldn't imagine what you'd collected."

I laughed because his laughter was infectious. "I've got no idea what you're talking about," I said.

In later years I learned that there'd been family talk about Taylor and a possible vocation, but in hindsight he dated the beginning of his apostasy to our moment in my pennanted room. As he explained it to me a decade later, something of the slippery quality of language and its power to undermine struck him, then persisted and grew, till the certainties seemed absurd and the mysteries mundane. His engagement with mystery, his deep gift for it, got transferred over, ferried by his genius across the religion/art divide to his fiction.

I could date a kind of apostasy of my own to that day, beginning our friendship and realizing, unconsciously, that my independence was just a show. Why not consciously? Because I couldn't yet handle the truth: with my pretense to self-sufficiency I'd been imitating my mother.

"Do you go to church?" said Taylor.

"Not really." It was odd, not simply telling him that I was Jewish, but it felt awkward.

8

P-e-n-a-n-c-e. My sonnets were penance.

It's easy now to say that the idea I developed for the sonnet sequence wasn't a simple accident. As persona I adopted a bit of a sad sack who spent his days listening to the CBC. Each sonnet referenced a different program. Each described a different stage in the speaker's relationship with his wife, and oh, that relationship was deep, loving, and in trouble.

However bad the poems were, I knew that if I sent them anywhere they'd be published. Even if the editors agreed that the poems were bad, they'd be published, but they wouldn't agree. Context always mediates reading, and the poem submitted by the famous novelist is laden with context. (Note, for example, the poems of John Updike—including sonnets, as a matter of fact—that appeared now and then in the *New Yorker*. I don't say that they're bad, not at all, but what would I say if I didn't know the author? What would you say?)

Of course, I didn't have to try to publish, but to refuse to submit seemed a refusal to *submit*, a sign that my penance would be incomplete. So, I sent the penitential sonnets to contests, to be judged the honest way: blindly. It gave me some satisfaction, pride in a literary culture that struggles to deserve it, when I didn't win, at first.

The Frum sonnet surprised with an honourable mention and publication in *Prism*. Perhaps a grad student on the editorial board hankered for old-fashioned form, however metrically clumsy. "She says I love *Ideas* more than her," which I'll save you from skipping here, took a blue ribbon from *The Antigonish Review*, along with two hundred dollars, quickly donated to PEN. I swear, I swear by my sword, that it wasn't part of the plan.

At that point I had to stop, because in the cramped community of Canadian poetry, I could no longer submit anonymously, even to a contest. My project would be known and subsequent entries recognized.

Then came an amused but laudatory mention about the two poems in the *Quill and Quire* blog, and then a call from Noreen, my agent.

People sometimes ask me what Noreen Weisgarten, Canada's oldest literary agent, is really like. Here:

"Just what are you up to?"

"Well, I'm writing again. I'm sorry. I know it won't sell, but at least I'm writing."

"Of course it'll sell."

"It's poetry."

"Nutbar. It's by you. It'll sell. What is it, exactly?"

"Twenty sonnets, a short sonnet sequence, the speaker in each case a man who's obsessed with the CBC and is describing the changes in his marriage."

"The CBC."

"Each sonnet refers to a radio program, or a CBC personality."

"And boy genius doesn't think his poems will sell."

"Explain this to me, oh worldly one. Have I been overlooking all the poetry chapbooks at the top of *The Globe* bestseller list?"

"Let me tell you about an illuminating moment in cultural history. It's before your time, but you should know about it. There was an American country rock group, charmingly named Dr. Hook and the Medicine Show. They recorded a song, 'The Cover of the *Rolling Stone*,' which is about—"

"I know the song, Noreen. Oldies radio."

"Oh piss, then I don't get to sing it for you. It got them on the cover of *Rolling Stone*. Let's say they made their agent very happy. Their agent loved them, not the deep way I love you, of course, but still. True love."

"What the fuck does this have to do with my sonnets, Noreen?"

"You're going to try to convince me you didn't have this all planned."

"I've no idea where you're going here."

"All right. I'll play along. One of the sonnets mentions Barbara Frum, who is unfortunately dead. I find I miss her. The other, which I had to stumble upon in *The Antigonish Review* because you didn't see fit to inform your agent, is about *Ideas*. It verges on cute, but that doesn't matter. It's about *Ideas*; I can at least see that. So, the others. Do you have one for Shelagh Rogers?"

"Yes, but it's not *for* her."

"Sook-Yin Lee?"

"Definitely."

"You're really going to try to tell me you hadn't thought this through."

"Noreen."

"All right. You've written the best-selling book of poems in Canadian history. Or you will have."

"Chapbook."

"Whatever, Gordon. I know what a chapbook is. It's a book. A little fucking book. And you'll be interviewed about your little book on every CBC show, national and local, that has anything at all to do with the arts. Your chapbook will be a stocking stuffer in every CBC-listening household in the country, because I will see to it that it's published at just the right time for Christmas shopping,

I promise you, not that you'll be grateful to your loving agent. Boy genius strikes again."

"Boy genius." I liked it when she called me that. But I should have remembered—I was supposed to be feeling penitential.

9

Young Taylor wasn't put off by my pennant collection, nor by the intensity of my loneliness, because he shared it. We were both bookish, socially limited, overcompensating with pretensions to superior feeling. Taylor was enthusiastic about sports but even more uncoordinated than I, always injuring himself, constantly limping from one gym-class sprain or another. So, easy friendship.

Then, one evening, "Would you like to invite Taylor to our dinner?"

Mum didn't have to tell me which dinner she was referring to.

My father was Jewish, my mother not, but the limitations of my Jewish identity don't have to do with matrilineal traditions. It was simply that my father was so thoroughly secular, indifferent to "culture" of all sorts.

My mother, in fact, took on the responsibility for teaching me about Judaism. We marked the holidays with meals and short readings from Arnold's *Judaism, from the Religious to the Secular*. Happily, the historical significance always involved a connection to the principles of social democracy and international justice.

The dinner upcoming was our celebration of the High Holy Days: Rosh Hashanah and Yom Kippur wrapped up into one observance, a true intellectual occasion, at least as organized by my mother.

"He's Catholic, Mum. He doesn't know I'm Jewish."

"Ask him when you're at his place," said Dad. "With his parents there."

Would this be the end of it—best friend found, then lost, casualty of old religious prejudice? Dad's suggestion certainly raised the possibility; Taylor would need parental approval.

Saturday afternoon, a few days later. We'd just finished lunch at Taylor's place—he, and his parents and I.

"I've got something to ask all of you about," I said.

"What's that?" said his mother.

"I've never told Taylor this. It's just ..."

Taylor was picking up on my tension, looking at me hard.

"I'm Jewish. On my father's side, I'm Jewish. We're not a religious family, but we do mark the holidays, just with a dinner. We have a dinner, and we talk about it, the history. So, next week—"

"Your High Holidays are coming up," said Taylor's father.

"That's right. We just have one dinner, on the Saturday, and I was wondering if Taylor could come."

Taylor didn't respond, but looked to his father. I could read Taylor's face, the hope there—surely, his liberal-minded, enlightened Catholic parents would not balk at this?

"What a generous invitation," his father said.

"That's very thoughtful," said his mother.

"Great," said Taylor.

Taylor saw me off, and we stood beside each other on his front porch, where we shook hands. I know, that's pretty funny. We thought so too. We laughed right away, then I took the steps in a couple of leaps and jogged home.

IN THE MIDDLE OF OUR NEGLECTED BACKYARD STOOD A concrete birdbath. Every year, summer's end, rainwater and leaves filled it, and every year, as far back as I could remember, the Rosh Hashanah/Yom Kippur combo-meal done, Mum would trudge outside and stand before the birdbath. She'd remain there for a long time. I always watched from the kitchen window, mysterious minutes passing, till finally she plunged her hands into her pockets and then took them out, to open them and drop whatever invisibles she was holding into the brown water.

The gesture was enacted over a few childhood years—I felt myself part of an ancient ritual: guardian, witness, even judge was I, but I couldn't explain to Taylor why this was so, because, of course, I didn't understand it myself. So I didn't try. So he didn't know he was interrupting.

"What's she doing?" he said.

"I don't know."

Taylor didn't say anything more, but he looked at me like I was stupid. I rather furiously resented that, but at the same time I could see it from his point of view. If I didn't know, why hadn't I found out?

"Let's ask her," I said.

We put on our ski jackets and joined my mother outside in the drizzle, standing a few feet behind her, and she turned to us after she had opened her hands over the birdbath, dropping, apparently, nothing.

"Why do you do this every year, Mum?"

"It's a tradition. We have a period of contemplation. We reflect on the wrongs we have done to God and to others. We atone. Then we empty our pockets into the sea, casting off our sins. It concludes the days of awe."

A pause, and then Taylor stepped forward, dug his hands in his pockets, found nothing, but opened his fists over the fountain anyway. He stepped back.

I wasn't quite ready to take my turn.

"But you don't believe in God," I said. See? I'm not afraid of my mother.

"That's true, Gordon. But I believe in others. We're nothing without others. I also believe in taking responsibility for my errors and trying to amend my behaviour. The ritual is useful to me because it reminds me to do that."

"It's like confession," said Taylor.

"It is, a bit. It involves absolution, for instance, though not granted by a priest."

"Why doesn't Dad do it?"

"He doesn't need to."

"Doesn't he ever do anything wrong?"

"Of course he does. Our difference is not that his behaviour is better than mine."

She waited, wanting me to take the next step myself, but I couldn't find it, so I asked. "What's the difference?"

"He doesn't need a reminder to atone."

10

■ ■

If selling books had been on my mind rather than penance, repentance, *teshuvah*, I could have predicted the chapbook's success as accurately as Noreen had. I didn't bring my motives up in the interviews that followed publication of *The CBC Sequence* (early November, perfectly timed as promised) and one host after another chuckled charitably when, careful not to protest too much, I tried to deny good-natured charges of calculation.

"You must have smiled, thinking, 'what a fine way to get attention for poetry.'"

"Honestly, Eleanor, it didn't occur to me."

I had no substitute explanation for this "new direction." Others filled the vacuum.

Arrogance, that explained it. The new take on author Gordon Bridge kicked off with a feature-length article in *The Walrus* that moved from the disturbing implications of the surprising terseness in the "famously loquacious novelist" to the poems themselves, bulging with evidence of the same arrogance, and then to each of my previous books. In one way or another, in every case, I was showing off, always: a fragment, a long sentence, any allusion, flamboyant diction, a goddamned omitted preposition (no matter how closely tied to character), emphatic simplicity, really any deviation at all from some purely neutral, unworked voice—proof of guilt. The problem was that everything I'd written appeared to have been *written*. Oh, the unspeakable audacity.

Most notable, suddenly, was my showing off with the review of *The Stendhal Effect*. At least the timid critics finally found the nerve to disagree with my shameful analysis and acknowledge the work's greatness. Taylor would know of this development. Would a note of forgiveness appear in the mail?

I could see the argument for the poems. They weren't very good. Also, I had no background or training as a poet—I agreed with that too. So, the arrogance? The arrogance was in publishing these mediocre poems at all, never mind in a print run unheard of in Canadian publishing (for a poetry chapbook, so that bar was set limbo low). Furthermore, the publicity was of a scope no true poet could ever hope for, crowding out the market and soaking up even the meagre bits of attention otherwise available for those true ones. Every interview I gave sucked up airtime that should go to someone else.

I agreed.

Except.

What about the attention drawn to Canadian poetry by the very debate about the merits of my little fucking book? What about the comments I made about poets I admired? I talked of Elise Partridge and Mark Cochrane. I caused a rare moment of diminished conviviality on *The Next Chapter* when, invited to read one of the CBC sonnets, I instead surprised even myself by reciting Cochrane's "Rescue." I declared it a masterpiece, which isn't news to anyone who knows it, but how many did? (Later, Cochrane offered gracious thanks in an email. In the week following my recitation he'd sold more copies of his last book, *Change Room*, than its entire sales to that point.)

"What do I do now?" I asked Jessica when *The CBC Sequence* was nominated for the Earle Birney Chapbook Prize.

"What do you mean?"

"There's a gala dinner in Winnipeg. In February."

"So don't go."

"That'll look great."

"You care about how you look?"

Well, did I? I didn't. I cared about Jessica's truncated responses, her impatience, so unlike the Jess of our early days, a grudge there still unresolved. I cared about the reality that not going on this journey would be arrogant, declaring that the award wasn't important to me. It wasn't, but it would be, entirely justifiably, to the other nominees, and my absence would be an insult to them. "I believe in others." Most important, the journey would complete my penance. Maybe the note from Taylor would be there when I returned home.

As soon as I'd boarded the plane and found my aisle seat I started on the chapbooks by the other two short-listed poets: Annie Nyo, daughter of Myanmar refugees who had settled in Cape Breton, and Fielding Nethercote, an English prof at the University of Alberta. I'd heard of them and had even come across a few pieces in the journals. It took only an hour to read their two little books. Then I ordered a Scotch.

Nyo's *Broken Feathers* is three long poems, each drawing on her family's history, as does most of her work. Harrowing stuff. It's prosaic for my tastes, the sort of free verse that makes one wonder, could one write an interesting narrative passage, exotic, rich with figurative language, and then chop it up? Is that a poem? Sure, the power of the material is undeniable. Perhaps anything more worked would just distract. There, that's the defence.

Nethercote's *Whatever Seven* is a single poem, about something I couldn't quite pin down. "Spatial practices" is the term that seemed to gather attention to itself. Perhaps a dream about a walk through a skateboard park that is also an urban mall. Every seventh word is "whatever." Not a metaphor or simile to be found. It's a funny book.

How could I criticize something that made me laugh, even if my confidence that the humour was intentional lapsed at points?

Anyone could read these books and note the contrast in their aesthetics. Not everyone would be aware of the deep hostility between the camps. Mensheviks and Bolsheviks, only less compromising. What would that mean for me? Maybe the two judges would represent each side. They'd be deadlocked. They would look for a compromise.

It meant I might win.

Before beverage service shut down for the descent I ordered a second Scotch, maybe dull the dread, clarify things. Nope. Swallow, then the familiar warmth, then a ferrous bitterness, taste of my doom.

I dashed from the airport exit to the cab, a few metres covered in seconds. The cold? A force. Pure hostility. Yet, in the hot taxi, it was just a hint, an idea, not concrete. Then the same from cab to hotel door. I checked in, unpacked, put on long underwear, wool pants, a heavy sweater under my parka, and, sweating by the time I hit the lobby, I headed out to a restaurant that Google Maps located just down the street.

Closed.

The map had indicated another possibility around the corner and two blocks on. At the intersection I turned and stepped into the wind. Shocked deep breath, my nostrils froze, my lungs threatened to crystallize and shatter.

I should have returned to the hotel and ordered in. But no. Onward—a character in a Sinclair Ross story, alone on the vengeful, allegorical prairie, staggering against fate's awful gusts, straining toward inevitable, meaningless death. I heard my relieved gasp when my mittened hand clawed the restaurant door open.

Inside, shown to a table, I couldn't read the menu at first. Something was wrong with my eyes. My nose thawed and began to run, reminder of snotty youth. With the napkin I wiped away tears, now melted and humiliating.

"From out of town?" said the waiter.

My useless tensing up for the return trip to the hotel, a desperate sprint, probably contributed to what followed.

"How was the flight?" said Jessica when I called.

"Something's happened to my neck."

"Your neck?"

"My neck's seized up. It hurts like hell. I can't turn my head. I was outside for a few minutes and I think one of my vertebrae froze and cracked."

"It's just muscle spasms. Take some painkillers."

In the morning, my neck a block of hot iron, I located a massage therapist with an opening and called a cab.

"It's muscle spasms," the therapist said.

"Ow! Fuck!"

"Sorry. There's not much I can do. The spasms'll stop in a few days probably. Then you can get deep massage. All I can do now is something general for your back. Try not to hold your whole back stiff like that. That'll make it worse."

I binged on meds all day, and by the time I arrived for the gala I still couldn't turn my head. The awkwardness increased when the meal began, Nyo on one side of me, Nethercote the other. Friendly, these poets were, complimentary, unpretentious, and relaxed, and in order to face one or the other to take part in the conversation I had to shift my body painfully. Finally, I just explained.

"I'm really sorry. It's my damned neck. It's seized up. I can't move my head. There's a pain between my shoulders that seems to be launching war on two fronts, into my skull and down my spine."

"Muscle spasms, I bet," said Annie.

"Got to be," said Fielding. "Don't try massage for a few days. It'll only hurt like hell and make it worse."

They were so congenial that my nightmare of victory as the compromise poet faded into implausibility. I'd exaggerated the conflict, obviously: between the writers themselves, no trace of animosity. I began to relax.

"The winner of this year's Earle Birney Poetry Chapbook Prize is Gordon Bridge, for *The CBC Sequence*."

I congratulated my new pals Annie and Fielding. I looked at the mic, and then at the crowd, and my speech came to me. It was time.

A few sentences. I would confess my old sin and plead for forgiveness, for another try at friendship. The speech would baffle but it would be reported and Taylor would be asked about it. He would respond, the silence broken, repairs finally begun.

I saw all this in one second, my fine redeemed life, and I could feel the audience feel the weight of my pause. I swayed and reached for the mic, another burst of pain in my shoulders and neck, sudden dizziness: you're drunk, Gordon. You're a stupid drunk.

My courage failed, I thanked the judges and took my seat. Twenty minutes later I left, after shaking all the hands that wanted shaking, trying, failing to do so without motion being communicated to my neck.

The sun shone bright and cold the next morning. The cabbie took us past the Manitoba Legislature on the way to the airport. "Look at that. Golden Boy in the sun," he said, friendly Winnipegger, pointing at the famous statue topping the building. "Eternal Youth."

"Great," I said.

His eyes met mine in the rear-view mirror. "You're not looking," he said.

"I can't turn my head."

He shook his. I knew what he was thinking. Arrogant.

Noreen called me from Toronto that night.

"Just what did you get up to in Winnipeg?"

"I won. I'm sorry."

"What?"

"What are you talking about, Noreen? I didn't get up to anything."

"I happened to catch the *Winnipeg Arts Review* on the CBC this morning. You know, just tuned in to see if anything was going on. Guess what. Joyce Malcom called you an asshole."

"She did not."

"She might as well have. She said you wouldn't look at anyone all night, wouldn't talk to anyone, you gave a crap two-sentence acceptance speech, you were drunk, and you left without answering questions. Obviously, you're too big for Winnipeg and the Earle Birney Chapbook Award."

These accusations wouldn't have made a dent, I would have smiled and scoffed, at the charges and at my pain, if only … if only those clumsy-gimmicky sonnets had been more. But they amounted to no penance after all. Publication satisfied at first, but then, the rush gone, just a watered dose of methadone, not the real junk. Not a novel. I'd broken out of my prison of silence, brought down a judgment, for what?

11

■ ■

I'm walking down Vancouver's Broadway—endless blocks of boxy, post-war, pre-fabby junk, interrupted every now and then by something more recent and worse. Who could design one of these cheap, post-modernish bad jokes, with their arbitrary arched windows, ticky-tacky faux tile, tinted glass, and still sleep nights? But I don't care, I'm bouncing along and even finding some warmth, some charm in the unrelenting urban shit. I'm so magnanimous.

IT HAD BEEN A COUPLE OF YEARS SINCE *THE CBC SEQUENCE.* I'd begun a novel, tried a bit of magical thinking: if I tell everyone that I'm writing a novel—well, if I tell Jessica—then I will be. And I did begin. The accusing voice remained silent. Punishing stiff necks cursed my life, but I got about twenty thousand words out, a year's slow progress, and then one night over dinner:

"How's the novel going? I mean, I don't need details, of course. I hope it's going well?"

"I'm giving it up."

I hadn't known those words were about to come out, but it was a relief more than a shame to speak them. Admitting things brings relief.

"Oh."

"It just never took off."

"I guess that happens."

"Yeah. It happens to most writers. The ones I've read about, anyway."

"You'll start another?"

"Soon."

Jess looked at Gavin and Leo in turn. They looked at me and back at Jess.

"Soon," I said again.

"I can't wait to read it," said Gavin. His reading had just started to take off.

"Me too," said Leo.

"Don't hold your breath," said Jessica, then a guffaw.

"Jess?"

"Well, novels take a long time, that's all. You boys'll probably be in high school before he's finished."

"Yes, probably. Your mother's right."

Soon took about another year. I retreated, in order to protect myself, to try to find a way to begin and then sustain. I canceled my subscription to *Quill and Quire*, I didn't learn what writers were winning what prizes, I stopped visiting the library and browsing the used bookstores, and I meticulously avoided the *Globe* book section. As I say, about another year, and then I began again.

As the second attempt ground along I made no comment. For days I'd write nothing, and I'd congratulate myself when I wrote something bad, pushing on, insisting that bad was fine, bad could be improved, just keep at it. Try not to hold my neck that way.

I wrote a paragraph, reread it, and found something to admire. It moved me. It sounded good. All the dull stuff that worked up to that paragraph, it could all go, but it wasn't a waste, because it got me there. I could start there.

I didn't want to hurry things, so early that afternoon I took a celebratory walk. Why did I end up on that insulting stretch of

Broadway? I don't know. Feeling generous with my success and wanting to include the worst of my city in my good spirits.

I LOOK AND THEN LOOK AWAY. BUT IT'S TOO LATE. I CAN'T pretend I haven't seen. There's a promotional stack of them in the window of Book Warehouse. A slim volume, a shadowy figure lurks on the cover, turns away from us, something disturbing in the posture.

Fairly Done, by Taylor Shepherd.

I stop and consider, watching the traffic, my back to the storefront. I blink a few times. I step closer to the curb. A thin and cruel thought cuts through my mind, and I push it away. My posture—why am I standing this way? I don't do this, teeter, some sudden, weird disease infecting my spine. I reach for the sky with both hands, put 'em up, insist myself straight, and then I turn, look again. That figure twisting also, away from me, furtive and indignant at the same time, and what I do, what I do is I go into the store and buy the book.

MY FIRST REACTION WAS MUCH LIKE THAT OF MANY OTHERS, maybe yours: did I want to read a novel written from the point of view of an abusive priest? No, I did not. But one does things one doesn't want to do.

Here's my response, offered up now, years later, no chance of doing any harm.

It's a hateful book. It's not sensationalist, reductive, moralistic, outraged or pat. Taylor had taken the time to get to know his man, perhaps had researched—prison interviews maybe—or perhaps he'd just plummeted into the depths of his imagination and his experience, and he'd lingered there, probably for years, because only years of study could have brought him to such understanding and to such wise, patient, generous … hatred. It's been earned; it's been paid for. I couldn't imagine the cost.

I read the reviews, none negative but many awkward, wanting to keep the novel at arm's length, preferring they had some other assignment. On a Saturday morning I heard Taylor on the radio: *North By Northwest*, CBC Vancouver's so dependably cheery Sheryl McKay finally regretful, defeated, and Taylor, apologetic for having written a work that holds our ultimate ugliness up by its greasy hair and shoves it in our faces, makes us stone.

I didn't bother rereading my paragraph. I didn't have to. I felt the hate. Vengeful. Once again, I just quit.

II

THE OTHER MAVIS

12

If this narrative could be said to have a sweep, that's more or less the backswing: me and Taylor, our success, my failure; me and Jess, our children, my silence, her threat; and me, my so-called penance, the origins of the legend of my arrogance, Taylor's dark triumph, more years of silence.

The moment of transition, then, the short, sweet pause when things hang suspended before events rush forward: the boys were in their early teens, Jessica and I were still hanging on, and we were in Lisbon, in the gardens of Queluz Palace, where I stood beside a pond and rested my hand on Gavin's back to comfort him as he threw up. I understood. The carp sickened me, too.

We'd risen early to make the most of our time, and we'd walked to the Bica funicular just to take the ride. Afterward, through the neighbourhood we strolled, stopped for coffee for Jess and me, soda for the boys. The boys were relieved that they didn't need to face another stained-glass window, a violation of the pact we'd made before launching our adventure.

"THE XYZ IN THE CHURCH OF THE XYZ IS A PARTICULARLY fine example of XYZ." Leo, at the kitchen table, awaiting dinner, read from the Frommer's he'd dug up at the library. The strenuous neutrality in his tone underlined the sarcasm.

"I don't want to look at stained glass windows," said Gavin.

"We'll stay out of churches," said Jessica.

"Paintings are okay," said Leo.

"Oh, sure, paintings are okay," said Gavin.

"We shall not linger in European monasteries. We'll walk *los vecindarios*, and we'll be sophisticated cosmopolitans, lounge in cafés, talk about literature and history," I said. "It'll be like hanging out on The Drive, only way better."

"No stained glass and no churches," said Leo, in his puritanical atheist phase, no stretch from the household norm. So, we'd all agreed that our spring break trip, while true to an excitement about history, would be free of the need to be impressed by the weighty sacred tradition that all the guidebooks took pains to detail. We all just needed to get away, which we'd realized as soon as Jessica had surprised us with the suggestion.

We flew into Porto, and after checking in at the hotel, we headed to the famous Café Imperial, not knowing what awaited. After the hilarity, I left it to Jess to lecture on the Imperial's surprise, which was not religious, but still: a diptych, high over the entrance, in stained glass.

On the right of this horror, lush tropics, a group of black men naked to the waist labour to load a ship. They stoop to the heavy crates on their backs, crates packed, it seems, with coffee, for on the left, the window's other half, elegant people at their leisure enjoy the labour's fruits; they lounge in a café and sip from delicate cups. These fine folk are white—us, in other words. Jess gracefully explained, offering a quick history, a relaxed definition of "colonialism," and an unrighteous glance at why we drink fair trade coffee at home. My coffee tasted like mud.

SO, JUST A COUPLE OF DAYS AND A SHORT TRAIN RIDE LATER, amused relief at a Lisbon café without stained glass. Then we cabbed to the palace. The day hadn't been strenuous, but we were still strangely jet-lagged, so maybe we shouldn't have launched straight into the self-guided tour.

The boys were more than troupers; they enjoyed themselves. We recalled the lesson of the colonial coffee trade and applied it to the images of 18th-century life, the implicit signs of the very power we'd seen crowed over in Imperial stained glass. Gavin and Leo tested us with questions, and between the two of us we did well, putting together the history and the paintings, trying to feel like a team.

Then, time-zone exhaustion coming on dizzy and overwhelming, out in the formal palace garden with its canal, its charming artificial waterfall, its absurd sphinxes dressed in old world finery—what was that sound? We could hear it in the distance as we strolled in the chilly afternoon, then more distinct, distracting us from the beauty as we rounded the fountain where Bernini's dolphins and tritons sported: a puckering, smacking sound, a thousand smothering aunts planting unwanted, exaggerated kisses on the cheeks of a thousand squirming nephews. We came to the pond.

Heaps of massive orange carp thrashed at the surface, a teeming mess of them on top of others thrashing below, crowding the shore, where an old man bent toward them, lobbing bits of white bread at the water's edge. The carp tossed and flopped over each other, and smack smack smack smack went their carp lips as they strained to gobble the soggy pieces of paste, some of the fish even wriggling onto the muddy bank, thrusting with their fins, as though drawn by the irresistible pull of disintegrating Portuguese Wonder Bread to evolve into amphibians before our very eyes.

I felt my own stomach turn before I noticed Gavin, ghostly and panicked, and I managed to lead him a few steps toward a giant magnolia tree, behind which he hurled, several times. I placed my hand on his back. It's such a loaded gesture, for me, its meanings so powerful, so apt at that threatening moment.

MY MOTHER PUT HER HAND ON MY BACK AS I THREW UP into the pail she'd provided, set by my bed so I could simply turn on my side to vomit. I had the flu. I was about eight years old. Maybe it was the spring after we visited Disneyland.

All night my mother sat, interrupted only by her trips to the bathroom to dump my liquidy puke down the toilet and to soak a cloth in cold water before easing it onto my hot forehead. The prospect of renewed relief every little while, delivered by the cold cloth, a whispered word or two—"there," "easy now"—and a simple caress, something realistic to look forward to rather than the impossibly distant morning—it made the long night bearable.

Years later, recalling that night and thanking my mother, she denied it. "I didn't sit up with you that long. You threw up a few times and then you fell asleep, and I went to bed."

She was embarrassed. She didn't want to be seen that way: sacrificing mother, sleepless, comforting her child, who, retching, felt all the while her hand on his back—it's all right; Mum's here; I love you.

I, in contrast, would not have been embarrassed. It was exactly who I wanted to be right then, in the palace gardens, shaded by the magnolia: father with meaningful hand on son's back. So, as usual when Gavin needed me or Jess, it was like he was giving something. He was giving me a second chance. I'd missed the first, with Leo.

"HOW'RE YOU FEELING, SWEETHEART?" SAID JESS. LEO HAD made his way downstairs for breakfast.

"I'm okay."

"You probably shouldn't have any cereal, dear." Leo was accustomed to helping himself to breakfast, always using two hands, just as he was taught, to hold the carton and pour milk over his granola.

"I heated up some chicken broth," I said. "It'll give you some energy, and it's the easiest thing to keep down."

"Thanks, Daddy."

Gavin was sitting on the floor, pretending to play with a truck while actually just watching and listening. When I turned from the stove with bowl in hand, Gavin quickly looked down at his toy. Jess had wrapped her arms around Leo and pulled him toward her as she sat in her chair. She kissed the top of his head. He let her.

"Leo," I said, but I didn't know what to add. Jess looked at me. She didn't know what to say either. Right then, we were a team, both flummoxed, honestly sharing.

What would you say? What if you awakened in the middle of the night and heard something, and you hustled childward, and then, more awake, realized what it was? You opened the door and your six-year-old son stood, bent over, throwing up into the toilet. He hadn't complained of feeling ill when he'd gone to bed early. He hadn't cried out in the night when he grew feverish, then nauseated, and then somehow knew what to do, and by himself had tried to be sick without disturbing.

Leo turned, looked at me, and then pivoted back, vomited one more time, little body lurch. He straightened up, chest still heaving. I poured some water into the toothbrush glass.

"Here, Leo. Rinse your mouth. It'll get the taste out. That's it. Spit it out in the sink." Jess was beside me by then. She walked with me as I carried Leo back to his room, and we tucked him in together and told him we loved him, and he'd feel better in the morning, and please sweetheart call us if you need anything, even just company. Jess stayed for a bit before coming back to bed and telling me he'd fallen asleep.

And now he sipped his broth and Jessica and I tried to find something to say. I found a joke.

"You know what they say in Australia?"

"About what?" said Leo.

"They say you were calling Huey on the big white phone."

He didn't get it, but when I explained with an extravagant,

puking, "Huuueeey," he giggled. Our first-born son, prematurely responsible like so many of his partners in birth-order precedence, giggling over his broth, and his little brother laughing too, not because he understood, but just because.

So, I'd said the right thing, the morning after. But at night, little Leo sick and alone, I hadn't been there, and in the morning my hand flapped around, wanting to rest on something.

NOW THAT HAND FOUND ITS PLACE, RESTING ON GAVIN.

"I'm sorry," said Gavin.

The guy who'd been feeding the carp had left, and the fish had receded. We could hear the splashing of the fountain.

"I was going to puke too."

"Me too," said Leo.

"Me ... me too," said Jessica, grudging, not entirely happy for all of us to be united in feeling.

I wouldn't put anything beyond Gavin's powers of empathy. I hugged him, careful not to worry him by squeezing too hard. It could have been one of his intuitions—first a turning of his stomach and then a flash that here was opportunity, better to puke than hold it down—an intuition that he could use this sickening moment to bring us together when only he could sense we were falling apart.

13

■ ■

We took the night train to Madrid, a Gran class double cabin on the Hotel Train Lusitania, exotic adventure. Leo and Gavin played Scrabble as we pulled out of Santa Apollonia Station, and Jess read. I, I opened my notebook, hand a-tremble.

I could taste it, a bitter solvent stirring in my mouth, and that old voice began to intrude, "Here's the asshole Gordon Bridge, thinking himself a writer." No. I would not accept that. I'd swallow that poison, ignore that accuser, recover myself. For it had come to me. An idea for a novel.

I kept the notes, of course. They're open beside me now. I remember writing them and pausing as I wrote.

The carp: conspicuously stupid consumption, overpopulation, colonialism's dead end. Capitalism's.

I looked up: Gavin and Leo concentrating—I couldn't tell whose turn it was. I looked at Jess. She turned a page, gaze fixed on her book.

The body's—the community's, the planet's—inevitable revolt, puke behind the magnolia tree, puke up a toxic history, something like that.

I looked up once more and waited till Jess turned another page, unwavering.

The brazen self-satisfaction: on one side the exploited workers, slaves; on the other the self-satisfied, the privileged.

The carp are decorative. They're not in their native place; they've been removed to this artificial life.

At other times, other places, it didn't work this way. I would turn a page, or make a note, look up—Jess reading. Resume, then Jess looks up, and this time I'm the one occupied, and then repeat, one of us waits, and the other looks, knows that the other has waited: recognition—we all need recognition.

Carp can live forever, it seems. Immortal animals. Reference Huxley's After Many a Summer? *They're also shit-eating scavengers: gorgeous, shimmering, and disgusting.*

Leo, managing a bad rack, played his word: "gat." I was surprised that he knew it. He picked his replacement tiles. Gavin looked up at me. He didn't know the word but he also knew that Leo wouldn't bluff—no point in a challenge. "Slang for 'gun,'" I said, and Leo smiled. I saw he'd scored a blank among his three new tiles.

A man in a café takes a sip of evil.

Jess turned a page, undistracted, eyes still riveted.

The Lusitania, sleek, modern, clanked us along at an antique speed through the industrial Lisbon suburbs. Jess had the window seat. Dark out and then yellow sodium lights, then darkness. The shadow and light moved across her face: gentle slope of brow, curve of soft cheek, lips, throat, and then a passing stronger light and her face's structure emerged, its elegant planes and lines. Leo looked up at her. Only his mother, maybe—not, to him, an impossible beauty.

MORE THAN ONE PERSON HAD COMMENTED. "I SAW HER AT the courthouse, hurrying along to some case, probably. She didn't see the people watching as she passed." "Man, Bridge, you lucky—shit, how does she do it?" "She's even more beautiful, after two kids. You probably don't even notice."

Did they think I was blind? Me? I was the connoisseur, from the beginning and always.

Her hair had changed colour. That was the even more beautiful, or at least part of it. It had more shades: something that was going to become grey, not soon, but eventually, and which would be beautiful then too, but at the time a mix of cooler blonde … inadequate to say highlights, but that'll have to do. Also, her face had changed, of course, lost a bit of fullness. She still looked young but there was a sign that she wouldn't be forever. She'd be old and beautiful one day.

She has a dimple, over her right eyebrow, visible only when her face tenses with concern. She doesn't have perfect, regular teeth. Her canines are long, and they curve away from the neighbouring incisors, creating a gap, a millimetre of soulful shadow visible there with a smile.

I get Jessica's beauty, I thought then, glancing at her while she read, the Lusitania finally gathering speed. I really get it. Don't ask me if I've noticed.

We still made love, true. We made love the night before we left, celebrating the beginning of our holiday. "What's wrong here?" I thought. Nothing at all. Nothing's wrong with celebrating by making love.

Maybe.

I thought about it while the boys continued their game and Jessica read on.

A few weeks passed once, perhaps a month, enough then to feel like a long time. We handed the boys over to Mum and Dad for an evening and took in a movie at The Hollywood: *Big Night*.

Driving home, when I wasn't shifting gears, Jessica held my hand. Smiles and laughter. It was such a relief and a delight to see a movie, hoping at best for a diversion, and getting hilarity, but also something so moving, such patience in the art. We made love and laughed some more afterward, amused that pleasure in the film supplied the erotic charge.

Was that a mistake? It started to seem so then, on the Lusitania. Did it begin at that moment, love after the film, or was it on some other occasion when sex first took its energy from elsewhere?

We went to parent-teacher day. Ms Illis, the grade five teacher from heaven, showed us Gavin's papier mâché *piñata*.

"It's really quite good," said Jessica.

"He has talent, such an eye for colour," said Ms Illis, exaggerating maybe, not knowing it struck us both wonderful that Gavin hadn't inherited our shared artistic ineptitude.

We loved joyously that night, celebrating Gavin and the *piñata*.

A federal election, the NDP made some gains—we weren't foolishly optimistic, not thinking that the neocons would now get taken down—but it was certainly enough lefty success for a sultry swinging of hips, a sturdy response, and love.

And how could I forget: the evening when I began to write again, my sonnet for Barbara Frum. Gold lamé revisited.

I closed my notebook. How wrong it was, how far away she remained while sitting beside me in the compartment. I felt her beauty like a force. I stood at a distance, in the next room, a courtier beseeching royal permission to enter, never granted evermore.

I resisted the force of that "evermore." I would find a pathway back. That had to be possible. The pathway would begin with a novel. I'd write a novel and I'd be the man I'd been, before my incomprehensible betrayal.

Jessica turned a page. The reason she didn't look up was that she knew she would be unable to keep her expression from showing disapproval. Of my writing. You threatened to leave me if I didn't write, Jessica, and now you're unhappy that I'm a writer? Or is it you don't believe anymore, you don't think I have it in me?

14

■ ■

In a restaurant a few doors down from our hotel on Paseo de la Castellana we relaxed, drinking *cafés con leche*. Then, outside, a scream. A man shouted, and someone else began to wail. The waiter ran to the door to look out, some patrons behind him, and then Jessica. We heard no blast. The room did not shake. I sat with the boys, and we put our cups down, looked at each other, wide eyes.

A piercing siren, and then another. More shouts. On the street people ran past in one direction, and then back, and the waiter stood in the doorway, yelling into the confusion. More people screamed. Jessica returned to the table, and we waited for the noise to subside, but of course it did not. Sirens wailed on, people shouted and cried, a hellish noise.

It was pointless to speculate. We were peripheral, of course; it wasn't about us. The screaming continued, unbearable: sirens, tires screeching, shouting. It wasn't about me. Nothing to do with me starting a novel, this cataclysm, whatever it was. Stupid for it even to occur to me.

The waiter came to our table and began to shout hysterically at me, saliva flying, Spanish much too rapid to understand. He could have been shouting at anyone—I'd been chosen at random. I put some money on the table and we left.

We spent the day in our rooms at the AC Cuzco, watching events unfold on television. I began taking notes, refusing to credit my irrational guilt, and I felt Jessica's revulsion.

Leo had the best Spanish of the four of us. He summarized what he could, the rest of us chipped in when we caught a word or phrase that he hadn't, and sometimes numbers and place names came up on the screen, making the horror easier to track.

Bombings on commuter trains. In the morning rush hour. 191 dead. 2,000 wounded. Basque separatists, said the government.

We ate lunch in the hotel restaurant, watched more TV and later returned to eat dinner at the same table where we'd had lunch. The waiter, obviously in shock, apologized: many menu items were unavailable. The Metro had closed and staff couldn't come in. We said whatever, whatever food they had to serve, with the least trouble. The stunned faces of everyone in the restaurant said the same. I was grateful that this waiter didn't single me out for abuse.

The next day we worked out the nearest location accepting blood donations and walked there, but they didn't need us. All of Madrid was giving blood.

"We should visit the Reina Sofía," said Leo, taking charge.

With other stunned tourists we stood in front of *Guernica*: Picasso's agonized Basques, crying their despair behind the bulletproof anti-fascist glass. A horse screams. A few lines—cubist terror. Hands full of pain reach to the heavens, a shattered sword lies in a dead hand, the slaughtered sprawl on their twisted backs, and our boys, I turn to see them behind me: Leo squats, his hands wrapped around his knees; Gavin looks but holds one hand up to shield his eyes as though a bright sun burns them. Why should I feel this is my fault?

We booked a new flight and returned home. I took more notes, and Jessica steamed.

It wasn't separatists, as we all know now, but Islamists seeking to punish for the Spanish participation in the invasion of Iraq. When the government lost the election three days after the bombing, its manipulative response to the catastrophe seemed justly to have backfired. I followed the reports, hopping from one station to another, wishing I could watch in Spanish even though I'd understand less. Soon the news cycle turned. I scanned the internet and picked up the last of the commentary.

Gradually we settled into the old routine. The boys returned to school, Jessica to work, me to writing. Jessica didn't ask and I didn't say. My energy for doing something, the conviction I'd had while riding the Lusitania that it was open to me to make an effort and just, somehow, shift our lives—gone, and if I noticed I found myself unable to care.

I took no pleasure in the crowds on The Drive and no amount of sleep could lift a sickening, grotesque fatigue. Jessica worked all the time. "How was school today?" I'd ask Gavin when he got home. "Great! Really great!" His forced smile was hopeful, so eager to think that I believed him and was unworried, and I accepted this charade greedily, excused myself for my failure of attention.

Then came Leo's underwhelming grade-ten spring report card, provoking uncharacteristic questions about homework, and uncharacteristic sullenness and procrastination in response.

"You'll regret it," said Jessica.

"I don't believe in regret," said Leo.

"Explain that," said Jessica.

We were finishing dinner. Jess had wanted to know how Leo's Buddhism project was going.

"Ironically, that's something I've learned from studying Buddhism. It's important to live in the present. Regrets are stories we tell ourselves about the past, and they create suffering."

"What if you do something wrong, like not getting a project done to deadline?"

"What's gained by regretting it?"

The worried look on Gavin's face showed that he suspected what was coming. I should've taken his concern as a stop sign.

"What's gained?" I said. "What's gained? Everything. Nothing could be more important than regret. *Je ne regrette rien.* Please save me from people who *ne regrettent rien.* Regrets show that you're committed to the person you are and the one you're becoming. Without that commitment you're nothing.

"You should consider how a decision makes you worse or better. If you have no regrets you're alienated from your past and uncommitted to others or yourself, which is the same thing, by the way.

"Think about this, Leo, this radical amnesia that the 'presentness' crowd pictures as an authentic life. Perform the thought experiment, and what you get is a grinning idiot, drooling meaninglessly in an empty present. But that's best. More reasonably, it means a life of panic as experiences come unpredictably from a strange universe.

"But even that's optimistic. It imagines this being who at some point has lived in time and been able to construct a narrative. You've got to have a narrative in order to have a self at all. Otherwise, you're simply an organism. A single cell. There's your 'presentness.' Is that your ambition, Leo? Life without regret. An authentic amoeba."

Leo, clenched and pale, left the table. Gavin looked down at his empty plate, his arms limp at his sides, his breathing ragged, and I knew he was regretting not having intervened with a change of topic. I didn't look at Jessica. I should have been happy: after all, I had another wonderful regret of my own to add to my collection.

I'd believed I had a novel on the way. Wrong. I tried, and nothing—no voice, energy, story. See, Taylor? Still, my guilt and my silence. I managed only an essay, which the *London Review of Books* published in its "Diary" spot. Gorgeous Jessica and the brilliant boys were in there, without being exposed in any way, really. The Café Imperial, coffee, colonialism, carp, puking, Madrid,

ETA, Islam, Iraq, government manipulation, blowback. I didn't mention the publication to anyone. Not a novel.

Leo picked up the mail when he got home from school, and he noticed two copies of the *LRB*, the usual subscription along with a contributor's copy, and he saw my name on the front page. If I'd just said not to mail an extra, would things ... no, hardly. Leo read the article right then, and next Gavin, before they showed it to me.

"Dad has an article in the *LRB*," said Gavin at dinner. "It's about Spain."

"Oh?" said Jessica.

She didn't read it that night, or the next day. Perhaps she intended not to, and maybe that would've been wise, but we were just postponing. Anyway, a few days passed, things grew colder, and I knew.

I appeared on some radio shows, which led to more appearances, and some TV. I hadn't imagined myself a registered pundit, expert on terrorism, offering my own accredited bites of sound.

Absolutely, I could have said no. I didn't because novelists don't get to be pundits and maybe they should, maybe I generously accepted these invitations so that, doing well, more producers would think to call on more novelists to add a little goddamned nuance. Nuance, Jessica.

Maybe I hoped that the introductions to my feature appearances, "novelist" Gordon Bridge, would total something, spill over, become true again.

"I'm going to be away for a few days next week," I said at dinner. "Really?" said Gavin. "What'll you be doing?" said Leo. Silent Jessica raised her glass of wine, looked at it and sipped.

"I'm going to New York to be on a panel."

"Cool. What's it about?"

"It's called 'Reading Terrorism.' They liked the *LRB* article."

To her credit, Jessica did speak, later, as we undressed for bed. She managed to whisper and eventually shout at the same time, as did I, straining with our fury and our need to protect the boys, asleep two rooms down the hall.

"I disagree with you on this. I can't say—I can't begin to say how much I disagree."

"I'll need to know a bit more here, about what your disagreement is."

"The bombings are not a metaphor. It's a disgrace, bringing your own little life into it that way. Gavin threw up because he was tired and jet-lagged, and the fish were disgusting, and that's all. God, how can you be so ... so ..."

"Arrogant."

"It's too weak a word, but it'll do. It's just ... what a stupid article."

"The *LRB* editors disagreed with you, obviously."

"Or they knew your name on the cover would sell papers, no matter how self-aggrandizing your so-called analysis."

"Sell papers? I'm not so big in England."

"What? Now? In the middle of this you're fishing for a compliment? Jesus, Gordon."

"Fuck you, Jessica. I don't need ... fuck you. That's what you think?"

"Oh, I'm sorry. I shouldn't be surprised at all. You do it all the time; it's probably just a habit. Why not now? I'll give it to you, too. You are so 'big in England.' There's no other explanation for their buying that ... that ...

"Not everything is a metaphor, Gordon. Don't you get tired of this? Doesn't it stop feeling like an insight after a while?"

"Of course everything is a metaphor. It's a matter of understanding what it's a metaphor for. That's the insight, Jessica, which you goddamned well know. That's what the *LRB* pays good money for and what puts me on a plane to New York."

"You can't believe that. Not everything is a metaphor."

"Every fucking thing."

"What about that idea, that everything is a metaphor."

"Exactly! And the idea that it's a metaphor, that's a metaphor. Give me a few minutes and I'll tell you what it's a metaphor for, no charge, just for you."

"So you have an infinite, meaningless regression."

"It's not meaningless! Nothing could be more meaningful!"

"It's disgusting … it's so—you can't see how reductive it is? God."

"It's the opposite of reductive. The bombings were a metaphor. Explaining it that way means understanding it."

"So nobody else can understand it but you."

"Why do you need to make me sound so arrogant? That's what all writers do. All artists. You don't think my writing is important?"

"I'm saying you're exploiting a tragedy."

"That's a metaphor. Calling it a tragedy, which is a literary genre, remember, is a metaphor, and it's not a bad way to understand Madrid if you've absolutely got to resort to a tired and used-up trope, forgivable for you, maybe, an ignorant, literal-minded lawyer, if we're going to start being clear about things."

"Oh God, there's no winning with you."

"That's because I'm right."

About metaphors, of course I was right. I'd written an article that was pretty good—I was right about that—and I was flying around showing off how subtle I could be about terrorism. I'd written a hit poetry chapbook. But I wasn't right because I still hadn't written a novel, not since Taylor. A chapbook and an article are fine, if they're done off the side of the desk, between chapters. Fine, but not a novel, not a novel.

I hated her. She'd begun undermining long ago, with her threat, those clever signs of subtle displeasure with the sonnets, and now this contempt. The article was so little, but it could be built upon, if I had some support. In bed that night, my stomach churned fury, burned with it, fury and fear. I would not cry. Jess would hear and she'd be glad. But I couldn't do it any more, just keep on keeping on, strung out, exhausted by my rage at her and crushed by the fatigue. I couldn't go on with this pretense that I was okay when I wasn't writing.

I needed to try something different. Taylor would've told me that. He told me the same thing once before, way back when, kneecapped by first failures and despairing.

15

"I've got news," said Taylor.

"So, tell me."

Taylor sighed.

"So tell me."

We were drinking at the Billy Bishop, the Legion down in Kits Point, after a quiet walk along the beach, quiet mainly because I'd lost the ability to hold a conversation. Earlier that week I'd heard from yet another agent unwilling to take on my second novel attempt. It looked to be sinking, as the first had. Taylor knew that, of course.

"The agency contacted me today," said Taylor. "I've got a deal for *An Earlier Encounter*."

"Really. Wow. Perfect timing."

"I'm sorry."

"You don't ... Fuck. You don't have to apologize for getting a deal. How big?"

"Gordon."

"How big? How big?"

"A lot."

"Wow. Really? A lot. That's a lot. No question. Congratulations."

"Okay."

"All right. I'm sorry. Congratulations. It should be a lot. It's probably not enough. It's a great novel. Really. Congratulations."

I got up and gave him a hug.

"Thanks," he said.

"Look. In a few weeks I'll be happy about this, probably. Okay?"

It was his second novel. His first, *Heart City*, was startling good, a magnificent debut—everyone agreed. *An Earlier Encounter* was another step, a knockout.

Taylor had finished a beer quickly and was on to a second. He's twice my size and can hold his booze better. He turned sideways from the table to stretch out his legs, took another long swallow, and then he tried one of his inclusive smiles—I loved his smile, like everybody—but he couldn't sustain it.

"I'm not sure what to say."

"You don't need to say anything."

"I've got two points. The first is that I believe in you. Our careers might go at different paces. Maybe I'll do better with my next, and again with the next, and you'll continue butting your head against the wall—yeah, I know, not just the publication stuff, but aesthetically, what we agree on. But I'm very confident that you'll get there. You'll write something that we both know … we'll both know what it is. You'll write a great novel."

"Well, I'm beginning—"

"Let me finish. I'm very confident. But I might be wrong. I could be. So the second thing I want to say is that I need you. I need you not to change. When you speak to me, you know that I know you're brilliant. You can't betray this in yourself or betray us by losing sight of the truth here."

I excused myself and took a trip to the men's.

"You Bridges and your sudden exits," said Taylor on my return. Really, only my mother and I had this habit of ducking out when the warmth got heavy.

"It's a little difficult for me. Okay, I accept what you say. Thank you. But I'm finding it a bit hard right now to start up again. Attempt number three. It's not offering itself to me."

He turned around to face me and pulled his chair toward the table. "I don't know, Gordon. Could you try something different? Is there something you could do, hell, I don't know, like a new desk, or writing by hand, or anything just … different? Maybe it's time, y'know, just an idea, but maybe you should move out. Think about it, anyway."

I'd been thinking. I was pushing my late twenties but still on the boy-child's subsidy. Still no rent asked for, no hint of it, just one hard-to-pay expense: bare-bones honesty. I guess, to be fair, Mum would have preferred to forget the whole thing, but we were too late. Years earlier we'd agreed that secrecy on such matters was soft and dumb. Not that we'd actually discussed it. The point got reiterated with each of her flat announcements about articles accepted or rejected, her insistence that there be no emotional deal here, just professional markers of persistence. So: "I've finished it. I've sent off my first novel." "I heard back. It's a no." "I got another no." "Another no." And, "I've sent it off. It's better. We'll see." "I heard back …" "I heard back …" She didn't wince, made no sign, but still, her intense effort to remain impassive, so clear.

I looked at my beer. If I moved out, I'd need to come up with rent money, which meant working, less time for writing.

"Perhaps you're right. My writing will develop a new maturity if I alter my juvenile circumstances. I can see a phrase like that in the inevitable biography, the story of my early struggles on the way to literary triumph."

"I don't know what else to suggest. I was just thinking, like I said, something new …"

Something new, sure. Primal scream therapy? Prayer? Maybe self-mutilation. Could I do it? Certainly. I'd hack off a hand if I thought it would get me an agent and a deal. If only it were that simple. Chop off the limb, write a novel that somebody would think worth reading.

But it was good advice. I needed to try something new, get over my self-pity, let the ridiculous jealousy ebb. In a way, I got lucky right then, seeing myself from the outside, so hateful, self-involved. Like certain literary characters that mean something to me.

BACK WHEN TAYLOR AND I MET, HIS FAMILY HAD A DOG, A yellow Lab, Mavis. I didn't like her much, though I didn't hate her in the active way I later came to feel about Joseph, always slinking about looking for a rub. Old Mavis lay around their place, sleeping. When Taylor passed her, he'd lean over and scratch her head. Mavis would wake, look up at him and thump her tail on the floor.

I was fifteen. I'd gone over to Taylor's house. We were going to head off together, maybe see a movie or just cruise around downtown. Taylor, recently grown fastidious, had decided at the last moment to take a shower. "Wait in the living room," Taylor's father said. "It's more comfortable." It wasn't any more comfortable than their den, but Taylor's parents looked for ways to show they respected me. From the beginning they were as happy for Taylor as my parents were for me when we became friends.

I browsed through the books in a big case, focused soon on a row of volumes by a single author. I was reading a jacket blurb when Taylor's dad returned. "Do you know her?" he said.

"No. Is she good?" Stupid question. They wouldn't have fifteen books by the same author if she weren't good.

"She's Canada's greatest writer," he said. He smiled, and I guessed he was thinking that I'd soon test that opinion out on my mother. "She'll win the Nobel one of these years, if there's any justice. Till then, she's got our dog named after her."

A few minutes later Taylor entered, done with his preparations. "Let's go," he said.

"I can't."

I was standing beside the bookcase. I hadn't moved since I'd pulled *The Other Paris* off the shelf and begun reading.

"Are you okay? You look a bit weird."

"Have you …? This … Here." I took *Green Water, Green Sky* off the shelf and handed it to him, then went back to my reading. I was reading as I walked across the room to a chair and sat down.

Every other writer I'd enjoyed and admired, even Fitzgerald, still my favourite then, was a child. That first story—what was going on? I barely understood, and yet I recognized. People were like this. They loathed each other. They failed. It had something to do with World War Two, probably. But not just that. How did she do it? What was the trick? How could a story be about its sentences and its characters at the same time? How could a writer hate people so much and yet … not? And be so funny?

When I looked up intermittently, I found Taylor in different postures, finally lying on his back on the couch, holding his book above his face. I thought I'd stop. Then I'd read just one more story. Another.

"Boys. It's getting rather late," said Taylor's mother. Taylor put his book down and stood up. I stood up.

"Yeah, I should be getting home," I said.

The next day I wasn't moved to seek out more. I didn't pick up another Gallant for weeks. Taylor raced through his father's complete set that winter, but I took years to complete the oeuvre. I'd reread bits, read sentences out loud. Just take my time. Each new story collection took months to assimilate.

WHEN I GOT HOME AFTER THAT SESSION AT THE BILLY Bishop with Taylor, I hid in my room. For a while I sat on my bed. I had a stack of books on a table, novels I'd been looking forward to reading. I tried a few and couldn't get past a couple of paragraphs.

I stood in front of my bookshelves, nothing close to a plan in mind. The spines came in and out of focus. I ran my hand over them. I pulled a few out an inch or so and nudged them back. I took Gallant's *In Transit* off the shelf and sat on the bed again, the book in my lap.

I flipped through the pages and then stopped at "April Fish." It's short, and I read it, not remembering at first, but then yes, of course. Such ruthlessness. What did the *New Yorker* editor who took it on think? "Ah yes, this'll do, three amusing pages to dramatize a crushing indictment of all of Western civilization. Lovely, really."

I set the book down on my desk, open to the story, and I began to write.

Why should it be so difficult? I knew nothing about grammar, it turned out. Parts of speech? I'm an ignoramus. But the project insisted on itself. I was rewriting "April Fish": my new version— syntactically identical to the original, word for word. My nouns replaced hers, my prepositions, verbs, substituted for the originals. My story would duplicate her rhythms, her patterns of summary and dialogue, but it would be new. Will this do the trick, Taylor? Fat chance. I should think, instead, about what it means, that I find this so difficult. An hour to produce a new sentence, and that sentence barely makes sense.

I would have given up again. But I had no other ideas. Failing here would just be too much.

I didn't call Taylor, and I didn't hear from him. He was giving me time to recover, to do as I'd promised and be happy for him. And then, after a while, I began to notice my anxiety shifting, even as I accomplished so little, one mediocre scene after another. I felt no better about the quality of the work I was producing, but I realized I was only pretending to care.

Mavis, this is for you. I should have done this long ago. A clumsy piano student struggles through some Bach, an unskilled painter copies a Rembrandt. A failed beginner imitates Mavis Gallant. Says "thank you."

At the end of another afternoon Kits Point walk, rapping about Taylor's new project, he at length with the thoughts and plans, me with the encouraging little interjections, we stopped on the beach and he turned his back to me. He picked up a few stones and threw them into the waves. Then he turned around. "If I could've left the room …" he said.

Two months later, when I'd finally reached the end, Taylor over for a visit, I told him about my rewrite project. He insisted on reading it, right then.

When he finished he danced a little jig, slapping his knees with the manuscript, laughing. A jig was not characteristic of lanky, injury-prone Taylor. No, Canada's hottest new novelist was not a man for spontaneous dancing.

"It's a hoot, isn't it?" I said, laughing with him.

"It's way better than a hoot." He slapped his knees with the papers again.

I guessed he was happy that I'd successfully completed the exercise, that the effect had amused, and that my persistence impressed. All true, but he also thought the new "story" had something special and strange. He said that it deserved to be published.

It took some convincing, but I sent it off. *The Capilano Review*, always open to this kind of thing, agreed with Taylor and took the story along with a brief account of my experiment. Not a novel, not a story collection, but still, a publication. Baby step.

Even when optimistic, I hadn't expected to learn anything concrete from my Gallant project. I just hoped. I began a new novel, drunk with longing.

I wrote a sentence. What was that? It was only a sentence. The next one, also, just prose, as usual. So, what was this change? I could hear it. As surely as I knew I'd discovered something important when I first read Gallant, I understood that a change had come. Every phrase emerged as a unit of sound, without my reading aloud, but as the words came and as they appeared on the screen. I didn't do a lot of revising to achieve an effect, I just … wrote differently; my identity had become the words and sentences themselves. Could it be a placebo? Who cares. Give me a placebo, please, doctor. Watch me gulp it down and write.

Taylor saw it when he read the finished draft of *Monica Documented*, and you know the story of the publication and the Ethel Wilson prize. It made things easier for the two of us, no longer a strain to find some way to share power. Everybody in every relationship needs to share power.

THAT NIGHT, BACK TO THAT NIGHT, THE BIG NASTINESS with Jessica, unprecedented worst. Jessica tossing and turning, frustration and angry disappointment. I, unmoving, locked into my cycle of questions and regrets, hate and anger. That different thing—it would have to be more than another clever writing exercise, more than an honest thank you to one of my gods. What? Then my old enemy, my neck, began to seize me once more, first an ache, deepening, a warmth, hot paralysis, my damned neck, a lot to do with what had happened and what would follow. Let me explain.

16

Post-Winnipeg and the Earl Birney affair, my neck hurt. Sometimes it hurt so much that if I sat, I had to steel myself to stand. The inflamed muscles would engage as my body shifted forward, igniting a flash fire across my shoulders and down my spine. Sneezing or coughing—just death; inadvertent sudden movement—Hell. During these attacks I simply had to wait, walking oh so slowly, turning my whole body in order to face someone not in my line of sight.

It was precisely the behaviour that had added up to asshole, according to the *Winnipeg Arts Review*. Take a look at the photos you can find on-line from my bit as judge for the Ethel Wilson contest. I'm at the gala, standing, facing the camera, while others just turn their heads. Or I look at someone while that someone faces the camera. In every shot, I look like a prick or a moron.

I took therapeutic massage. I thought it did me some good, but I hadn't received the last scheduled treatment before my neck seized again. The therapist suggested I see a chiropractor.

And so, down the months—chiropractor, acupuncturist, chiropractor, physio, a better physio, new and better acupuncturist, on, on, and on: failures all. I tried yoga, Feldenkrais, and tai chi. We installed a massage attachment on the showerhead, changed mattress and pillows. On an anti-inflammatory diet I curried up with scary quantities of turmeric and achieved nothing.

Finally, intramuscular stimulation, IMS for short. It's like acupuncture, a bit, but one feels the needles. It was all the thing for intractable necks and backs.

People's pain is boring. More detail risks entirely derailing any narrative momentum. But one scene, please: me and the boys.

I signed up for the prescribed ten sessions of IMS. I would experience some discomfort, said the eager young woman poised to stab needles into knotted neck muscles. She smiled.

When I staggered out the first time, a guy standing by the door gave me a curious look. I wasn't in the mood. "Did you want something?"

He peered around me. "I wanted to see what she looked like, you know, the *beeitch* who made you scream that way."

She assured me the treatments would work. So confident. My body rebelled, and I hurt everywhere.

"It's normal. It's a muscular adjustment. With a few more sessions, you'll notice a big improvement."

Four times, I submitted. Now, my passivity shames me. But perhaps it's helpful for us to encounter our horrible weakness before the figure that embodies so much, the publicly insured practitioner—science and the state, vicious partners in evil.

I arrived home after the fourth appointment. Through the door, down the hallway, into the living room: to my knees I fell, then over on my side, fetal. I wish the memory were less clear, the trauma not so enduring. I could observe myself observing that sweat soaked my shirt. Pointless to try not to weep.

A few sobbing minutes, then Gavin and Leo arrived home from school.

"Dad?"

"Dad?"

I forced myself together. Still lying on my side, invalid, I gave a few instructions, and the boys prepared dinner. By the time Jessica came home I had made it to the breakfast nook, and the boys said nothing when they served the meal. Of course, Jessica could tell something was terribly wrong, our sons looking at me, at her, scared as hell. But they waited, Gavin and Leo, for me, until I explained.

Maybe I don't wish for forgetfulness. I remember the agony and I can feel the greasy pain-sweat. Sobs burst out of my gut. But I see Gavin and Leo. And I need to say this, in my defence, for you to keep in mind as you read what comes next; I need to say that I do not underestimate. Them. What they mean to me.

The obvious analysis occurred to me, as it has to you—I'm confident of that. The neck onset, you'll recall, coincided with a reward for my return to writing—mediocre, jokey sonnets, but still, writing, and a reward, the Earl Birney Prize. This new flare-up, that same structure: an article written, praise and recognition following, and ouch, ouch, ouch. Want to cure your neck problems, Gordon? See Taylor. Deal with the years of loss. Show some courage, man.

Or the courageous thing to do was to live with it, accept that pain, because if Taylor wanted to hear from me, I'd have heard from him, or I'd have heard from Yvonne, an update on that note gouged in ballpoint.

I LIVED WITH IT THROUGH THE NIGHT OF MY BIG METAPHOR argument with Jessica. I got out of bed and shuffled through the house, trying to move without moving, failing to sleep while sitting in my office chair. In my slippers I stepped outside and journeyed down the dark street, cautiously, not lifting my feet, not thinking or dreaming, just suffering into the night.

The swooshing of a few cars on The Drive, the night-sighs of the city, and then, out of the quiet, an ambulance siren. It wailed faintly in the distance, and I was still on Kitchener Street but I was back in Madrid: sirens, shouts, the waiter hurling Spanish curses at me, the televised horror. *Guernica*, the boys so wounded. Jessica withdrawing.

It all mixed up there in the night—the terror, my dying marriage. Were my feelings about Madrid just projections of despair over what Jessica and I had come to? The reverse? Were we each mistaking a shell-shock loss of joy and will for the other's failure?

As best as I could, I hurried home. I'd wake her. Insist that we be kind and honest as we talked to each other. But in our room, my neck screaming now, I looked down at her sleeping so deep, relaxed long breaths, and my resentment took me again. It was her. Her fault.

Before anyone else got up in the morning I left, an excruciating bus ride over to Douglas Park.

"I'm going to be on a panel, 'Reading Terrorism.'" At the Y."

Pause. The pause extends. Then laughter, Mum's and mine, because "the Y" can only mean the YMHA on Manhattan's Upper East Side. I'm not much disappointed by the contrast here: no celebratory laughter marked earlier successes—book contracts, prizes, the novels themselves.

Nobody else I knew would've understood without some elaboration. Maybe, right then, we were closer than we'd ever been, closer than when she stayed up with me (all night, I say), closer than when she said "sure, you can buy a pennant," even closer than when I sat across from her, and she sat on her couch, and she finished it, my first published novel, put it down, got up, walked out of the room.

"You're a snot-nosed kid," she said.

My mother's laughter was much more important than the muscle spasms that still gripped my neck, at takeoff, New York bound.

"I'VE GOT A STIFF NECK, SO I APOLOGIZE FOR NOT BEING ABLE to turn to face people."

"You should get a massage," said our moderator.

Afterward, all my nuances having been shared and appreciated, came the obligatory milling, down there in front of the stage. I tried to say with my frightened eyes, please, be careful, don't shake my hand vigorously, don't touch me at all.

People were pretty considerate. I told myself, it'll pass, Gordon. You'll survive. I told myself this and then I could sense someone standing behind me, too close.

But there was no danger. Or … there was. There was!

I froze, embodied vengeance inches away from my back. Some trick of synchronicity had dipped into my sorrow, my failure, my deep culpability, and conjured up an assassin.

My neck burned. Paralyzed, I waited for the knife blade. The fearsome memories rushed into that moment, images from a time when so many had wanted to hurt me, and worse.

17

◾ ◾

"Fill out your organ donation card, asshole. Your time is coming."

"You'll be donating your own organs soon."

"Kill yourself and donate your organs. Your books are shit."

"Of course you should be afraid," said Jessica. "Jesus."

This was back in my glory days, Gordon Bridge the shiny new thing on the Can Lit scene. Leo was only a few months old, and fatherhood and fame puffed me up, so I'd ignored the first threats. When they kept coming, I showed them to Jessica. She took my face in her hands, cool hands on my cheeks, and she looked in my eyes. "I'm your protection. You need to tell me these things, right away."

She dialled and then handed me the phone. "The police. Tell them." She stood beside me, hand on my arm, while I did just that.

I could understand the anger. These are heavy, emotional cases. If you read *Vancouver Flood* you'll remember the bit where it's early June, and Royce, his illness advanced, is teetering, and Andora is stricken, and together they're reading the papers and watching the news.

The material leading to that moment is the strongest in the novel. The reader doesn't know. Understanding emerges, and then, despite sympathy, horror: Royce and Andora, near the crisis, hoping to hear of fatal car accidents. Early June, high-school grad season, let's face it—it's the best time of year for such nightmares: healthy teens, celebrate their pending release, overestimate their road skills, and then, brains dead, bodies pumping along for a few machine-supported minutes, they offer up fresh, pink organs to the dialysis-dependent, the lung-frozen, the heart-clotted desperate ones. It's a sad truth, but the truth part is not enough justification for some. It doesn't excuse saying such things, in print, in a novel everyone could read, exposing them.

A police detective visited—rather smart guy. He asked to read the passage upsetting so many, which I thought a very sensible place to start. He sat on the couch for about ten minutes. You could read those couple of pages in much less time, but he took care. I saw his lips move slightly, but you'd be surprised how many people do that; it's no sign of illiteracy. Near the end, his eyebrows went up, and then he showed himself a sophisticated critic indeed.

"This bit here, at the end—that's what's causing the problem, isn't it?"

He put a finger on the spot. He'd read on from the passage I'd shown him.

Andora and Royce aren't happy about what they're doing; they feel just sick about it. But they feel justified too. They say to themselves that they're not hoping for people to be killed. They're only wishing that if people die, they've thought to donate their organs, so Royce can get a liver and live on. They don't go out and try to cause accidents, flashing mirrors into drivers' eyes, nothing like that. But still, they need to apologize to themselves for what they're doing.

"The thing is, you're sort of doing the same thing, what you say right here."

"I don't understand, Detective."

He read: "'Thus our longing, to be to others what we are to ourselves. To be ends. Thus our society, our world that forces us to use others as means.' These characters here, Royce and Andora.

They're a means to you, aren't they? You use them to get the point across."

Correct, okay, but they're fictional. He was probably also right about the other, what really ate at people. I'd like to think so, that at least something subtle provoked the murderous thoughts. Full disclosure here: the worst thing? The passage. What embarrassing crap. Such pretentious, awkward, intrusive didacticism, and it could get me killed. It was a rather extreme way to get the lesson that the metaphor must always speak for itself.

The messages stopped, and the police never found any suspects. I grew pretty scared there for a time. So, Salman, I know it's not on the same scale, but I understand a little. You too, Philip.

In fact, Philip Roth was the more germane case, to me, at the precise moment of my more-than-panic, fear-frozen at the YMHA. Years back he was a self-hating, anti-Semitic Jew, according to a few jerks who felt accused by those great stories in *Goodbye, Columbus*, and for such a sin he did not deserve to live. Imagine the person who takes this imagined insult to his dignity so deeply. This person is crazy and dangerous.

For too long Roth's public appearances were terrifying. One was worse than the others. The cold-sweat-inducing, paranoia-building crusher. At the Y.

ON A BETTER NECK DAY I WOULD HAVE HAD THE COURAGE to turn and look over my shoulder. As it was, I just stood there. Hey, Philip, my sweat too. It's cold. Also, my lungs. Shit! My lungs! They're not working! I'm trying to breathe. What's wrong with my damned ... my lungs?

The conversation lapsed when politeness called for a pause and then my contribution. People stared at me. Would someone protect me? Would I faint? Wouldn't someone see, and leap to my aid? C'mon, a chance to be a hero. "Bystander Saves Novelist." Somebody!

Then I felt a hand, light touch, on the back of my neck. Soft voice: "Let it go now." The hand stayed, and I didn't move. "Let it go," she said again.

Things can change so quickly. The fear, gone. My neck—the pain, dissolving.

18

■ ■

I turned to face a very short, plump woman of about my age, smiling broadly up at me.

"Thank you," I said.

"You're welcome."

"I'm Gordon." I stuck out my hand.

"I know." She laughed. "Trudy."

The relief dizzied me.

"You fixed my neck."

"It's not permanent. You need more treatments." She gave me a card, which identified her as a "healer." I looked from the card to her.

"I'm not allowed to call myself a massage therapist. So I'm an exotic healer, from The Islands, you know. Trinidad."

"'When the Yankee come to ...'" I said.

"Ah, yes, that wonderful song celebrating the prostitution of our women. The original, you know, is rather more political than your Andrews Sisters version."

"I'm sorry ... I didn't mean."

"It's all right, Gordon. I will try to find a way to make you pay."

"I'd like that."

She laughed some more. "You do need to come to see me. For your neck."

I made an appointment for the next morning. I had three more days in New York, and I would make the best of them.

She was right about my neck, which started tensing up again not long after the Y business wrapped up. I squeezed into a Tribeca wine bar that I'd found on a list of *New Yorker* recommendations, and by the time I'd finished my duck confit and most of a litre of Cab/Sauv that was probably great, my exclusive train of pain had come in again, picked me up at Just Functioning and dropped me off at Agonyville.

A bit of jostling on my way out the door, nothing at all rude, just the inevitable in such a crowd in such a place, and Christ-oh-Christ, had it ever been worse? Was it connected to Trudy, a devil perhaps, already exacting the ultimate price for the cursed wish granted? My soul certainly seemed at risk, as I was ready to bargain anything to make this piercing, raking pain go away. I confess! I distributed the pamphlets! I said the host is just bread! Yes, my doctor, my accountant, my wife, they've all helped Al-Qaeda! I take it back! The earth does not move! Make it stop!

I think now that this episode was probably no worse than others had been. The difference lay elsewhere, in me. I couldn't, couldn't bear any more. No more.

A cab pulled up without my signalling, and, sure it would take me on a downward journey, I hunched my crippled self in the back.

FACE DOWN ON THE MASSAGE TABLE. TRUDY PLACED HER hand on the back of my neck, and the pain eased. She wasn't doing anything at all, that woman, just resting her hand and talking to me.

She set her other hand down alongside. She moved her hands down my spine, slowly, stopping each in place. "I'm going to move my hands again, Gordon. Now, you'll feel my hand on the back of your head. I'm going to hold your arms now." And, every few minutes, "Be good to yourself, Gordon. Let it go," and "You can let it go now."

When she asked me to roll over I did so without pain. With a cloth she wiped tears from my face. I told her about the episode I'd had, beginning the night before.

"It won't happen again, but don't drink tonight. Don't have anything to drink for the next few days."

Temperance: I pledged it from that moment forward.

"You aren't cured," she said when the hour ended, and I sat up on the table, experimentally turning my head.

"I'll do anything you say."

"Just no drinking, and nothing, oh, nothing such as, no handball, no karate."

"No. Of course."

"You should see me the next two mornings. It would be wise even to go on longer, if you can."

"I can't," I said.

"All right then, but Gordon."

"Yes."

"For now. Also, for some days, it would be best if you did not have sex."

19

■ ■

No self-medicating immediately after take-off. Soda water, ice, cool reflection.

Trudy and I hadn't really been flirting during that first encounter, with my cringe-inducing song quotation, her joking threat. It was just parody. Or is flirting always parodic? It's imitation of romance. Flirting is pretending to flirt. "I don't know how far you can go," says Bogart. "A lot depends on who's in the saddle," says Bacall. They're joking. But it gets to the point where the joke will lead to an imitation of a kiss, a caress, and then an imitation of sex that strains to be seen as imitation. Consider the point where it produces true children.

This shift happens in all kinds of exchanges. Take my argument with Jessica, a good example for me to be taking as the plane crossed westward over the Rockies. Jessica is no kind of ignorant, literal-minded lawyer and has never thought about my work what she said she thought. We'd been collaborating on a parody, the way those who flirt always collaborate. We parodied an argument, a last-ditch effort to shift the weight crushing us.

What I saw on my return is that I didn't feel like taking anything up again, and neither did Jessica. We avoided each other. We did it the common way two people who have been close for a long time can continue to speak and be together, and yet agree to matter to each other very, very little.

Trudy's voice stayed with me. "Let it go." What might "it" be? Jessica, ghosting around in some other dimension I didn't want to reach, passing through walls, through me? Certainly not Gavin, all gentle affection, asking me for advice about an essay. Not Leo.

Gavin suggested a Trout Lake walk one evening. "I'll pass," Leo said, not distant like his mother, not anxious-empathetic like his brother, but angry, confused, huddling up to protect himself. "I've got too much homework."

He headed upstairs, and I followed soon after.

"What?" he said, sitting at his desk, books indeed at the ready, looking up at me standing in the doorway.

I had never recognized myself in Leo. He was sixteen, much taller than me by then, nearing six feet, broad shoulders and a frame that would eventually fill in to be muscular, like Jessica's father. So, obviously, not like me physically. But oh, Leo, in those final days I hoped I hadn't passed on my emotional stupidity to you. Had Mum ever looked at me and shuddered the way I was shuddering, some flaw of hers reflected back so cruelly? Don't do this, Leo. Your father's not the right model for you with crisis looming.

"Nothing. I just wanted to make sure you were okay."

"Why wouldn't I be okay?"

Because of how much we're alike.

THE SIMILARITY HAD BEEN CLAIMED YEARS BEFORE. I JUST hadn't accepted.

Jessica and I took a few days, leaving the boys with Mum and Dad, the first time we'd been away from them overnight. Leo and Gavin were so excited when we told them they'd be spending the weekend with Grandma and Grandpa that we were a little perturbed. Sure, Mum and Dad were great with the kids. Mum went so far as to be silly with them. A lifetime of effort and concentration could be shifted aside, to be taken up later without worry that it would have weakened or diminished her.

"Won't you miss us even a little bit?"

"Maybe a little bit."

"Maybe a teeny-weeny bit."

I insisted that Mum do the driving if they went anywhere by car, and that whatever she said to Dad while they were travelling, his only response would be "keep your eyes on the road." Dad was a terrible driver—nervous, second-guessing himself into near catastrophes. Mum transformed behind the wheel, became overconfident and weirdly voluble. She whipped her head around to make eye contact with everybody, talking, all while changing lanes, turning left, passing. But she could be okay if all her passengers refused to respond.

Their incompetence behind the wheel had become clear to me over the years following our Disneyland trip. As I grew up and took the occasional ride with friends' parents, I learned from the obvious contrast that something was wrong with motorists Mum and Dad, and I began to nag them. I insisted that they take a taxi to their concerts—night driving, for them, was insane. When I got my licence at sixteen I drove them myself.

"Mum drives. Dad shuts her up and she keeps her eyes on the road. Promise."

"We promise."

"Swear by my sword."

"We swear it."

Off to Seattle went Jessica and I, Experience Museum bound.

On our way home, calling from the border to predict an arrival time, my cell died, and Jessica hadn't brought hers. The wait at the crossing took a tedious hour, and traffic through the Massey Tunnel crawled. Three more hours altogether, but the dying cell had killed our opportunity to warn of delay.

Gavin rushed to us for a hug. "You're back! I missed you!" We gobbled this up and then looked for Leo. He was easily found, reading in the living room. He wouldn't speak to us. His silence continued on the ride home.

Jessica persisted. "Come on, Leo. What's wrong?"

Finally he deigned—clearly he was deigning—to reply. "What took you?"

Jessica tried to explain, and then I took a turn. No dice. Each time, indignant: "No. What took you?" Finally, Jessica just said that she was sorry, and on our next trip they'd both come with us.

That did it, a deluge of tears, but then, through his sobs: "No. Next time I'll go, and I'll leave *you* behind, and then *you'll* know how it feels." He actually wagged an index finger at us.

After they were in bed, Jessica asked me, "Is it genetic or learned?"

"What?"

"Leo."

"What?"

"You don't see it?"

It had been a long day and I was a little irritated. "I'm not going to say 'what' again."

"He's just like you. He's you. Gunnysacking his feelings. Then it all comes out. The pain. The need for retribution."

"And that's me."

"I thought you knew."

"I'm not ... I don't really think of myself as, y'know, a horrible, immature person."

"You think Leo is horrible and immature."

"I think he's six years old. The standards for me are a bit different."

"Were you"—she began laughing—"were you anal retentive? Did you do that thing?"

She wasn't laughing meanly. I wasn't angry. "I've never asked," I said. "I was snot-nosed, like Gavin, remember? I haven't sought to confirm the other label. You can see, can't you, that I wouldn't seek it out."

Leo had a retentive phase when he was very young. (Sorry, Leo. You can take this, right?) A day, another day, a third: no action. Leo getting rather moody, not easily motivated to eat, play, talk, bathe. Then, he gathers a few toys. He wedges himself into a corner, between the wall and a stereo speaker in the living room. He's at attention, face tense, I note from a distance.

"Daddy, bring me more toys," he cries. I grab his Brave Daniel doll, his xylophone, and his rock collection (three gorgeous rocks, delightful gift from Taylor). I drop them all into the magic semi-circle he's created—a little, protective, coherent barrier between him and the disorganized, unowned world. I discreetly withdraw till I hear him cry out again, louder now, "Daddy! More toys!" and I obey, and again later, at a high pitch of sharp urgency, "Toys! Toys!" I come running with handfuls of whatever I think might count, stuffed animals, books, anything, dropping them for him to arrange in the deepening redoubt he's constructing, then skedaddling out of sight to let him battle his existential foe in private.

And so, protected by the solid substance that affirms his place against the threat of what must be given up, shielded by the aura of his possessions, he shits in his diaper, a real giant crap, I can attest as a direct witness.

SO, I WONDERED, THOSE DAYS FOLLOWING MY RETURN, WAS it some ancient anger that I was gunnysacking in my damned neck? Had I sought, less successfully than little Leo, to surround myself with marks of my presence in this world, hoping they would accumulate enough substance and weight for me to gain the courage to release? Go ahead, Gordon, launch a heaping big steaming one, right here, right now. You'll feel better.

Leo always felt better. He'd soon be laughing and singing, a delight, shining away. I fed him mashed-up stewed prunes to try to sustain that delight, and it sometimes worked, a bit.

ON MY RETURN FROM NEW YORK I DIDN'T SAY ANYTHING about the change Trudy had wrought. Would somebody notice me swivelling my head around, looking over there, then there, rapturous with the ease, the lubricated, frictionless, free-swinging facility of my liberated neck? No.

With my neck pain smacked down, would the emotions responsible for it pop up elsewhere, maybe crippling plantar fasciitis, or a burning sensation, or some disastrous autoimmune attack? I could only wait and see.

Through the course of the week I began to lose my appetite, and I noticed that Jessica too was serving herself ever-smaller portions.

It was no surprise that Gavin took the final shot at repairs: "The fish is really good, Dad. Why don't you have some more?"

I took a small piece. He winced.

JESSICA SAT ON THE BED, DISTANT, WAITING TO GET IT DONE. I closed the door behind me and leaned back against it. "I …"

"Go ahead, Gordon."

"I have to leave."

She looked down. She kneaded the duvet on either side of her. She looked at me and sighed. "I think it's your job to tell them."

"Tomorrow, after school."

The next morning, I walked up to Trout Lake. I could have paused several times a block, remembering moments, conversations, and jokes.

Such failure. I was not just a person who had failed, not so much as any kind of person, rather an empty … a thing, a thing that should have been a person but was only and entirely just … failure.

Impossible that my body could carry on, that I breathed, the blood flowed, my muscles moved, my neck continued free and easy. Why was there no stronger connection between my physical self, which continued to live, and the dead moral me?

I stayed at the lake for a while then trudged back.

Jessica phoned from the office. "Wait till I get home, okay? Let's do it together."

"Thanks."

"I'm not doing it for you."

"I know. Thanks."

We ate dinner, in a manner of speaking. "Hey, guys?" I said when they'd cleared the table and were about to leave. Maybe they were hurrying, hoping to avoid.

They stood side by side.

"We've got something important to say," said Jessica.

My turn. Gavin clamped his hand over his mouth. Leo stared at me. Get it over with, Gordon. "Your mother and I are separating. I'm going to be leaving. I'm moving out."

Leo gripped Gavin's shoulder with one hand. He extended his other arm toward us, palm up, straight-arming a tackler, a stop sign before I could begin the explanation. "Gavin," he said. He turned Gavin toward him, stepped forward and pivoted so his back was to us. "Gavin!" He stood between us and Gavin, interposed, facing his younger brother and cutting us off. "C'mon!" He put his other hand on Gavin's other shoulder and moved closer. "This isn't your failure! Gavin!"

I couldn't see Gavin's face, but I could see his body shaking. Jessica and I remained silent. Disqualified.

"Gavin! You're my brother!" Leo pushed him now, gently toward the door, and Gavin shuffled backward, Leo's hands still on his shoulders, his face inches away. "We're brothers," Leo said, crying, voice choking. "They did this, Gavin. Don't, don't, don't," and then they left the room. I looked at Jessica. She had turned her frail back to me. She was leaning over as though to catch her breath, hands on her thighs. It was done.

III

JOSEPH IS
HAVING DIFFICULTIES

20

■ ■

"Change," said my father. The red light changed to green.

My father the magician made the light change. Later, after further demonstrations of his power, in a grand leap toward cynicism, I thought only that he magically sensed when it would change.

I wasn't disillusioned when I figured out how he did it, watching green turn to yellow in the signal facing the intersecting traffic. If anything, that simple trick impressed me even more. Achieving mystery with such a device: better than magic, or maybe magic itself.

My first attempt to replicate the trick with Leo and Gavin flopped. They didn't watch the light, didn't care, and so my power registered not at all.

I tried again later, hoping that a few months of child development would lead to a better result. Why did I want to fool my young sons and also impress them? Wanting to imitate my father and so affirm to myself my own adulthood, I suppose, which is not that bad a desire to have, but such a trivial expression of it? A bit embarrassing.

"I can do that too, Dad," said Leo.

Then—whisper, whisper—"I can do it too," said Gavin.

Perhaps the difference had to do with their having each other. They were, compared to me, less focused on their parents. Each of their child's worlds buttressed the other's, giving them more power, me less. Entirely healthy. Something to be grateful for, not frustrated by.

Recall, if you will, the scene of Mum's silent critique of my youthful story about marital discord. Picture me again, in the hallway, outside her study, in my hands the manuscript freshly wrested from the dot-matrix printer. I stand poised at Mum's study door, waiting to enter, when I regard her small movements, her shift in posture, and infer a judgment. My story is not good.

Did you pause at that point in the narrative? Did you detect some unintentional irony? Maybe you didn't share my confidence that I knew what Mum was telling me. You suspected she wasn't telling me much at all, in fact, so my response revealed stuff about me as a child, but little about my mother—not her judgments, mood, anything.

Sorry. I disagree.

I knew that she didn't know what I'd written. She didn't have ESP. She hadn't snooped on me. But she knew what I'd been up to—that wouldn't have been hard to figure out: the fever the first night, her glance at the manuscript on her way out of my room, all my writing in the days that followed, my young artist's intense silence at mealtimes, and of course the urgent request for a typewriter.

She knew how long I'd been working on the story—not long enough. Most importantly, she knew why I'd ventured down the hallway to see her. Why? For encouragement and praise.

If I wanted praise, I didn't deserve it. That's what I understood from her shrug, the arch of her back, her unwavering gaze on the paper in the Selectric: no acknowledgement for you, Gordon. If the story were good, you would know. You wouldn't need anyone to tell you so.

Asking means not deserving. Harsh doctrine.

ONE WAY OR ANOTHER, FOR YEARS, SHE'D BEEN TEACHING me that central lesson: the important rewards are internal—a key point for her, an obscure, underpaid book reviewer. And I, I'd been focused, oh boy, keenly focused on my mother. No siblings, Dad in the gentle background. No distracting friends, pre-Taylor. Could I detect meaning in a shrug, judgment in a shift in weight? Could I? If you're an only child, please, go ahead, answer that question for everyone else. Don't shout.

Now, at this moment, I'd like to argue with her. Mum, there is no such thing as an absolutely internal reward. Satisfaction in an accomplishment is empty without some sense of that accomplishment in relation to another. We're nothing without others, Mum; you got that one right. Was that what you were doing, standing in front of the birdbath? Silently atoning, once a year, for yet again forgetting about all us others?

I'D NOT PLANNED ANYTHING, AND I HAD NOWHERE TO GO. I walked over to The Drive, wandered south, and from The Calabria I texted the boys. I ordered coffee, but I couldn't drink it. I plodded up the hill past cafés and restaurants then walked back to where I'd started.

Leo replied an hour later to say that Gavin was okay, which meant, I guessed, that Leo's intervention had taken hold of his brother and brought him back from the verge of some devastating decompensation. Good buttressing, Leo.

My neck still felt fine. It felt permanent, even though Trudy had said I needed more treatments. Well, if we follow up on that psychosomatic business, here we have it, I thought, the new expression of the old hurt: deny the problem with Taylor; get a stiff neck. Make the stiff neck disappear; lose my family. I'm playing whack-a-mole, and the moles are getting vicious.

Had the moment arrived? Take all this despair and run with it, over to Taylor, probably still with Yvonne in their West End place. Take advantage of the evident pain, let him see me at my end, tell him that I've suffered enough, my writing block, my neck, and now this: a heavy payment, biblical suffering, earned forgiveness.

I could do it. Taylor would be overwhelmed, would have to listen and respond. And then, what changes might follow, what would come? I told myself that I thought of no reward and knew that I lied, saw myself at the computer, writing, novelist Gordon Bridge writing again, free of the old accusing voice, guilt-free.

I hailed a cab. I gave the driver the address.

The rather Hollywood vision, me sobbing, on my knees perhaps, and Taylor too, breaking down, forgiving, friendship restored—well, it faded pretty quickly as I headed west. A big scene was not the way to approach Taylor. Years had passed since Yvonne's threat of catastrophe had commanded my silence. I could see her note before me still, could see that something I didn't understand was at stake. If ever I were to contact him again, I'd need to be careful. I could reference these losses, sure, but not with the emotional circus—desperate, bad novelist grabbing a reader by the lapels: "sympathize with my character!"

So, where would I go? I had nobody else to turn to. No brothers or sisters. No friend. Only child said to cab driver, "Um, sorry, I need to go somewhere else. Twenty-third and Willow. It's just south of Douglas Park."

MUM WEPT. SHE WAVED HER HAND NO, KEEP AWAY, THOUGH nobody was moving, and she wept some more. Dad turned grey.

"I had no idea," said Dad. "You never said anything."

"I know it's a shock."

Mum got up and went to the bathroom, from where we heard the honk as she blew her nose.

"How did the boys react?" she said when she returned.

"You know. Leo helped Gavin."

Joseph walked in and slunk over to me, asking to be petted. Stupid, indiscriminate cat. He rubbed against my leg and I ignored him.

"What are you going to do?" said Dad.

"I don't know."

Mum looked at me and then looked away. Acknowledgment? Not quite. Judgment? Look at her, shrinking back into the chair. And Dad, defeated by her, probably wanting to say more, but just defeated.

So, I'm humiliated and sad, coming on despondent, and I discover the answer to Dad's question. Nothing here for me. You want someone, Gordon? Go where you'll find.

Out on the street, waiting for a bus, I used my phone and booked a flight. Then I called Jessica.

"I'm leaving late tonight for New York. I'll be back in a week or two."

"I see. Fine. We can work it out then." There was a lot in her neutral "I see." I was returning to New York, and there had to be a reason, and she could see that reason gathering form in the distance.

"Where are the boys?"

"They went out."

"I'll be back in a few minutes to get some stuff."

"I'll be here."

Such judgment. Such unfairness. All right, I screwed up, sure I did, but so did you, and we're both to blame, for Christ's sake. And does this failure erase everything? Was I never a good father? Are we the first family to split? Other men have left wives and have found that the line they crossed didn't put them on one side, humanity on the other.

I texted the boys again, burst of words. I was going away but I'd be back soon. I was still their father. My distance wouldn't mean anything less or different, not really.

A promise and a claim. By the time I was done I found myself gasping, like I'd just run a sprint. I sent the message without rereading.

A few minutes later I got a reply from Gavin:

Thanks, Dad. I love you.

I was back to Gordon Bridge, failure. I didn't deserve my sons; I deserved nothing, I had lost any right to any kind of place, function, or dignity. Stumbled home.

The boys returned before I left. Leo kept a hand on Gavin, gripping his shoulder or his arm, even while we hugged on the front steps as the cab waited. My knees fluttered, ready to give out. Only a striking view of how selfish this would be kept me upright.

"I'll see you soon. We've got lots to talk about."

"See you, Dad."

"See you soon."

I texted Trudy from the departure gate, asking for an appointment, and then I slept through the flight, a strange, deep slumber that I found on waking still numbed me—a welcome enough sensation. It persisted through the disorientation of baggage claim and customs at Newark Airport in the early morning.

A message. No, Trudy couldn't see me at her studio. She didn't work Tuesdays. But she could see me at her home, in Brooklyn, not far from her work.

Her message didn't express any surprise at my being back so soon, nor did she say anything about it when she greeted me at her door. Just "Gordon!" and reaching up, taking my cheeks in her warm hands.

I can't now remember a feeling of anything at all being celebrated as we rolled around on her futon, skinny little Gordon, plump little Trudy, laughing out of our clothes and into love. Just a glimpse—of what? A flash of austere beauty, in retreat.

21

"How do you know where to place your hands?"

"I don't mean to sound mystical, Gordon, but it feels as though my hands place themselves."

"And 'Let it go'? I don't suppose you've got any thoughts there. A hint perhaps of what I should be letting go of?"

"I have no idea of any of these things, Gordon. You tell me. Do you need to let go? Let go of what?"

"Could you always do this?"

"One day I'll tell you."

I could see through my frustration to a gladness that she should remain mysterious.

When Trudy had an opening, I showed at the studio for a free treatment, and when she didn't, I arrived at the end of the day and took her to dinner, or we returned to her cramped one-room apartment, where a meal I'd cooked simmered for us. Love each night turned out a simple and brief bit of fun, little resemblance to the intense, exhausting, obligatory works of high art on which Jessica and I had collaborated. Only weeks earlier I might have come up with something critical to say against that past, but now it seemed only the past, and the jolly, let's-get-to-the-essentials approach was the new me, and I liked it.

That apartment. Cramped, as I said. Also, overflowing with books. Bookshelves wherever they could be squeezed in, every wall space, up to the ceilings, fiction to the north, non-fiction, politics mainly, to the south. Those looming towers made me nervous, but inspection revealed pretty heavy-duty bolts and brackets, so a surprise Brooklyn tremor wouldn't see Gordon come to a poetic end, crushed by a library.

Yes, I conducted a search, not the first day, but soon after, and I found them quickly—the Bridge oeuvre tucked in on the left, second shelf from the top of the bookcase by the entrance, one side Elizabeth Bowen, Brontës the other, impressive company.

I didn't look for the "S" shelf.

"You have all my books."

"You sound surprised."

"Well, I don't assume. You were at the 'Reading Terrorism' evening, but I wouldn't assume ..."

"I'm a fan, Gordon. I suppose I thought you knew, but of course you wouldn't."

"So that's why you were there, to see me?"

"Well, no. It was the topic. You weren't listed when I bought my ticket. I think you were added at the last minute."

"Oh."

"But they were lucky to have you. Oh, Gordon, don't look like that. They were lucky to have you. They were probably thrilled when they saw your *LRB* article and thought you might be willing to appear on short notice. I was certainly thrilled."

She was so obviously trying to ease any injury to my pride, and succeeding at it, that it was funny.

"I believe they found getting speakers difficult. I heard somebody saying so afterward. People are somewhat fearful. A topic like that—they're concerned about who might appear."

"They thought a discussion about terrorism might draw terrorists?"

"Just unpleasant opinion. Anger."

One evening, dinner done, we traded childhood stories, sharing smiles at this obvious move to get to know each other.

"I've been to Canada. I was twelve. We have family in Montreal, and they wanted us all to join them, so we visited, to see."

"How was it?"

"I got sick and spent the entire vacation watching TV. It was most fascinating. *The Beachcombers*. My father wanted to make the move, but my mother said no. She found Montreal … unfriendly."

"Unfriendly."

"Yes. Not … welcoming. My mother observed that we weren't welcome."

"Montreal? It's got a pretty friendly reputation."

"Gordon. It was racist. That's what made me ill." A sudden leap to intensity, narrowed eyes, impatient because I'd needed it spelled out. And assessing. Would I resist the idea? One of our so-proudly celebrated models of Canadian diversity is racist enough to give a girl the flu?

"I'd like to meet your mother," I said. Won a nod, impatience gone, from the gaze, at least.

"I've been here two weeks," I said.

"That's true."

"I need to go back."

"Clearly."

"I want you to know …"

"I think we should wait, Gordon. To consider what we need to know."

AIRBORNE YET AGAIN, I CONSIDERED THAT I NEEDED TO know about Jessica, just how angry she would be when she learned of the plan I was forming. Outraged, almost certainly.

I said nothing to her at first—just the obvious practicalities, both of us calm. We sat at the computer, and we divided our money and our investments in half, creating new accounts and portfolios. I'd pay support for as long as the boys stayed with her.

We scanned the real estate listings for recent sales of similar houses in the neighbourhood, and we came up with a formula, and then we arrived at a price. Jessica paid me half, emptying a bunch of her investments without a blink.

"Do we need to do anything else?" I asked. "A separation agreement?"

"God, no. Nothing involving lawyers."

Then I blinked. Then she did. That is, I sniffled, once, and then again, and in seconds I was weeping, and Jessica set in to howling, and we harmonized our horror and sorrow, what a lot we'd managed to lose, the mourning that needed doing still.

The enraged Jessica I'd been imagining—that vision felt so unfair to her. She knew me so well. She had loved me. Perhaps, imagining her anger and doubting me and Trudy, I'd been projecting my own second thoughts, my lack of confidence.

"Jessica."

She was standing, wiping off smeared makeup with a tissue. She glanced down at me, sitting at her desk. Her eyes, not wide, but guarded, fearful.

I'd need to say something reassuring and tread carefully now. It was frightening, of course. No matter that she'd be able to hire help for the house stuff, that the boys were independent, that work would continue as always—she would be alone. Terrifying.

"Are you okay?" she said.

Her voice trembled. Eyes, so anxious. Wanting something so much. Fearing.

"Gordon? Are you okay?"

Fearing! Jesus!

It was her repetition of the question that did it, the tone so anxious and yet hopeful, positively yearning.

She wasn't afraid of life alone; she was afraid that I wouldn't go through with it. She thought that now, logistics taken care of, the boys, Christ, the boys … she thought that I might back out. This woman wanted me gone, and she feared that here, the finish line before us, I was going nix the deal. She wanted her solitude. Gordon Bridge—no more of him.

"I'm going to be living in Manhattan, or maybe Brooklyn, at least for a while."

Relief buckled her knees, and she dropped back on the bed. I let her take some time to reflect, measure up the costs—maybe some inconvenience, maybe some parenting challenge—and the benefits—he'll be gone, gone, gone.

"Leo and Gavin are going to be okay," she said. "But New York? That's a long way away, suddenly."

"I've thought about that. They could come out this summer, or we could take a trip. I'll be back, too."

"Sure. Fine."

"It'll be hard. It would be better if I were here—"

"We can do this. Just don't … don't think it'll be easy for them because they're smart kids. Leo helps Gavin. And Leo? How were you at sixteen? Need a father much?"

Much, I said, but to myself only.

"Don't get pissed off, Gordon. I need to be able to tell you this."

"I'm not pissed off. I'm grateful, in fact. Tell me again, whenever you like, okay? I agree with you, and if you come up with anything else, say that too."

"Fine."

"SO, WHAT DO YOU THINK?"

"It's lovely."

"I think so too. It's perfect."

"You're planning on buying it?"

"That's the idea."

"We'll be neighbours."

"Trudy, for us. I'm thinking of buying it for us."

"What?"

"I'm ... I'm thinking—"

"You're not serious."

"Well."

"You're not serious."

We stood in the kitchen of an ample Brooklyn brownstone. Vancouver property prices had been soaring for a decade, and, my savings account now big with the cash-equivalent of half a house off The Drive, I could simply shift from one glamour city to another.

"We need to talk."

She turned and left. I watched for a second before following. She let the front door close behind her, and in the moment before I opened it I thought I might have to hurry after, that she might be rushing down the stairs and along the sidewalk, but I found her sitting at the top of the steps, off to the side, by a row of planters leading down. Space for me beside her.

Trudy looked at me, held my gaze, then turned away, faced into the street. "We need to talk," she'd said, but now, silence.

The sun wasn't setting yet, just lower in the sky, light less intense.

All right. I'd met Trudy. Mere days later, I'd ended my marriage. Then the return to Brooklyn, and, immediately, our affair, happiness of a couple of weeks. To Vancouver to arrange the house sale. Back to Brooklyn yet again.

Trudy glanced at me once more. The shadows under her eyes were darker—a different sort of writer would say they looked bruised. But just ... darker. She rolled her shoulders back, once.

A young couple came along and ascended the steps, plenty of room for them between me and the bay window on the far side. The woman looked down at us, one second, quizzical. They entered without knocking.

I was about to speak but stopped myself—good move—when I realized I didn't yet have anything to say.

Minutes on, the sun really setting now. What's the moment when the lowering sun can be said to be setting? Again, a glance from Trudy, eyes darker still, and her lips, too, shading now to black. It wasn't just the trick of the light. Anger building in her. Blood, in her face. I'd just left my wife and my boys, and I was proposing to buy a place, be a couple.

What foolishness was this? What love-at-first-sight, worn-out fairy tale? Wounded soldier and nurse. No. Literary celebrity and groupie. Please, no.

Or perhaps just her difference—short and brown, not like tall blonde Jessica, or, sure, not like Mum. The similarity had been remarked on before, Jess a young look-alike for my mother. Some had even claimed they shared certain mannerisms.

No, no, no, I was not just mistaking love for a rebuke of that old jokey accusation of being one of Sigmund's boys.

But I didn't know her, her life. I hadn't met her friends. She didn't know me. Well, she knew my work. I'd just left my wife and my boys. Just.

"*Monica Documented* is my favourite of your novels," she said. "I don't mean the best, but my favourite."

She patted my thigh once, looked at me and smiled. Narrow smile, darkness remaining.

"Your piece on Madrid reminded me of it, actually."

She exhaled, shook her head gently. Trying to accept something.

"They both tell unexpected stories. They're quite lovely, I think, which is strange, isn't it, a strange thing to say. A lovely article on terrorism, a topic I'm interested in, because ... well, never mind. I'm interested. And your novel about Monica, a woman so constrained by ... all the ways the world registers her. And they both become other things. It's quite beautiful, the way I begin to see and think that 'what to do about terrorism' isn't really the question. And the novel is about Monica and then, somehow it's not about her at all. In thinking about her that other way, we've been doing the very thing that limits her so. Documenting. Oh, I'm not explaining myself very well. Gordon, how can I explain how disappointed I am?"

22

■ ■

I could return to Vancouver, rent a place in the apartment block just west of them on the other side of The Drive. I wouldn't drop in on them, or expect to have dinner with the three of them, or join in on family weekends. But if the boys wanted to hang out after school, if they wanted company for dinner on nights when Jessica worked late, I'd be there. They'd know I was just down the street.

Then I spoke with Leo on the phone.

"I guess I'm glad."

"Yes?"

"You were both so unhappy."

"Well, you're right about that."

"It was killing him, y'know. He felt responsible. Like, forever."

I understood the moment he spoke that what he said was true. Why didn't I know it at the time—"the time" being a period of years? It would be misleading to say that I was thinking anything then, but if I let the word stand as a placeholder for some more vague and primitive feeling/cognition, then perhaps what I'd been thinking was that of course Gavin would know he wasn't responsible for his parents' unhappiness. So, I wasn't responsible for ensuring that he knew. What a delightful convenience.

Such a stupid, insultingly stupid, story to have been telling. And now, that lovely aesthetic moment when the skilled writer allows me to see that all along, I've been misunderstanding. It's the very moment Trudy said I had managed, in *Monica Documented* and my Madrid piece. I look back to see that all along when I was worried about Gavin, he was more worried, more honestly worried, about me and Jessica. A different, more important story.

I'd damaged him. My focus needed to be on damaging no more. Maybe make some repairs. If I returned now, what would Gavin's response be? His project would resume, restoring the parental couple. Looking out for my unhappiness.

Another delightful convenience of a story. Maybe. I'd see. I could return any time. Just not now, not days after I said I was moving east—destructive to bounce around like that, crazy father doesn't know if he's coming or going. Trust big brother Leo, more deserving of trust than any of my intuitions. He's glad I'm gone.

So, can this narrative with Trudy be picked up? Taken in a more intelligent direction?

My opening move in the revision, written in an anxious hurry—gotta clear out that rom-com disaster right here, right now—was a place, one bedroom, large enough to squeeze the boys in here and there when they visited. Not far from Trudy, but not too close either. I thought about going ahead with a purchase, but getting into a big brownstone seemed a passive-aggressive move, emphatically waiting on her. A rental, half-hour walk away, clearly the thing.

Noreen thought it was exactly the thing.

"This is great news. Great news."

"Well, Noreen, I appreciate that you're not upset with me, leaving my wife and my children."

"I'm sorry, Gordon. Do you want family counselling from your agent? I thought you had friends for that. You still have some friends, right?"

"Okay, what do you mean, 'great news'?"

"It's great that you're in New York. It frankly still makes a difference. You'll get more reviews. More TV. Set your next novel there and you'll kill. You'll be very surprised at how much room remains at the top."

"I can't just stay here. I'm Canadian, remember?"—an objection that had escaped me when I'd formed my beautiful plan to homestead with Trudy.

"Leave it with me, Gordon. I know just the right lawyer for a famous novelist looking to take up residency in New York."

One trip to Value Furniture. Then cheap dishes, supplies, done in a week. A mere day to sit around and build up the nerve for the phone call.

Initial chat, banalities forced up and out my throat.

"I've got a place, an apartment, and I was hoping you could come over for dinner, any night this week. My schedule happens to be entirely free. It's not far. You could walk over after work."

The tension built in me, all that I had riding here, so that when I said, "You could walk over," my throat tightened, a potential to choke.

"That sounds lovely, Gordon.

"Great!"

"Could I bring a friend?"

23

■ ■

"It's delicious, Gordon."

"Well, I know you must have had better."

I'd succeeded, while shopping, chopping, and sautéing, in shutting down speculation, putting "friend" thoughts out of mind, though maybe—spilled broth, dropped knife, broken bowl—maybe not out of body.

"I'm not comparing. It's very good. Don't you think it's good?"

Mulligatawny soup. I knew Trudy wouldn't find it authentic, but I'd hoped she'd appreciate the gesture.

"It's wonderful. Trudy wasn't lying when she told me what a good cook you are," said Cynthia.

Cynthia Winston. English Professor at Brooklyn's Medgar Evers College. Specialization in Creative Writing. She'd heard about Trudy from a colleague, gone to her for a sore back, and they'd become friends.

"Trudy recognized my name. She'd read my YA novel. *Heart Forty*."

"She's very well read."

"Raather," said Cynthia, an accurate, comic-posh English accent, comic especially because of the contrast with her African-American Mississippian.

"It's terrific," said Trudy. "You'd love it."

"It's now at the top of my list. I'll get it tomorrow."

If I sounded anxious to please, I didn't mind. I was. How anxious?

"So, Gordon, how'd you like to visit one of my classes?"

"I'd love it."

"WHO'S YOUR FAVOURITE AFRICAN-AMERICAN NOVELIST?"

I'd been ready to answer questions about my work, talk about the business, tell some war stories, but I understood.

Second query: "Who's your favourite after Ralph Ellison? Anybody who's alive?"

Third: "Do your novels have any black characters?"

Cynthia grinned from her seat at the back, enjoying watching me cope. Had she planted the questions? Had Trudy?

I left with a good list of contemporary African American novels I needed to read. Maybe the best thing was just walking through the crowded main building off Bedford, a first for me, racialized minority for a minute, sort of—not the same, of course, not at all; I knew full well I'd shed no privileges—Douglas Park, etc. But still ... worthwhile.

Trudy reported to me that Cynthia reported to her that the class thought I was great.

"All I did was compile a reading list."

"What about at the end?"

"What about it?"

"You responded to their work."

"Well, sort of."

"That's not what Cynthia told me."

"A couple of them told me the premises for stories they were working on, and I said they sounded good. That's all."

"You did say something about them, Gordon. You explained why they 'sounded good.' Was Cynthia making this up? She said you took them seriously."

"Anybody who tries to write a story should be taken seriously."

A WALK WITH TRUDY IN PROSPECT PARK. SHE BROUGHT HER pal Ronnie, an electrician, and, like Trudy, a member of Trinidad's South Asian diaspora. Older than us, but fit, a wiry former middle-distance man, brisk walker.

"Trudy tells me you used to run in university," said Ronnie.

"Jog. I jogged with a friend. Slowly."

"But you're not doing so now."

"No."

"I run in Brooklyn Bridge Park three mornings a week. You should join me."

"Ronnie, I don't know what Trudy has been telling you, but I'm not a runner. There's no chance I could keep up with you, even if I was in shape, and I'm not in shape."

"That's why you should do this. I run the park loop. If you're as slow as you say, we'll start out together, and you can take it easy. I'll run at my normal pace and we'll meet up at the end."

"How far is it?"

"Two miles. I run it twice, so perhaps your one and my two will have us at the end at the same time."

"That's a challenge, Gordon."

"It's not a challenge. I'm just suggesting to Gordon that he can run at his own pace, even run-walk, and we can still be social. I'm tired of doing this on my own. We could have coffee afterward."

Another plant?

A DANCE SHOW AT BAM, VEERING TOO CLOSE TO performance art, for me, but not for Trudy's more avant-garde dancer-friend Jane, whose feet Trudy had repaired. We had drinks afterward.

"I could walk, I could even run, but if I tried in any way to dance, they just—they cramped on me. Instantly. It hurt like shit. Trudy saved me."

"I believe it."

"Saved me."

"If it's not giving away a confidence, do you remember whether Trudy said anything, while she was working on you?"

Jane looked at Trudy. Trudy shrugged permission.

"She said 'Forget it.'"

"Really. 'Forget it.' Did you figure out what you were supposed to forget?"

"There are lots of possibilities."

THEN, DINNER AT MY PLACE AGAIN, THIS TIME AN ELDERLY couple, Auntie Agnes and Uncle Suraj, visiting from Trinidad. On Trudy's request, no faux Island dishes, just roast chicken and veggies.

"They didn't like me."

"Auntie Agnes doesn't like anyone. She just approves or disapproves."

"Uncle Suraj?"

"He's hard to read."

I was walking with her to Cynthia and her partner Al's apartment, where Trudy was staying while aunt and uncle bunked at her place. A month had passed since my blunder at the brownstone.

A bit of jangly nervousness, an edge. "I've enjoyed meeting some of your friends. Uncle and Auntie too."

"That's about all of them, Gordon. But they're good friends."

"Well, three good friends is a lot. Thanks for introducing me around. I'd say I'm an introvert, obviously, but still, I don't know anybody here. So ..."

"What have you been doing with your time?"

"My agent wants a blockbuster New York novel. But I haven't got anything. I sit at the computer for a while, then I go out. Touristy stuff. Walking, mainly. Central Park. I bought some books at The Strand. I saw the Senior Concert Orchestra at Carnegie

Hall. It's a seniors' orchestra—well, clearly, and I just wanted to see something at Carnegie Hall, and, uh..." Relax, Gordon.

She slipped her hand in mine and gave our arms a youthful swing. My mouth was dry. What was I going to say?

"It was tremendous. I've never been to a better concert. Free at Carnegie Hall."

We stopped in front of the building. She turned to face me.

"How can you write a New York novel when you don't really know the city? I don't understand your agent. You don't know the city, and you don't know the people."

"It'll have to be from the point of view of someone who's not a New Yorker. One way or another."

"Ah."

"It's still a problem. But I'm telling myself I'm trying to do something about that, walking around. Shopping. Going to Cynthia's class was good. Medgar Evers College."

"Gordon, this isn't really my business, but ... how are you doing? How are you? Are you talking to them?"

"Yes. I think they're okay. We talk, every couple of nights. They haven't got a lot to say right now. I think that if there were serious problems Leo would tell me. He'd call on his own ... in private."

"He sounds mature."

"He is. And I think if there were ... if Leo weren't doing well, Jessica would tell me. We talk too, Jess and I."

"Good."

She was waiting for me. I realized that I didn't want to kiss her, that I hadn't felt anything physical for ... not since my stupidity, the plan to move in together. I hadn't observed my desire gone. Odd, not to have noticed. I guess because a different desire remained, romantic still, but ... different.

"I'd like to do something together. Just the two of us."

"Something touristy?"

"Broadway show?"

"Not that touristy."
"Yes. I mean no. Not that touristy."
"Okay."

24

Trudy and I were back on, friends at least. Dinners out, sometimes with one of the trio, sometimes just us. Patience, Gordon.

Noreen posted an author update on her impressive website. I suppose that not having any literary Gordon Bridge news to share, she thought my change in locale would have to do. Without saying anything directly she managed to convey that literary news would be forthcoming, that my shift to the U.S. was indeed a step up to the big time.

I got a few concerned calls, people figuring out what this change meant for Gordon Bridge the father. I emailed some people I hadn't heard from, trying for preemptive. Their strained reactions previewed how my new life would play. Then some references in the papers followed, oblique, the false Canadian politeness that makes me want to pull the sweater over someone's head, hockey-fight style, and whale away with my honest little fists. Worst of all of my crimes, certainly worse in the puritanical Canadian hierarchy of sins than leaving my wife and children, was where I'd landed. Joni Mitchell moved to California, and also Wayne Gretzky. David fucking Frum went from a good conservative Toronto boy to renouncer of citizenship and writer of nasty, grandiloquent distortions for George

W. Bush, and still he was forgiven. Any number of hip Canuck comedians morphed into American stars. But Gordon Bridge, novelist, he moves to New York? Hang him for a traitor.

I talked about it again with Noreen. "It doesn't matter, Gordon. Canada doesn't matter to you anymore. They might care in Vancouver and even Toronto but they won't give a rat's ass in New York or London. You're a New Yorker now. Write me a New York novel."

Earlier times, I would've whined to Jessica. Taylor. Now?

I gunnysacked for a couple of days. Then Trudy asked me what was wrong, and I poured the whole bitter brew on her after another post-work repast at my place: the anger abroad, Noreen's ambitious enthusiasm.

"Big deal," she said when I'd run down into silence.

"That's not quite the response I expected."

"Big deal."

My stomach lurched. Already? A step back when we'd only come such a short distance?

"Gordon, you know so much better than this." She looked at her watch. "You could call right now. They're probably home from school."

Trudy rested a hand on my shoulder as I dialled. Then she took herself to the bedroom, leaving me to talk in private, set up the dates that would work for Gavin and Leo. I tried to sound just like me on the phone, make my voice sound like me instead of the vulnerable, shame-filled catastrophe I'd been burying, while the boys cheerfully pitched in to nail down the details of the summer visit.

I hung up. Exhausted but lighter: all my irritation with the world's take on Gordon Bridge's move south dispelled.

Trudy returned to the living room.

"Now I'm nervous about their visit," I said.

"It's a very big deal."

I stepped in for a hug. Trudy hugged me back. I stepped away, my hands still on her waist. If I kissed her, would it all return, would we be on my bed in moments, easy fun once again?

I let my hands fall. "We haven't seen Cynthia in a while. Why don't we invite her and Al over for dinner at the end of the week?"

Spring and into the summer, a romance, really—I felt at the centre of Trudy's life. Did she make everyone feel that way? At night, alone, I longed for her. I imagined that next time, the next time I saw her, there'd be a moment, it would happen easily, she'd turn her face up to mine. Not only did the moment fail to materialize, however, but the desire for it didn't persist from those dreamy nights into our time together: weeks of walks, Scrabble, her friends, dinners, talk of books, weeks of trying and not succeeding to begin a novel.

THE CITY IN AUGUST STEAMED, SO WHEN THE BOYS ARRIVED we ducked the yuppie exodus to the Hamptons and rented a cheap place upstate for a few days, on Lake George.

We walked the windy shore, echo of Trout Lake strolls. I said, "I want to make some things clear here, but I want you to be patient and forgive me if this stuff seems obvious, okay? When we set this trip up, I told myself it would be obvious and didn't need to be said, and then I thought, I need to say it anyway. I'm confident you know it already. I covered some of it in that text I sent you. On the day.

"You're in my life. It's hard because I'm in New York, but you haven't got any less of my attention, really, and you're still at the heart of things. People say that I'm a writer, I'm a novelist. All that stuff comes after you. I think, 'I'm Leo and Gavin's father.' That's the absolute me. Everybody who gets an important place in my life knows this. So, wherever I am, whatever I'm doing, you guys are first.

"Imagine … do this thought experiment with me. Imagine your dad's a candidate for the Nobel Prize for Literature. I'm in a meeting. You're outside. You're thinking, we need to talk to Dad.

You knock on the door. That meeting is over. I say to the Nobel Committee (at this point Gavin started laughing), 'this'll have to wait, okay, because I've got to help Leo and Gavin with their fucking homework.'"

"You can't say 'fucking' homework," said Gavin, grinning.

"Yeah," said Leo. "That sounds like you're complaining." He wasn't smiling.   Gavin looked at his serious big brother and lost his cheer, and then he just looked down. The Lake George breeze died and my sweat poured in the sudden humidity. Of course, a short speech from Dad does not restore us. What, then?

The weather broke in time for a week back in the city, and the next step. Introductions.

Gavin and Leo treated Trudy politely. They had probably heard plenty of wisdom from Jessica about how to manage things, and that would've included a healthy dose of expecting Trudy to be uncertain and their needing to give her a break.

The four of us A-Trained to Harlem and caught Amateur Night at the Apollo, where a kid sang a knock-out "When a Man Loves a Woman." With his last triumphant, soulful shout of love and humiliation I leaped up and roared my joy. The boys remained seated while they applauded.

Gavin and Leo tracked our underground journey south across Manhattan, checking subway stops on the map they shared. I didn't try to get a conversation going. The problem—the look in their faces when they glanced at me, curious, distant—the problem was that this was a holiday. *I* was a holiday. Not a father. Just diversion. I had left them and now they were leaving me. "Leo," I said, just as a northbound train screamed past. He couldn't hear me and wasn't looking at me, so he didn't see that I'd spoken.

Trudy surprised with a suggestion that she and the boys head out without me. The boys agreed. Off to Central Park.

On their return, Leo and Gavin plunked themselves down on the couch, and Trudy trucked off home.

"How was the day?" I said.

"Really, really good," said Gavin.

"It was great," said Leo.

"Why so serious?"

"Trudy took us to the Dakota," said Leo. "And Strawberry Fields, y'know, in Central Park."

"That's serious."

The boys had never been Beatles fans much, or Lennon, so this surprised. "That had quite an impact on me the first time I went there."

"Trudy did this thing," said Leo. "We were standing out front, looking up at the building."

"At the Dakota," said Gavin.

"She held our hands," said Leo.

"Oh."

"I never really got it before, y'know, the whole Lennon thing," said Leo. "I know you and Grandpa like him and the Beatles, and they did some good songs."

"'A Day in the Life,'" said Gavin.

"Right," said Leo, "and Grandpa's tried to explain about it, but we never got it before."

"So, let me get this straight. You went to Strawberry Fields, and then you went to the Dakota, and that's where Trudy held your hands."

"That's right," said Gavin, surprise in his voice, as though it were weird that there wasn't anything more.

"Yeah," said Leo.

"She's pretty cool," said Gavin.

"Did she say anything when she was holding your hands?"

They looked at each other, confirming. "No," said Leo.

"She just held our hands," said Gavin.

"John Lennon ..." said Leo.

"Jesus," said Gavin.

They looked at each other, sharing their amazement at Trudy, maybe their indifference to me.

The day before departure the boys headed into Manhattan alone. I would've been happy to tag along, but I was happy too that they wanted to do this by themselves, The Natural History Museum. Maybe it would help make the city theirs. Next time, they'd be visiting me, and Trudy, and their New York. They were bagged when they got back, and they had an early flight home, so we all turned in before it got late.

After I bunked down on the couch I could hear the two of them in the bedroom, talking for a long time. It made me curious, but I wasn't going to ask. All right, more than curious. Anxious. Awake, dreaming, awake again, I worried through the night that a judgment was surfacing and Pa Bridge wouldn't do well by it.

In the morning, in the cab to the airport, just pulling away from the curb, Leo said, "Gavin, tell him about your science project."

25

■ ■

"I did a science project on drift nets," said Gavin.

"What are drift nets?"

"He's about to tell you," said Leo. Good use of tone. If he'd added "dummy," his meaning wouldn't have been any clearer.

Gavin glanced at Leo, then he focused his gaze on the info-sheet on the back of the driver's seat and took a breath.

"Back in the fifties they came up with this new technology. There weren't as many fish, because they'd been catching too many. They came up with a new system. Drift nets have floats on top and weights on the bottom, and they hang there. They're vertical. It's like a curtain of net in the ocean.

"They can catch more fish because the nets are big." He looked at me for a second to confirm that I was paying attention. I nodded, and he looked ahead again. "They're *really* big." He turned back to me, frustrated, as though I didn't get it or my attention had already wandered.

"Fifty K, all right? They made drift nets as long as fifty kilometres, hanging there, trapping fish. You'd have this huge net and this huge ship with these monster hydraulic winches to drag the nets in, weighed down with fish. You can't imagine how much fish."

He turned to me again. "You *cannot* imagine how much fish.

"With a drift net, you don't control what you catch. You're fishing for herring and mackerel. But when you pull the net up, you've got other fish, even squid and octopus. And sea turtles. They let these nets hang there, filling up, and then they pull them in and see what they've got. The ship, it's a factory ship. They cut the fish up and they freeze them right away.

"Y'know what they do with the squid? Guess. Guess what they do with the squid and everything that isn't the fish they want."

I might have guessed, but nothing could be clearer than the need for my silence, so I just shook my head.

"You don't know." He put his hand on the plastic cover of the info card and tapped his fingers on it.

"They dump it. They call it the 'by-catch.' It's just by-the-way. By the way, we killed a bunch of octopus and turtles and fish we don't want." Another look at me. I nodded.

"That's not all." Still looking at me. What was I to do or say? I just looked back. I'm paying attention, Gavin. You have *all* my attention.

"They kill dolphins. Okay? Even whales. You know how they die? They drown. They drown! They're trapped in the net, and they're thrashing and drowning, and they get cut by that plastic netting. It's sharp.

"So, they're thrashing and bleeding in this huge net, and then you get what's next."

I wasn't ready for what was next. I'd never seen Gavin like this, my cheerful, ever-giving youngest. I was sweating in that air-conditioned cab, trapped, terrified. What's next? I forced myself to shift in my seat to face him.

"There's blood in the water and the dolphins are thrashing. Thrashing, bloody dolphins. So that brings sharks. They're not cruel, they're just animals doing what they do. They eat the dolphins as they drown."

I nodded some more.

"Then the sharks get tangled in there. The sharks are more by-catch, because they're not fishing for sharks."

The car went dark. What? What eclipse, what apocalypse? What?

Nothing. The Holland Tunnel. Nobody spoke. I could hear my boys breathing.

"They're just by-catch," Gavin said when we came out into the light of Jersey City. I'd thought maybe he was done, and I'd been wishing an appropriate response into being. He wasn't done.

"They began to make rules, about what size the nets could be, mainly. They could see what was happening. Really that started a while back, in the sixties. But it didn't work, because the rules were just for ships from certain countries. The owners, the big companies, they registered their ships in other countries. Those countries don't have regulations. That's called flags of *convenience*."

He sneered the word "convenience." I'd never heard Gavin sneer. If you'd asked me, I would have said that Gavin could not produce a sneer, but there it was, contempt-filled, hanging in the cab air.

I thought, perhaps now, a time to speak up, but I glanced past Gavin and caught Leo's eye, and he shook his head just once: shut it, Dad.

"Here's the worst part," said Gavin. He looked at me again, but even though the worst was coming, he seemed a bit easier now, more confident that I was listening as I should.

"Sometimes there was a problem, like a storm maybe, and they had to cut the net free, and they lost it. The net isn't worth much, and it was less trouble to put out another one than to search around the ocean for the net they lost.

"So that net just hangs there, filling up with fish. And dolphins.

"They did finally get enough rules passed that it stopped. Nobody uses those big nets anymore. They're banned. But guess what?"

Was I supposed to speak, finally? I looked from Gavin to Leo and back. Yes, it's now my line. "What?"

"Those nets are still there. They're called ghost nets. They hang there, killing fish, for years. Years! They're hanging in the ocean. They start to sink, because the floats break up and they lose their buoyancy. But they're still hanging vertical, these huge ghost nets. They're in the ocean right now.

"Think of that. They've been there for years and years, sinking. Some of the fish rot away, but more fish get caught, fish that live deeper. They're strange fish. You haven't even heard of them.

"They do that on and on, till finally they hit the bottom. The nets lie on the ocean floor. They're full of the skeletons of fish. Ghost nets."

Gavin leaned back. Leo looked out his window, watching as we crossed the Hackensack River into Newark. Not much farther.

We rode the last minutes to the airport in silence. Also no conversation beyond the necessary through check-in, and then up to security.

I gave Leo a big hug and squeezed hard. He hugged me back. Then I turned to Gavin, who was waiting for me. He stepped toward me. His gentle, caring self was resuming control and he didn't understand what had happened. I could see an apology coming, so I needed to speak right away.

"Thank you. I'm so glad you took the time to come to New York. You two were so nice to Trudy."

He was holding on to me hard.

"I'm so glad that you told me about drift nets. I needed to learn about that. I'm going to read some more about it. Send me some book titles in an email, and I'll get the books."

They stepped through security and passed out of sight on the way to their gate. I turned, lost my balance, staggered and recovered. And I knew. Gift from Gavin. A novel. Oh Gavin, ever-generous youngest son.

26

◼ ◼

"What's happened?"

"What do you mean?"

"Something's happened."

"Nothing. I just saw the boys off and ... well, I've got an idea for a novel. Set in New York. Gavin gave me the idea."

Trudy had just come over after work. She gave me a hug. "I suppose now the dam should break, as they say, and all our sexual tension should finally spill over, and we should make passionate love. Like in the movies.

"Oh, Gordon, if you could see your face! You look like a teenager who's been caught ... doing something. So, tell me about your novel idea."

HERE'S A CHARACTER FOR YOU, GORDON. THIS CHARACTER IS drifting, killing, and sinking, and he's being killed, and he is abandoned, and he's an ocean that contains multitudes and is dying, and he sits at table, forking to his mouth a chunk of fish. He chews and swallows with pleasure, no thought to where the fish came from and how many like it are left, if any. Such is this character's interior life. Here's your character, one to anger people, enrage them, remind them of themselves. Can you build a novel from this character?

I told Trudy about it, trying to pin it down a bit in the process. When we made love that night, well, it wasn't like in the movies. Nervous. But good anyway.

I wrote, ambled around Brooklyn, wrote, rode the subway up to the Village to stroll some more, and then back to the Financial District to pace home with the hip pedestrian commuters, over the Brooklyn Bridge, and I wrote.

Three mornings a week I ran with Ronnie. It turned out that neither of us was really interested in coffee afterward. He did, in fact, complete two loops more quickly than my one of walk-run, shouting "Track" when he'd lap me, and then he'd wait for me, we'd shake hands and head on our ways. Convivial, somehow.

I visited another of Cynthia's classes when her new term began: Ta-Nehisi Coates, Jacqueline Woodson, Tayari Jones, Brandon Taylor, and yes, still, Ralph Ellison. Ralph makes every list.

Trudy and I were a couple—sometimes a gallery on her day off, sometimes an artsy happening that Jane guided us to, perhaps a double date with Cynthia and Al.

My neck was cured, and the boys and I seemed fine—Gavin's rage expressed and received. The writing slowed before I visited them in the fall, but the trip went well and I picked it up on my return. Coming up to Chanukah/Christmas, I couldn't concentrate, but the holiday brought joy and renewed focus. Once more, before the boys flew out again for spring break, I began giving in, frustration overtaking, why was this going on so long?

The boys and I emailed and called, and that was no duty, no sacrifice, not something to be proud of, just a fact, a fact that I did not abandon my children. I didn't leave behind an aging wife who had supported me when the times were tough.

I called Noreen, not for advice, but just looking for something. Distraction. She came up with some suggestions, and then, calling back:

"I've got you on NPR. This could be really good."

"I don't know, Noreen. It's been so long since the last novel. And NPR isn't going to be interested in *The CBC Sequence*."

"They'll be interested in *you*. It's a thoughtful show. You won't be expected to hawk a book. That's not what they do."

I agreed. I supposed it could be helpful, responding to questions about my current project. Maybe create focus.

The chat, in studio, began innocuously enough. I talked about my work-in-progress without really saying anything, but won that enthusiastic NPR interviewer response. In answer to the inevitable question about autobiographical elements, I reviewed my dull middle-class bio.

"Have you ever felt at all limited, or maybe even trapped, as a novelist, by the privilege of your life? Salman Rushdie referred to John Updike as 'parochial,' writing about 'wife swapping,' and I'm wondering if the safety and relative comfort of a life like yours ... does it ever make you feel limited, or even jealous of those writers whose work engages with matters ... that are more obviously *urgent?*"

"Like Rushdie."

"Indeed."

"I suppose not. If readers want to find that sort of work, they can find it. I haven't felt that I should seek out experience like that, put myself on the front lines in order to write fiction that *matters*, in some obvious way."

"Is fiction of that kind necessarily 'obvious'?"

"Not necessarily, but it can be. It can become a kind of terror-tourism."

"Terror-tourism."

"Yes."

"Could you name a writer, or a work of terror-tourism?" His tone had become saccharine, supersaturated with condescension and aggression. I should have ignored. I tried not to sound haughty with my reply, but I could hear my failure in my headphones.

"I'd rather not. I'm not trying to diminish any individual writer. I'm just saying that I write out of my imagination and my experience. If I observe sensitively, my characters should reflect the deep issues in our world, even if the scene of my work is 'parochial.'"

"Can you be sensitive to terror if you've never felt it?"

"I have, though. I've written about it, though not in my fiction—I was in Madrid with my family when the city was attacked."

"That must have been terrible. Were you hurt, or was anyone in your family?" The false concern now, feigned sympathy, designed to enrage.

"No, thankfully."

"Did you feel targeted?"

And I was back, in Madrid, in the restaurant. Not in the studio anymore. The sirens wailing. Gavin and Leo shocked, the waiter shouting at me. Screams from outside the restaurant. What? What?

"Did you feel singled out?"

"What? No, of course not, but affected, certainly."

"You left the next day. I think I remember reading that."

Guernica. Unspeakable pain in the twisted torsos; disembodied, tortured faces. Gavin and Leo, so vulnerable. All of us, assaulted.

"You returned to Vancouver?"

"Yes."

"Back to Vancouver. Did you feel safe after you left? Did you feel guilty for being *able* to leave?"

"Guilty?"

"I'm not saying you were guilty of something. I'm just … I can imagine one perhaps feeling, in a moment like that, being able to escape so easily …"

"I felt glad to have returned with my family. Perhaps I should have stayed in Madrid with my children, hoping for more bombing, so I could become a writer of more urgent fiction? Should I have made some public statement that would have made me a target? I experienced something important in not being a target, I think, and not being injured. There's a randomness in the threat we face. I've felt that."

"Does that give you a special insight, as contrasted with, for example, Rushdie, or other writers, the ones you refuse to name?"

"Nothing *gives* anybody insight, okay? It gives me an opportunity. The opportunity doesn't produce the insight. That's up to the writer, obviously."

Relaxed agreement, a sentence or two to expose the obvious ignorance of the assumptions here, about what is traumatic and what surprising shapes our challenges can take, that's all the moment called for, but what I produced was in turn whiny, then angry, finally defensive.

Did I need to let go of Madrid? I stumbled out of the NPR offices, dazed, beat-up, lost.

Later, the retransmissions, summaries, internet commentary, the whole blabberverse's reduction of my original stupidity, all added up to one damning slur: I believed that what happened to me in Spain was worse than being killed or injured. I'm more deserving of sympathy and attention, and that's mainly because, of course, I'm Gordon Bridge, famous novelist.

Sure. Famous novelist. Unable to write a word. It all came to a stop. No scribbling, no experimenting, nothing.

I told Trudy.

"I know. I know. Give it time. Try not to worry."

Not exactly helpful, no healing wonder, but at least it wasn't a threat.

Yet I failed badly at not worrying. Would my crime of long ago overpower Trudy's healing power and bring my neck to pain yet again? Would the old excoriating voice return? My reconstructed world, still delicately new, would it shatter? Would I then see, though nobody else could, that the destruction was again the result of my old sin and the evasions that followed?

Would I lose her?

27

We were shopping at Boomer's, a supermarket around the corner, crammed, packed to ceilings. What peaches and what penumbras! Shuffling along in the cashier line, we passed a rack of organic granola bars with catchy names. "Lotta Apricotta," read Trudy. "Is that a play on that woman's name, you know … Lotta Hitschmanova? Remember? Those ads for the Unitarian Service Committee?"

"Probably not. It's just a funny rhyme."

Then I wept.

We had a cart full of groceries, we were standing close to the front of a long line, and picture me, tears pouring, pouring, unable to speak or explain, streaming tears during the crush of late afternoon traffic at Boomer's.

"Gordon! Gordon, what is it?" Then she simply held me, no magic words, a comforting embrace while I cried. We shuffled along in the line that way, and I pulled myself together sufficiently to help unload the cart. I sniffled still while we humped our grocery bags up the street and home.

After putting away the groceries, I turned to Trudy. "Jesus."

"Do you know why you were crying?"

"No. No, I … Do you?"

"Maybe you can figure it out. You might let yourself, over the next few days, try to picture it exactly, take some time, and then perhaps you'll understand."

I took some time, days, waiting for an insight, and got nothing. I told myself to let it go.

Trudy, at dinner, out of nowhere: "You can't let something go if you don't understand it."

I sipped some wine.

"Gordon."

"Maybe it's not very important. I was … raw. A lot has happened. And my writing has stalled."

"Mmmhmm."

She looked at me, not exactly angry, but not pleased, and when again I reached for my wineglass, she put her hand out to hold mine, stopping me.

I could picture the scene, hear her voice. Her hand lay on mine, and I heard her ask that question, about Lotta Hitschmanova.

"You sounded so innocent," I said.

"Yes?"

"When you asked me about the granola bar. You sounded like a child. You were wondering, even hoping. You hoped I'd have the answer."

"Sure."

"If you're a child, I'm a parent."

She released my hand, sipped her wine, and then when I moved to drink as well, once more she stopped me.

"Maybe it surprised me. When I talk to the boys I'm ready for it. I can brace myself."

She nodded and stroked my wrist.

"I can deal with what's coming when I talk to them. What's coming. I suppose that would be a reminder of my failure."

"Go on, Gordon."

"If I'm a parent to you, then I'm going to fail again."

"Of course you'll be a parent to me. Of course you'll fail."

"Mmmhmm."

"Mmmhmm."

I got my reward, a big gulp of that wine, and I began to get up.

"Oh no, Gordon."

Back I sit, child to Trudy.

"Picture it."

A bit of frustration. "You're there, I'm there, and I'm crying."

Trudy's smile. "Picture what you pictured, Gordon."

"You know, you know what I saw? Lotta Hitschmanova. Yes. I could see her in those public service ads, her nurse's uniform, I could hear her."

"That voice."

"That voice, that's right, appealing for help. Her Czech accent. Appealing to me, so the Unitarian Service Committee could help. I was a child."

"You couldn't help."

"This is getting ridiculous."

"There's nothing ridiculous about it, Gordon. You know better than that."

I did know better, but I hope you can be sympathetic, little Gordon so done in by a public service announcement. Big adult Gordon done in by the recollection.

"I've never thought about this."

"Think."

"I felt injured. Those starving children on the screen. Wounded. I was so ... Douglas Park, our beautiful house, my food, my clothes. It stabbed me, so guilty, so powerless. I wanted to run to Mum and Dad. Had no idea what ... Shit."

"You were how old?"

"Ten, maybe."

"Who is this like, Gordon?"

"Who?"

"Picture yourself, so moved, so hurt, wanting to do something about all this suffering. Who do you remind yourself of?"

"Well, it reminds me …"

Again she laid her hand on mine. "It reminds you …"

"This makes no sense."

"It makes all the sense in the world."

"Gavin. That makes no sense."

"Why?"

"He's nothing like me. He's a mystery. A gift."

"What's at the heart of this mystery, do you think?"

"His empathy."

Trudy clasped her hands under her chin and sighed, waiting for me now.

"This is crazy. I am not an empathetic person. I'm not."

"Please help, through the USC, fifty-six Sparks Street, Ottawa." The voice, the Czech accent—perfect.

"I'm not! I've always known—you know, Gordon Bridge, neurotypical, but down there, the skinny non-empathetic end of the bell curve."

"Such lies. Why did you cry? What really happened to you?"

"This is stupid."

Trudy got up. I wonder sometimes if she thought right then about hitting me. Probably not. Getting up and clearing away the dishes was violent enough. Disapproving.

She stacked the dishwasher. I stood behind her.

"I felt I'd lost something of myself. All of that scene, your question about the granola bar, what I remembered, watching that ad by myself. There was a potential back there that got screwed up and twisted somehow. That was it. That made me cry."

"You're a very empathetic person. I knew this reading your novels. Cynthia and her students knew it after a single visit, if you want a recent example. You deserve to know this. But perhaps … well, Gordon, that potential shows itself so well in your novels."

"In my novels."

"Breathe slowly," she said.

"You're going to make me cry again."

"So you should."

You'll be able to guess here, project the dénouement. Back to the manuscript, unblocked. Relief so intense that it hurt.

And then. Only days later. I'm at my student's desk, and Pamela Henderson at the front of the class, and Taylor, intensity radiating, waves of it. I open my laptop, —hurry, hurry, open the document—something I need to catch, to be there when it arrives, and it does, the final stretch opens up for me, the startling yet fitting resolution takes enticing shape in the near distance.

28

I raced. Usually, the final stages really slowed down, but this time, words came more quickly, no irritation, no anxiety for speed, but still, such a pace, one jingle jangle morning after another.

What eased the novel along to its conclusion? Trudy, the evenings we shared at her place or mine: "Will you read to me?" She'd sit in an easy chair, legs curled under her, and she'd close her eyes, listen. Afterwards, simple thanks, no commentary, a smile.

She read fiction always, set out often for literary events like the one at which she had freed me from my pain. So, an educated audience, but she didn't bring that education to bear, not in any way that she shared.

Why was reading to Trudy so good? She'd stopped telling me to let go of something but maybe that's what I was doing. There were lots of candidates. Taylor, of course. Jessica. Madrid. Perhaps a lifetime of stuff I'd clutched to myself without knowing—little constructs, nuggets of shit cathected for no reason other than retentiveness, which is always about fear, a need to protect a narrow idea of self.

On an early July evening I completed the final edit of *Volley through Eternity*, the New York novel. I slept on it and flipped through the manuscript again in the morning. I wrote a short email to Noreen, attached the document, and then my routine pause, a short, weighted moment.

Then not so short. The walls of my room were receding, and I was shrinking, occupying less and less of the vacant vast surrounding. I stood, moved around to dispel this nasty illusion, and then I strode to the computer, novelist Gordon Bridge, and hit "Send."

A JOURNEY IS MY WAY TO BEGIN MARKING THE LITERARY event that most matters to me, which is the completion, to my satisfaction, of a novel. Solitary journey: an example of Mum's training in action, internal reward. Off to Central Park.

I sat on a bench at Strawberry Fields, not reading, not thinking or planning, just allowing myself to be done. I felt it in my muscles: relaxed, slack, and satisfied. But I waited for any sensations of doubt or sorrow, whatever it was that had gripped me before sending to Noreen, and even though my mind seemed stable again, the apprehension spoiled things a bit.

I walked by The Dakota: clouds mottling the sky, people making their way along Central Park West, lots of them hurrying, a handful just turning their heads and looking, probably as always, as they passed, maybe not remembering anything particular, not humming a few bars of a song, but just … The Dakota. I paid attention. I could put the details in an email to Dad. I'd remind him of Leo and Gavin's trip here with Trudy.

Then home. The radio on. The news. Bombs. The London Underground bombed.

The assault had come in the morning rush hour, just like Madrid—middle of the night New York time. If I'd bothered to turn on the news in the morning, or checked online, I'd have known. Instead, while I'd been hanging out on the Upper West Side, indulging, in London they'd cordoned off streets, they'd begun the suspect hunt, they'd pulled bodies from wreckage. As

I relaxed in Central Park, dazed Londoners walked homeward through their stricken city. I saw the images, ghostly crowds flowing over the bridges—so many, I had not thought death had undone so many.

Nobody could say this was my fault. All right, I'd submitted my novel. That doesn't bring terror across the Atlantic. The waiter who cursed me in Madrid had no idea who I was or even what he was saying. My stiff neck, okay—punishment I'd brought on myself. But the rest of it, even to think of it, just stupid, negative egocentricity, if you want a fancy diagnosis. I'm not that important. I'm not.

The phone rang.

"Hello?"

"Hi, Gordon."

"Jessica."

"You must've heard by now."

"Only just now. I've been out all day."

"Are you okay?"

"I'm fine. Well, I'm not fine, but I'm fine. You know what I mean. You?"

"Same."

"The boys?"

"They're out. They should be home soon. I don't know if they know."

"I'll call later."

"That'd be good."

That's as close as Jessica came to acknowledging that my article had been something other than nasty self-promotion. I wished that this sign of her understanding, of what I could even consider an apology, meant more to me. It only felt strange. Who I'd been then, so angry with her, so vulnerable and hurt—who was that?

"What's wrong?" said Trudy. She'd just let herself in, expecting dinner. But one look at me ...

"They bombed London," I said.

"Oh no."

"Just like Madrid."

"Oh no." She fell back on the couch.

I was relieved that the news hit her. I wouldn't have wanted her concern to be for me, though maybe she showed that concern and helped me by directing her attention elsewhere.

We turned on the TV. She continued to watch an hour later when I phoned the boys.

Leo said he was following online. He knew a bit more than I did and filled me in on some of the details, many of which proved in a few days to be false, though the brutal basics didn't alter: bombs on the Underground, and one bus, suicide attacks, Islamist extremists.

After Madrid, I'd followed all the reports, but this time around I couldn't face it; I watched a couple of hours of TV news, and then I heard and read next to nothing. I called everyone I knew in London. It was a no, in every case but one. George Connor, Noreen's English co-agent, had a good friend whose father had been badly hurt. I knew someone who knew someone who knew someone.

"Would you tell everybody, George? In the agency? I'm thinking about you. I'm so sorry about your friend and his father. I'm sorry about London, your home."

"I will. It's good of you to call, Gordon."

Trudy knew more people in London than I did. From Trinidad, many had found their way to England. She didn't check. If someone she knew had been killed or injured, someone would contact her.

"The news is bad for all of them. I don't need the details."

"Of course. Yes. The entire city."

"Gordon."

"Yes."

"Lots of the people I know there are not Muslims. Some are. But they look ... you know."

"They look like Muslims."

"Yes. That Muslim look. There'll be a reaction. Here too, an echo of 9/11. It'll be months before it goes away. Some of my clients will cancel. They'll say they're better and that they're busy and thank you so much, Trudy. They'll repeat that they're so much better thanks to me, several times, so that I know that's not the reason."

She began to weep.

Before I moved to her, I felt and rejected my inadequacy; I couldn't do what she could, know the right few words, the place to touch—so what, she wouldn't expect that at all; don't be an ass, Gordon. I sat beside her, put my arm around her, and she sobbed once, said "Thank you."

I understood. I also wondered. Would it be as bad as she said? Could there be some understandable sensitivity here, exaggerating things?

It's no pleasure to me to admit that at the same time, I felt a certain relief. I wasn't responsible; this latest eruption of evil wasn't a symptom. The bombing in London, a horror, but not another pop-up punishment timed to coincide with the novel's completion, nothing that could be connected to me and my old crime.

29

■ ■

"Two adults," said Trudy.

"I beg your pardon?" said the man in the ticket booth.

We were trying the restaurant-cinema on Bogart Street, seeking cheer.

An anti-Muslim, anti-brown wave of nastiness had been breaking over Trudy for weeks. Or so she said. She'd directed my attention to the looks she was getting, the hostility. I hadn't contradicted, of course, but I hadn't confirmed. How could I confirm something I couldn't see?

"Two adult tickets," said Trudy.

"Sorry? What?" He put on a falsely puzzled expression, pretending, and wanting to be clear that he was pretending, that Trudy's request made no sense.

Trudy looked up at me, intense challenge in her eyes. You see, Gordon? You've said nothing, but I know that you've doubted. Do you understand how you've ignored, how you've refused?

How stupid I'd been, thinking that she hadn't noticed. I took her place in front of the booth.

"Yes?" the guy said.

I gave him silence and a stare.

"Yes?"

I clenched my fists. There were a few people behind us in line. I glared at the guy.

"What do you want?"

Trudy took hold of my wrist, and I waited for her to tug a signal that it wasn't worth it. I put my other hand on the counter. No move from Trudy. How far was I prepared to go here, confronting him, but angry really at myself, my own blindness?

"It's twelve dollars," he said.

I passed over the money, relieved that I hadn't been called upon to do more, and he slid the tickets across. Still I stayed where I was, anticipating a complaint from behind us in line now, but wanting to make this jerk squirm, to show Trudy … something.

Trudy tugged my arm. "Gordon. It's okay."

I nodded my inadequate apology to her.

Some of Trudy's clients oozed into the frightened racial distances, just as she'd predicted. Out with her, walking Brooklyn and Manhattan, I now saw the accusing looks: How dare you! Why don't you leave! Murderer! Muslim!

Why had I been unable to see them before?

"This is just the shits," I said. "What is it with people? This city …" Trudy had returned early from work—more appointments cancelled.

"That's the question. What is it with people?"

"Let's get out of here. Let's have a holiday in Vancouver."

A pained Trudy sigh, then the wash of relief.

STOWING OUR CARRY-ON, SETTLING INTO OUR SEATS ON the plane, looking over the list of movie offerings, my orientation shifted: turn from New York racism to face Vancouver … stuff coming up.

"Yes. I'll have a Scotch, please."

I and little, brown Trudy would be two rooms over from Dad and tall, blonde Mum: Childe Gordon's old bedroom.

"Gordon?"

"Yes?"

"How did Jessica and your mother get along?"

Rattle the ice cubes and take another sip. "Fine."

"I see."

"Well, they weren't close. It was rather cool at first. Things improved after Leo was born. And then Gavin. Mum saw that Jessica was a good mother, and Jessica knew she knew. That's how I read it, anyway."

"That makes sense."

"So, she knew Jessica was a good mother."

"Sure. And once they got that far, some other stuff. I suppose Mum didn't mind that Jessica was tall and blonde, like her."

"No."

"Excuse me? Could I get another Scotch?"

"You're going to get drunk."

"You're right—Excuse me? Sorry. Just a soda water, please."

"You can get drunk if you like."

"I'm being stupid."

"So, she didn't mind that she was tall and blonde."

"Also successful. A big-time lawyer."

"A trophy daughter-in-law?"

"Well put."

And then, the annoying insight that no acknowledgment of Freud's sexist twistedness can take from him or deprive of power for us. Hey, Mum, meet Trudy. Note that she doesn't resemble you at all. Mummy, Mummy … I'm through. No longer do we have a thing going on.

"Gordon?"

"Yes?"

"You're confident?"

"I am. Honestly? My mum's a piece of work. Everybody would say that. But she's not a bad person. She's not racist."

THE TAXI DROPPED US AT THE FRONT DOOR. ABOUT TO PICK up a couple of our suitcases, I noticed that one of my shoelaces had come undone. Bend to tie it. Take the two ends in two hands, and … nothing. Helpless, untrained infant can't tie his shoes.

It took only seconds—look up, down again, tie shoelace—but it signalled that part of my brain was misfiring, some other region more recently evolved and less efficient taking over. I stood, and Trudy grinned at me as Leo and Gavin materialized to grab the rest of the luggage.

Mum and Dad came down the front steps.

"Trudy," said Dad.

"Trudy," said Mum.

"Linda. Michael," said Trudy. I hustled along with the suitcases.

I helped Mum serve the food, did so without dropping anything or messing up despite my new clumsiness.

Dad toasted Trudy as the meal began. The sound of eating for a few moments, and on, and the awkwardness grew, glances travelled around the table.

"Leo can speak Arabic," said Gavin.

"Really?" said Trudy. "How did you learn?"

"I didn't know that," said Mum.

"Leo's always been good at languages," said Dad, addressing Trudy.

"It wasn't that hard," said Leo, and Gavin, sitting beside him, snorted—younger brother derision that's admiring at the same time.

"Everything's easy after Gavinian," said Gavin.

"Gavinian?" said Trudy.

"When I was little I didn't speak English," said Gavin. "I had my own language, and Mum and Dad couldn't understand me, but Leo did. He translated for them."

"You don't know. You were too young to remember."

"I do so remember. You were really proud of yourself. You knew stuff Mum and Dad didn't."

Leo had produced complete, careful sentences by twenty months. "I like it when the sun shines on the dust," he said, motes shimmering in the morning light that filtered through the curtains on his bedroom window. "It's beautiful, isn't it, Leo? Here, let me just check, does your diaper need changing?" But Gavin was different. When little Gavin wanted something and Leo wasn't right there he would toddle off to get him. Leo-the-Linguist looked perplexed at first, uncertain why we didn't know what he knew, not wanting to be a four-year-old condescending to his parents.

I can sense a reader's creeping dissatisfaction with this continuing rosy depiction of the boys. So what. I hate the work that tries for sophistication by debunking romantic myths of children. The child character who is consciously cruel or deceitful does not make a narrative hip; a knowing, sexually manipulative preteen gains a frisson of edginess only for readers who mistake a pose for a position, a new cliché for a new reality—those readers. Idiots. Not you.

"Why Arabic?" said Mum.

"So I can watch Al Jazeera," said Leo.

"Isn't there an English version?" said Dad.

"You get a different perspective in Arabic," said Leo. "In the English version they're talking to us. In the Arabic they're talking to each other."

"Can you give an example of how that shapes the reporting?" said Mum.

"Well, for instance, in the English version all the stories involve the West. But not everything important on the Arabic Peninsula involves the West."

"I suppose not," said Mum.

"Yes. And, in Arabic, they don't have to prove certain things. So, when an American official says what's happening, then that's on the English networks. So, it's on the English Al Jazeera, but they show that maybe it's just the Americans saying things. But on the Arabic

Al Jazeera it might not be there at all. It's American, so probably …
they can just ignore it. They present something different."

"I see. And you can understand all that."

There was something in Mum's eyes then, it dropped over
them—a film of opacity, resistance. Where had I seen it? Where?

No. I hadn't seen it. I'd felt it. The resistance in Mum's eyes
reminded me of the way I'd felt about the way I'd felt, at the ticket
booth with Trudy, understanding that I'd looked but not seen,
unwilling to acknowledge what confronted her.

"It's not that hard, Grandma. Reporters speak really clearly,
and the stories get repeated. It's a great way to learn."

"Very impressive," said Dad.

"Very wise," said Trudy.

It should have occurred to me that Leo's summaries of the
news from Al Jazeera came from the Arabic version. He'd been
using the same software program that had worked so well with his
Spanish before our fated trip—all the thing with diplomats and
gifted teens.

The conversation rambled on from there, and we got through
dinner. The only problem belonged to me and nobody else. Dad
reached for the pepper, and his hand shook. Mum put the grinder
in his hand. It seemed only I noticed.

30

■ ■

" "Trudy and I can give the boys a lift home," I said. "Gordon, why don't you take Gavin and Leo, and I'll stay and help clean up."

It was still light out, a gorgeous, soft blue Vancouver summer evening, but I wasn't feeling that gorgeousness. Dad shakes. Why had nobody said anything?

"All buckled in?"

"Yup."

"Yup."

Had the grim diagnosis been delivered weeks ago, and they'd decided not to tell me until I arrived? Had they agreed that Mum and Dad would let me know when we were alone? It would be unfair to question my sons. I'd be asking them to break a confidence. Or showing them that their father was a frightened fool.

I shared a hug with Jessica. Dwarfed. I glanced down. Nope, not wearing heels. I've forgotten how tall she is. How short I am. Jesus. Try to cope, Gordon.

I considered stalling over a coffee at the Calabria before returning, but that would've been cheating.

Mum and Trudy sat in the living room, Mum's long legs extended to rest on the ottoman, Trudy's, as usual, curled under her: tall vs short, blonde vs brown. Dad had slipped off somewhere, wise man. I plopped down beside Trudy.

"Trudy was telling me about her work," said Mum.

"It's not a very interesting topic," said Trudy.

Joseph smelled my entrance, trotted into the room and started rubbing against my ankles. I handed him to Trudy, who stroked him as he clawed at her lap.

"It's most interesting," said Mum. "I'd just asked if there were an element of faith in what she does."

"Of course," said Trudy. "All healing involves faith."

Mum doesn't like it when the answer to a question she's posed begins with "of course," and she looked at Trudy, then at me. I raised an eyebrow back at her.

"You're right about that," Mum said. "Certainly, my dermatologist expects me to have faith, or it seems so when he can't provide explanations. You don't have experience with eczema, by any chance?"

Or neurological illnesses?

"No," said Trudy, thoughtfully shaking her head while looking down at Joseph. Joseph rumbled as Trudy scratched under his chin. I've never heard a cat purr so loudly.

"What is it again that you treat?"

"Oh, aches and pains, like Gordon's stiff neck. Joint problems. I work quite a bit with people recovering from injuries, but also with chronic pain."

"You don't do tumors."

Tumors? Dad? Could she ask it like that, matter-of-fact, as though nothing were at stake? Jesus.

Trudy chuckled, choosing to consider that a joke had been made. "No, not tumors. I don't cure cancer. I can't make the blind see. Sometimes the lame will walk." She smiled at me to share the jest.

"Half the writers in New York are seeing Trudy," I said.

"How remarkable," said Mum.

"It's one in the morning New York time," I said.

"You must be exhausted."

Trudy handed Joseph over to her. Dad still hadn't appeared. Maybe he was already in bed, easily fatigued now, battling a tumor, or a merciless degenerative disease.

I was exhausted indeed, just thrashed. Bits of trivia had knocked me out: a stubborn untied shoelace, a mere look in Mum's eyes, a tremor that a rational mind would know was nothing, blonde vs brown. Could I make it to bed without passing out?

I could. I could even fail to fall asleep.

It had been a while since I'd lain in bed at night, anxious, insomniac, unspecified stuff driving my wakefulness—hadn't happened at all, since Trudy, but it was like riding a bicycle, like I'd never stopped.

Trudy was relieved to be out of New York. Mum was unhappy about Trudy. Dad had the shakes. The boys had obviously anticipated awkwardness, or maybe worse, and had planned the dinner-table conversation topic—Arabic Al Jazeera. All of them, they pissed me off. What was it about, this buzzing anger keeping me from the relief of sleep?

I had a novel, for Christ's sake, at long last. It should have been the important thing. These post-completion days should have been the finest time. Instead, everybody's got other *issues*, and I'm not allowed to celebrate. Not that I would have told anyone, even if they hadn't all had their urgent shit preventing them from giving my accomplishment its due. I would have been silent. But I would have enjoyed knowing, not a petty pleasure in a secret, but just … knowing. Permit me, if you will, a sense of myself apart, as an artist.

Before, the only person I'd have shared with was Taylor. Maybe I'd run into him over the next few days. Vancouver isn't so big. I could just happen to take Trudy to a café where I stood a chance of seeing him. I could be casual, as though the entire review-trauma was something I'd long ago forgotten and that I'd assumed he too had put behind him. "Hi, Taylor! What a surprise! Oh, not much. I just sent the next novel off. Thanks! Hey, this is Trudy."

Of course, Trudy knew, but it wasn't the important thing for her. The London bombing overwhelmed everything.

There! The explanation. Back in Brooklyn, all that racist anger I refused to see. The bombing had shoved my novel off centre stage, and I'd resented. Mum's eyes glaze over; it's a sign of resentment, of what Leo's tale of Al Jazeera implicitly demands she make important. Not as bad a case as my own, but similar, the structure of it, the blinding self-centredness.

On into the night, still sleepless. Recognizing my selfishness doesn't solve the problem quite yet. Meditation fails. Can I feel something in my neck? No. Thank you, Trudy, for that mercy.

THE NEXT MORNING I GOT UP EARLY, STILL ON BROOKLYN time, and found Dad in the kitchen. "I'm making coffee," he said. He had one half of the Moka in each hand, and, embarrassed smile, he held both up to me as though he needed to demonstrate the truth of his statement.

I dumped some beans into the grinder, because he couldn't. He ran the grinder, watching as it roared, avoiding my gaze. His hand shook as he filled the Moka under the tap, and he held the filter cup out to me, so I took it from him. Measuring out my life, I was, and I dawdled, took needless care to level off the coffee. This would be the final moment, the instant before I knew. Later, even years on, the sound of a coffee grinder, the smell of freshly ground beans, the brush of stray grains from the threads of a Moka, and I would be back here, before Dad's announcement changed everything.

Dad managed to screw the top to the bottom and set the pot on the stove.

We stood together and watched the pot. He turned it off when the coffee bubbled up. I poured and took our cups to the table.

Dad reached for the sugar, but his hand shook and he gave up.
"One teaspoon, right?"

"Yes. Thanks."

I dumped the sugar in his cup and stirred for him. Dry mouth. Sip of coffee, and again, my mouth is dry. Force out the words: "What's going on, Dad?"

"It's nothing."

"Well, you shake."

"It's intentional shakes."

"What's that?"

"It's nothing. Really. Lots of older people get it. Even middle-aged people. You intend to do something with your hand, and your hand starts to shake. The doctors say that there's basically no treatment, which is a drag, but it also doesn't mean anything. It's not connected to anything else."

"I was worried. I thought ..."

"I should have said something right away, but it's embarrassing, y'know? And I try not to think about it."

"Jesus."

"I really should've said something. Your mother worried at first, but once we learned what it was, well, what's to do? She's fine about it. She just hands me things."

His hand did not shake as he reached to stroke his beard. I, on the other hand ... shaking all over.

"Gordon! Oh, man, I should've said something."

Trudy joined us soon after and of course saw immediately that something was up, looked back and forth at the two of us.

"I have intentional shakes," said Dad. "I was just telling Gordon."

"Yes. I saw that last night," said Trudy.

"I didn't know what it was."

"It's quite common."

"So Dad was telling me."

THE NEW YORK SUMMER STICKINESS HAD INTENSIFIED IN the days before we left, and now Vancouver offered its early August special: clear sky, temperatures hovering at perfect; the ocean air soft, a balm; purple and pink sunsets forever; grey-green sea and dark blue mountains. After our coffee, Trudy and I headed off to be tourists. Stanley Park.

"Would you like to move back here?"

"It's not like this all year. We're a lot farther north than New York. It gets dark. In mid-October, it's going to start raining. Those mountains? You won't see them for seven months."

"That's hard to believe."

"Believe it. People move here to get away from the snow, and a year later they kill themselves to get away from the grey."

"Gordon!"

"All right. The truth? I hadn't anticipated this, but no, emphatically not, I don't want to move back here."

"I see."

"I'd love to be closer to the boys."

"Yes."

"You see what it's like, with Mum and Dad, the past hovering over everything. I prefer life in Brooklyn."

"I see."

"Look. Right now I want to be where you are."

What? Was this too heavy? I looked at Trudy but she seemed unperturbed.

"If you want to leave Brooklyn, I'll go too if you'll let me. Toronto. Hell, London—Noreen would be okay with that. Take me to Trinidad, if you like. Just not Vancouver."

"Brooklyn will be fine. People will forget again. I'll get new clients."

"Okay."

"The hovering past."

"Yes."

I hadn't told Trudy the Taylor story. The idea frightened me. The way she said "yes"—maybe I was making stuff up again, but it felt like she knew something needed disclosure. I'd have to find the time and the nerve.

We had dinner out on The Drive with Jessica, Gavin and Leo, having decided against an evening together at the Kitchener place. We found lots to talk about, Jessica and Trudy were interested in each other, and kind, and nobody wanted to stay for dessert.

"Waiter? The bill, please? Now?"

A couple of days later, back at Douglas Park, Mum had brought the conversation back to Trudy's healing powers again, clearly some irritation driving her. But Dad didn't share it.

"Trudy, I've got this … can you do anything for elbows? I get this pain in my elbow when I'm playing squash. I'll pay your usual rate, of course. Oh, this is horrible. You're on vacation. It's when I serve, or when I hit an overhead. Ouch."

"You're too old for squash," said Mum.

"Michael. I can heal your elbow. You get the family price, the same price you've charged us for your wonderful hospitality."

"Just like that? You say you can fix his elbow, and you haven't even examined it?"

"Well, I can, Linda. I'm not going to say I can't if I can."

I was proud of her for that answer.

After, Dad couldn't tell. "I don't know," he said, windmilling his arm around. "It only hurts when I play. Otherwise it's fine. I'll set up a match."

OUR LAST MORNING, I'D BEEN SAVING IT, NITOBE GARDENS, and Trudy was knocked out, just as I knew she'd be. I was finally getting some joy, mainly, I knew, because we'd be leaving so soon. So, we were cheerful as we returned to Douglas Park.

Dad burst toward us as we entered. "It's gone! It's … it's gone! I've been to a doctor, a physio, a massage therapist …" He mimed a squash serve, bounced on the balls of his feet, smashed an imaginary return, and then raised his arms in victory. "Trudy, you're a miracle worker!" He hugged her, lifting her off her feet.

"Perhaps I should've asked you to test your skills on my eczema after all," said Mum at dinner that night.

"I could try, Linda."

Mum didn't answer. She took a bite of the baked salmon I'd made, the thank you dinner. "The fish is very good, Gordon."

"Do you want Trudy to take a look at your eczema, Mum?"

"It would be unfair to ask her to go to work again."

Trudy took this for what it was, a refusal—of help, maybe more.

At the end of the evening, with Trudy getting ready for bed, Mum already having retired, I found Dad in the den, reading.

"Hey."

"Gordon, it's been so lovely having this time with you, and meeting Trudy. I'm so happy for you."

"Dad, did Trudy say anything? Do you remember, when she was treating you, did she say anything?"

Dad put down his book. He swallowed. "She said, 'you don't have to.'"

"'You don't have to' what?"

"Just, 'You don't have to.'"

I considered then telling him about my novel. I considered telling Mum. Sit them down in the living room in the morning. Announce it. Dad would have been so happy for me, automatically happy, and really, what does an automatic response amount to? Mum ... she would have been surprised that I'd bothered to say, would have been, perhaps, disappointed in such weakness in me. For the rest of the evening a fantasy gripped my imagination. Each of them, confronted by so undeniable a contrast in the other, would learn something of themselves. But it was just a fantasy.

I got up in the middle of the night. Returning from the bathroom, I almost tripped over Joseph; the bastard had awakened and rushed down the hall to see what he could gain by rubbing up against my ankles one last time. I shoved him away with my foot, and he meowed. Then I heard Mum and Dad, very softly behind their closed door. Three a.m. The tone suggested argument, and I didn't try to hear more.

Everybody up early for the departure, Mum and Dad fending off all protest, both of them insisting. For once, Mum didn't talk while she drove. Both hands stayed on the wheel, her eyes on the road.

They didn't come in, just pulled up to the curb at international departures. Dad stayed in his seat while Mum got out. She'd been silent all morning, not sulking, just reserved. "It was a pleasure meeting you," she said to Trudy. "Thank you for giving us so much time."

"Oh, Linda, thank you for having us stay with you; it was so generous."

Trudy bustled off to look for a cart, leaving me behind, curbside, with our luggage.

Mum hugs me. She holds on.

"'Bye, Gordon!" Dad leans out of the window and waves.

"'Bye, Dad!"

I should've tried harder. If I'd taken Mum on a walk and talked to her, even if she'd said nothing in response, I could have spoken my mind, challenged her. Accepted how much I owed her and yet forced her to admit things, what she had wanted to make of me. She wouldn't have agreed or even understood, but at least she'd have known I resisted. I should have figured out what I needed to say to Dad that made me ache a bit every time he looked at me.

31

■ ■

"I swear, not a hint, not a passive-aggressive sigh. I will not ask for a reason. I swear by my sword, if you want to leave, the only thing I'll give you is any help you ask for."

"I believe you."

"There's room ... there's room ..."

"It's okay, Gordon."

"Your rent is extortionate. So's mine."

We were in another brownstone, another open house, much like the first one. I hadn't sprung anything on her. I told her about it, asked if she would like to think about it, and she'd been fine.

"Let's look at some more. It's not smart just to jump on the first one we see."

So, for a month we were a couple on the hunt for real estate. It didn't make sense to check out other boroughs, what with Trudy's work being in Brooklyn.

The place I'd shown Trudy more than a year before came on the market again. We didn't look at it. But, soon after, another one, nearby, similar. Why not?

GORDON BRIDGE, NOVELIST, IN LOVE. PARTNERED UP AGAIN. I strode along 7th Avenue, the charming centre of Park Slope. I don't look at myself in shop windows, but I looked. Ridiculous. Head back, chin up, chest out, arms swinging—I'm a skinny little middle-aged man pretending he's fresh out of marine boot camp.

I'd been attempting a do-over, back in our new home. But I couldn't conjure up the old feeling, the satisfaction—novel done. Trudy had confirmed that the post-London ugliness had begun subsiding. The Vancouver trip with its attendant emotional junk had also receded, late summer easing into fall. But the time for my private triumphing after the novel submission had been lost. London is bombed, my celebration is spoiled. Out on my walk, I'd made a method-actor's last attempt to call up that old smugness, tried to draw it out by finding the right posture, and, there I was in the reflection of the Da Nonna Rosa window, and I could only hope the diners digging into their pasta lunch specials hadn't glanced out and wondered why that weirdo was walking that way.

The obvious thing was to put it behind me and start a new novel, but I had nothing there. That didn't worry me. The big thing was to have broken through, even if I had to postpone more joy till publication. I read a lot. Into the winter, dutiful son still, I called Mum and Dad and reminded them about their driving. Trudy worried that I was being rude, nagging them that way, till I explained the necessity.

Some energy returned in the summer when publication neared. Then the boys came out for a visit, and then the book arrived.

A reader, of this and of *Volley*, might reasonably ask what happened to the ghost net metaphor. You have to look carefully, but it's there, when you first see that Carson has no memories, only acute anticipations. The destructiveness of his amnesia is broadcast so casually, and his disorder produces such indifference to suffering—that's just one trace of the drifting, death-dealing net. You can also see a trace in the dedication, "For Gavin." Leo had his already. It was Gavin's turn and he'd earned it.

I opened the box, pulled out a copy and handed it to Gavin. "Take a look inside."

He opened it, saw the dedication, and left the room. He'd acquired the family habit: exit rather than play the emotional scene. Holding the novel to his chest, he ran down the hall and into the room he shared with Leo, closing the door behind him.

He came out only a few minutes later, grinning, sheepish. "I'm famous," he said.

Leo, sitting on the couch, witness to the whole thing, glanced up nonchalantly from the *LRB* he was reading. "Don't let it go to your head," he said. Gavin knocked the paper out of Leo's hands, so Leo had no choice but to stand up and accept Gavin's hug.

Noreen will be pleased with me if I say what's true and is no strain to acknowledge: she's always right. About my New York novel, for happy example—*Volley through Eternity* killed, with loads of interviews, readings, all that extra New York attention, months of it, on into another summer, fall. If I'd been writing I could have found it irritating, but I wasn't writing. When prize season rolled around and *Volley* hit all the short-lists but never won, Noreen fumed, but I delighted, something *raffiné* about not winning. Governor General's, Giller, Booker: finalist, every time.

Back home in Brooklyn, after an end-of-season appearance at a writers' festival upstate, the last in a series of shows stokin' the star-maker machinery behind the popular novel, Trudy and I headed out into the cold so I could clear my head and enjoy the neighbourhood with her again.

"The reading went well. They all went well, but this one was particularly good. I'm glad there'll be a break now."

"Me too."

"I'm glad I didn't win any prizes," I said.

"So you told me," said Trudy.

"Winning is kind of crass. It's like saying my novel finished in first place."

"I can see that."

"I was really pleased with the reviews, not just because they were positive, but because ... well, you read them. That one in the *LA Times*, for instance. It's affirming to be taken seriously that way."

"You should be pleased and you should be taken seriously."

"I took that royalty cheque seriously."

"Me too. Let's go someplace expensive and tacky for drinks soon, to celebrate."

We headed into Brooklyn Bridge Park.

"You know, the most important thing, I feel like I've given something to Gavin."

"He certainly felt so. It meant so much to him."

"Yeah."

"But, Gordon ..."

"Yes."

"You're working very hard to be happy about these matters."

A romantic snow had begun falling on us, and on the Park, and the East River and Manhattan: snow was general all over the five boroughs.

"Is this usual for you? Do you get depressed once a novel is out?"

"Am I depressed?"

"Well, you're busy with all the book things, but you're sad."

"Okay."

"You've stopped cooking. We get takeout for dinner. You eat pistachios for breakfast. You've stopped returning phone calls. You're not even reading anything."

"Okay."

"Aren't you supposed to be calling your parents? Last winter you reminded them constantly, and now, you're silent."

"I see that."

Trudy's questions dispelled a fog that I hadn't noticed, emotional fog of my own creation. It went back at least to that summer trip to Vancouver, after I submitted the novel, my failure to enjoy that moment, my failure really to enjoy anything, my creeping depression.

The hole—enormous, unfilled, loss still felt.

"WHAT'S BEST HERE IS THE HANDLING OF TENSE. IN THIS novel, verb tense is a triumph." In his hands Taylor held his copy of *The Legal Tender*, dedicated to him, while he looked down at the front cover, and as he spoke he shook the book a couple of times in emphasis. We had no official arrangement, but always, soon after publication—his, mine—we'd come to this debriefing.

"Verb tense," I said. "I'm relieved that you noticed. I couldn't believe how all the reviewers overlooked it."

"I'm serious. It got to the point where I was more interested in the shifts in tense than the characters. Well, as interested—and I was damned interested in the characters," he said quickly, before I could object. "I'm not surprised you don't think about this when you write. It'd be impossible to achieve that kind of success with a conscious manipulation of time."

He began to explain, and his explanation evolved into one of his intense, virtuosic rambles. The ramble found its way back 2,500 years to Heraclitus and his river, the heart-breaking, beautiful stream into which no one can step twice. For Taylor, the novel's mixture of tenses—sometimes relating flashbacks in the present tense, sometimes the past, sometimes shifting within paragraphs—gathered momentum and made him breathless with the mystery of impermanence.

Sometimes, when he'd started talking this way, I'd tried to take notes, but he'd refused to let me.

"Taylor, c'mon, just one of these sentences, sometimes you come up with a sentence, and if I don't get it down, just as you said it, its power is gone."

Nope. Never. It made him too self-conscious.

This time, I hadn't asked. I hadn't reached for my notebook, and Taylor continued, explaining how my shift to the present in the midst of a flashback transformed the memory into a *tableau vivant*, somehow eternal, and then he stopped himself mid-ramble.

"What's that in your shirt pocket?"

"It's a pen."

"A pen."

I looked down at my shirt. "A pen," I said.

"Since when do you carry a pen in your shirt pocket?"

"I don't know. I hadn't thought about it."

"Can I see it?"

"No."

He reached for me, but I moved back. He rose from his chair. I got out of mine and darted behind it, and he came for me.

He let out a comic-book, triumphant "aha!" while he sat on my chest—he was fit and he outweighed me by about sixty pounds—and he held the pen aloft, and then he yelped, a sound I'd heard before, ending tennis games, basketball shoot-arounds. "Shit," he said. "I've torn something in my shoulder. Damn."

Later, the pain-killers gobbled, the ice-pack in place: "How do you work it?" I explained, and he played back what I'd recorded on my specially purchased secret-agent recorder-pen.

In an eternal *tableau vivant* Taylor holds up the pen in one hand, my book in the other, grin on his face, just before his cry of pain.

I'D NEVER FOUND THE RIGHT TIME. I'D BEEN A COWARD. NOW, to respond to Trudy's comment that I was working hard to be happy about my book, clearly there could be no further postponing. Did she know already? Had she already understood and forgiven?

We'd been standing a few minutes, watching the snow. Trudy put a mittened hand in mine and squeezed.

"There's something I need to tell you about," I said. I looked at her. She was gazing at the river, waiting for me, the snow falling.

The night growing colder, I confessed my miserable past.

"Do you think he'll ever forgive me?"

"I don't know. You haven't tried to contact him for a few years now?"

"More than a few."

She knocked her arms against her sides to shake off some snow. "I don't know, Gordon. Even if he does forgive, it may not mean what you hope. Heraclitus says—"

"I know. You can't step into the same river twice."

FOR THE RECORD, AND TO RESPOND TO SOMETHING LOTS have been curious about, Mum and I never talked about my books. I was on the scene when she finished my first novel, and when she turned the last page we simply made what we wanted to out of each other's silence. Too much complicated stuff was at stake for us to repeat that performance, so farther on down the road she would simply congratulate me on publication. I assumed that she read and she assumed that I assumed, and we knew, didn't we, that I didn't expect or need praise.

It cut both ways with Mum and me, and I'm not complaining. When very young I read her articles in *The Literary Review of Canada* and sometimes asked her questions, but I learned that explaining held no interest for her. I never wondered, of course, whether she wanted comments. What would have followed if I'd merely said, "Hey Mum, terrific piece in the latest *TLRC*. Really smart stuff."

Some of those articles are worth very little. All right, she had to get them out to deadline, and the material she worked with didn't always help. When she found something good, she identified it and clarified why it merited attention. A small collection could be made of those articles, worthwhile for reviewers learning the craft and for readers of all sorts: an aesthetic carefully expressed is a valuable thing.

When the material was bad enough to make her angry, that too could lead to good work.

"NO!" SAYS MUM. I'M DOING MY HOMEWORK AT THE KITCHEN table, which in my social moods I prefer to my bedroom desk. Mum strides into the kitchen from the living room, where she's been reading, and she yanks open the back door. The cold air crashes in. She steps onto the porch in the pouring rain. It's early evening but it's Vancouver in November and it's dark, dark out. I get up, go to the door, and I see my mother hurl a book into the drenched night.

I take note of that book each of the next several days when I come home from school and push my bike through the back gate. I admire my mother's throwing arm: the book made it all the way to the fence. It lies on the lawn, swells up with rainwater, fatter day by day, and then it's gone. I know that Dad would have done nothing, not wanting to take any action that could count as interference, so it's Mum who has bothered to drop the soggy mess in the garbage, I guess.

I was fourteen and I sort of understood the long feature article that followed a couple of issues later, which discussed five recent novels and touched on a bunch more, published over the last decades. I went back to the piece a few times, wanting to get it because I wanted to get my mother.

What angered her was flattery. Specifically, each of the novels she discusses and connects to a shameful pattern in Can Lit features a protagonist who is selfish and narrow. Each main character discovers a capacity for generosity and breadth. In each case, moreover, the novels manage to show that the selfishness is superficial; it's a quality misunderstood, a response to conditions over which the characters have no control—reaction formation.

But it's flattery. The novels tell their assumed-to-be-selfish readers that the qualities in themselves that they know are bad are not so. They're off the hook. They can believe that when they finally meet demanding circumstances like those the protagonists encounter, those circumstances will reveal the fine truth of their own truly expansive hearts. Until that happens, they can relax. They can go on insulting the other members of their book clubs behind their backs.

Readers gobble up these books like crowds of scavenging fish sucking down sodden bits of refined white crap.

From Mum I learned the lesson: never flatter. A flatterer is a liar and a coward. A flatterer's book finds its judgment lying against a fence. It swells and rots.

32

"Hello?"

"It's Jessica."

"The boys? Is it the boys?"

"Oh God, Gordon, no. No ... your parents."

"What?"

"Your dad. There's been an accident. Gordon, he's dead. Your mum's in a coma. I'm at the hospital with Gavin and Leo. Lions Gate Hospital."

"I'll get the first flight I can."

Trudy offered to come with me, but it made more sense for her to stay on in Brooklyn. She'd fly out for the funeral. If Mum had been awake and we could've done anything for her right then, it would've been different.

I arrived in Vancouver mid-morning, carry-on only, straight to car-rental row.

Minutes before, taxiing into the gate, I'd seen snow falling heavy past the window, starting to accumulate on the tarmac. Snow, Vancouver: try now to think, Gordon. It's Vancouver, wet snow, New Year's Day.

I ditched the rental plan and caught the Canada Line downtown. Rode the SeaBus across the pretty inner harbour gone grim in the storm, and, through the slush, a hike up the big hill to the hospital at the foot of the mountain. I wanted to get there and wanted never to arrive. Into neurological intensive-care, down a corridor that looped around a nurses' station from which all could be observed.

Mum's room, I'm looking down at her. Jessica, Gavin, and Leo stand with me.

Mum had a brain injury. She'd also broken an arm and twisted an ankle, but that was nothing. After the surgery the doctors had induced a coma to try to control the bleeding and release the pressure. Bandages swathed her head.

They were waiting for her vital signs to stabilize, so they could take her off the medication that kept her under and she'd gradually gain consciousness—they hoped.

The accident happened in North Vancouver, where Mum and Dad had gone to a New Year's Eve party. That's why Mum ended up at Lions Gate. Who'd been driving? The nurses didn't know.

Gone. He's gone. Moment by moment I forgot and then remembered and staggered again.

Somebody had to know about the accident, but I couldn't think who to ask. I latched on to it, needing to believe something would make a difference.

When I called Mountain View to book Dad's cremation, and then the papers to place the obit, I stepped out of Mum's room, remembering stories of people in comas who heard the conversations around them. I didn't want Mum to know yet that Dad had been killed.

I took my laptop along, opened it, created a new document. I would defeat this. Right there, bedside, I'd alter reality. By writing, insisting that I was still a novelist, everything else would realign. I'd no longer be in the hospital; the accident would not have happened. I didn't believe that I believed it, but I did. And I wrote nothing. I was nothing.

A man and a woman, uniformed, came along and hovered by the door.

"Can I help you?"

"Is this Linda Bridge's room?"

The ambulance drivers, first on the scene, now at the end of a shift and checking on the shattered woman they'd delivered here, and they looked at me, hoping.

I told them what I knew and thanked them for what they'd done and for thinking to visit. They thanked me, and they prepared to leave.

"Wait," I said.

Suddenly it wasn't so easy. Maybe I shouldn't know. But now they were concerned about me and waiting to see how they might help me.

I asked.

They exchanged glances, surprised nobody had been able to tell me.

"Your mother was driving, Mr. Bridge."

"It wasn't her fault."

Not her fault? Hell, no. Whose then?

I'm an ass, sulking back in Brooklyn. I'm a petulant child. Oh, poor me, I can't celebrate my new novel the way I want to. Boo fucking hoo. Too woe-is-me stupefied to think of anything or anyone else. Like what? Like call your parents! Fuck! It's winter! Call them! Nag them! Don't drive at night! Don't drive in the snow!

"Here's the patricide Bridge, guilty and useless at his mother's hospital bedside."

Four days passed before I remembered the cat. I checked out of the hotel by the hospital and got a cab to the house, picturing Joseph at the door, hungry and desperate.

He didn't show. I put some food and water out, and still, no Joseph. He could've been anywhere; cats can find places to hide. I looked through the house, angry now, stomping around, useless. But he was in the house. He was an indoor cat. It would take a cat more than four days to starve to death, wouldn't it? What about water? Now, now I'm full of concern, wanting to save the damned cat.

MOUNTAIN VIEW. I WAS THE SECOND TO ARRIVE. FIRST, sitting at the back of the room, head down, statue-still—Taylor.

I watched him from the door at the front entrance. Would he speak to me if I addressed him? He must have considered the possibility and decided he could handle it. Or maybe he assumed I'd keep my distance. No. You can't do that. You don't show up here and expect me to ignore you. My father's death governs us here.

My footsteps echoed as I walked toward him, but he didn't move.

"Hi, Taylor."

"I loved him," he said, looking up, first words to me in nine years.

"He loved you."

Taylor nodded. "And he missed you," I almost added.

Trudy said nothing, didn't even look at me questioningly when I returned to the front of the room. I was distracted through the short service, failing to think properly about Dad, not grieving the way I wanted to. He'd ruined it, showing up like that.

I stood at the door, shaking hands with Dad's friends and colleagues and thanking them. Taylor remained in his seat till I'd received the last offer of condolence. I strode toward him, footsteps echoing again, he again looking down. What would I say? Ask him to join me for coffee? Go for a walk in the cemetery and reminisce?

I turned around and echoed on out. Oh, how I should have taken care of this by now. So much time had passed since Yvonne's blistering order to stop communications, her threat of consequences I couldn't imagine. I should have contacted him and tried to get us going once more, or at least, yes, found it, much as I hate the word. Closure. If I had done so, then Dad, then Mum …

Trudy stayed for a week after the funeral, sitting bedside with me and taking her turn holding Mum's hand. She kept holding it when she stood up and leaned over the bed, stroked Mum's forehead with her other hand and said "Oh, Linda." No response, no miracle.

After Trudy left I set up my desk in my old room and made another attempt, saner now, utterly unambitious: just try writing something. It doesn't have to go anywhere. Nothing.

It snowed again, the snow turned to more days of rain, and I willed myself into the safety of a mindless rut. For a while Joseph remained hidden, but he drank the water and ate the food I put out, when I wasn't there. Finally, some cat judgment being exercised— don't go near that guy, not to be trusted.

Sitting beside my mother, waiting and hoping, but also, God, also bored, even bored with my guilt, my thoughts returned to Taylor. Maybe I should have spoken to him at the funeral. I could have suggested only that I'd call, later, in a week or so. "It's time now, Taylor. We need to talk."

Joseph began to appear, mornings, always at the moment I was preparing to leave. I'd hear him galloping from somewhere as I started putting on my boots and my coat. He'd meow, desperate for contact, and he'd try to rub against my legs, and I had no time. I'd shove him away, open the front door and close it quickly. As I walked down the steps, he howled.

IV

CHARLES'S EXPECTATIONS

33

The trick I developed of just refusing all affect, keeping my head figuratively down and trudging through, one morning broke down. I got my SeaBus ticket, tramped along the long enclosed ramp over the drowning railyards, past the rain-splattered helipad, but I stopped before the door to the loading platform. The boat chugged into its dock, people got off and walked by me, and I stood, and then I retreated.

This could not be: Dad dead, Mum comatose, everything over this way and yet not over at all, everything … pending.

I hunched into one of the cabs lined up outside the terminal. "Stanley Park," I said.

ONE MORNING DURING OUR SUMMER IDYLL IN VANCOUVER, Trudy and I had risen early, taken the car, and headed to Stanley Park.

The sun hadn't yet come up as we crossed Burrard Bridge, ahead of the rush hour traffic. I drove the Beach Avenue route, Trudy counting the freighters coming into view on the inlet as dark sky shaded toward morning turquoise. We parked off Pipeline Road and had the forest-filtered dawn, the waking birds, and the short Beaver Lake trail to ourselves.

Beaver Lake is not a lake but a pond at the centre of a little wetland, grown over with lily pads, cattails and bulrushes packing its shores. Central Park is extraordinary, of course, but New York has nothing like this—the morning joy chorus and the wind picking up, stirring the trees, the mossy rain-forest smell, the sense that the world of the city has just … vanished. We watched the ducks coasting through the lily pads, dipping under and bobbing up with dripping leaves in their bills. I held Trudy's hand and didn't worry about how the time with Mum and Dad was going.

"My, it's gorgeous," said Trudy.

"Nothing gold can stay," I said.

She dropped my hand and looked at me.

"Those lilies are taking over. They're not a native species. When they die they sink and rot, and they're filling the pond in."

"We need more ducks," said Trudy.

"It's not just the lilies. All lakes do this. The vegetation around the shore dies and pulls soil in after it. It can take eons, or just decades. This one'll be decades, at most. The lake flattens out and dies."

"Couldn't we just say that the water flows elsewhere? Gordon?" She gave me one of her gentlest smiles.

"Sure. Hey, see that tangle over there, on the other side?"

"Yes."

"Beaver dam."

"Really?"

"Yup. Also, there, beside it, that's a stream that runs down to the inlet. Salmon spawn in that stream."

"Really?"

"I tell no lies."

"Well, this is an important place for you, isn't it? My." She turned away, giving me some space for recollections.

LOSING SHEPHERD

THE SUMMER AFTER GRADE EIGHT, ONE MORNING A FEW days into summer vacation, Taylor and I rode our bikes to Stanley Park. Neither of us had ever ridden downtown before, so it was a coming-of-age moment, a self-conscious one, which didn't make it less significant.

We pedalled around the trails, enjoying being free of school and on our own. Arrived at a clearing above Prospect Point, we stopped for lunch, eating our sandwiches, watching the sailboats, then riding on.

Taylor had been a couple of inches taller than I when we'd met, but in just the last few months those two inches had become four. Also, his voice had changed. This difference had begun to unsettle us, but riding through the forest, stopping at forks in the path to discuss which way to go, balance seemed for the time restored.

We found ourselves at Beaver Lake, and we got off our bikes.

Neither of us could remember having seen the place before.

"I feel like an explorer," said Taylor.

I started to respond with a joke, but I stopped myself. I still remember the feeling, reaching for some witticism and then thinking, hold it, be serious, and then also thinking that this decision to be silent was mature of me. I felt proud of that maturity for just a second and then I thought the pride itself wasn't so good. It was more grown-up to feel humble, looking at the pond that we'd reached after a day's riding.

Taylor took out the orange left from his lunch and peeled it. Showing even then his talent for the graceful symbol, he broke it in two and offered me half. When done eating, he knelt by the water's edge, dipped his hands in, and swirled them around. I took his place, plunged my hands in the water, and then I cupped some of it up and passed it across my lips. It tasted good, slightly grassy, after the orange. I can close my eyes now and still capture the citrus sweetness and the cool water.

A crow cawed at us. Taylor put one hand on my shoulder and shoved me, not hard. We rode home.

An important, beautiful memory, sure, but also a mere prelude—the little dumb show before the full drama, the scary stuff of real maturity.

A year and a half later, and Young Taylor had a crush on Janice Evenson. Impossible. A grade ahead, popular, pretty, and a reputation: boys from other schools, boys in university. An interesting choice for my handsome, brilliant, shy pal. His intense suffering was nothing unusual, but so what? We cheat ourselves when we look back at such first journeys and chuckle at our young selves.

"She doesn't know I exist. It's a cliché but it's true."

"How's she supposed to? She's in grade eleven. She's not in any of your classes. You're not on Student Council together."

Taylor looked at me—oh, the pain in his eyes, his friend stooping to sarcasm at such a moment.

I didn't have to stoop for Taylor to look down on me. He now stood six feet tall. I'd stalled at five-four, and the limited expressive capacities of my little boy's soprano blunted the effects of my wit. I was fifteen and battling to keep my impatience from exploding into despair.

"So, the first step is to make her aware."

"I thought of writing her a letter. You know, a note."

"No, no, no. Too heavy. You give her the letter, she doesn't even know you, one of her friends sees you doing it, and they ask her and she's all embarrassed ... death."

"Okay, what?"

"Do you know her timetable?"

He sighed.

"So, I assume you also know where her locker is. You plot a route from her locker to her last class of the day, any day. Make an early exit from your class. Go to her locker. Walk the reverse route to her class, and when you cross paths, no matter who she's with, what she's doing, you say it."

"What?"

"Hi, Janice."

"Then what?"

"That's it. Keep walking. Mission accomplished. She's aware of your existence. She asks her friends who you are, and they tell her."

He did as I suggested, after only a week to work up the courage, and he reported her reply, a cheerful "Oh, hi, Taylor." This text got the impressive Taylor close reading. She knew his name already—good sign. And if, as he'd said, the tone of her "Oh" registered positive surprise, and of "hi" a hint of promise, well, the portents were good.

He created other accidental meetings, and each time a prepared sentence—the greeting, the comment on something innocuous—won its positive response. A couple of weeks of this dance, and Taylor grew certain that Janice knew that the encounters were planned, and she didn't mind. She liked it. They were sharing a joke.

I could see a change coming. Here, we have Taylor, bass-voiced, lanky tenth-grade six-footer, not cool, not athletic, but definitely now handsome, with dark wavy hair and that big friendly smile, and nice, and winning enough academic awards that Janice Evenson and actually, probably, everyone in the school was aware of his existence; over here, Gordon, five-foot four, six significant months younger, a so-charming, smooth-cheeked lock for the prize role of Ophelia in the upcoming King's Men's spectacular: we would lose each other for a while. I would lose my friend.

Taylor couldn't manage his way into membership in one of the shifting social groupings that sexy Janice flowed through. No opportunities for casually getting to know her presented themselves. He simply had to ask her on a date.

Over days he crafted his line. It needed to be short, to take advantage of a brief opportunity when she'd be alone. It needed to be casual but unambiguous: a date. He settled on "Hi, Janice. Would you like to go to a movie with me this weekend?" and then, at the last minute, a fine edit to achieve a more relaxed tone, "Hi, Janice. How'd you like to go to a movie with me this weekend?"

She would. Saturday night.

SUNDAY MORNING. TAYLOR KNOCKED ON MY BACK DOOR. I hadn't finished my granola.

"Gordon," he choked out, and then he retreated onto the porch. Nothing could have been more urgent.

I dumped my dishes in the sink. "I'm going riding with Taylor," I shouted. Then, to him, "meet you out back."

When I pushed out into the yard, Taylor was standing over his bike by the open back gate, watching for me over his shoulder. He rode into the lane, and I followed.

I had a hard time keeping up, and ascending the south slope of Burrard Bridge I just let him ride away from me.

He was waiting when I got to Beaver Lake.

Taylor looked at me as he spoke. Face contorting. Licking his lips. Waving his hands around, then noticing them and holding them at his sides.

They took the bus downtown, had a good time, held hands at the movie. They bussed back and he walked her home. Kiss on her front porch—incredible.

Janice's parents had gone for the evening and she invited him in. They necked on the couch, and then she led him to her bedroom, where they undressed. They necked some more. She produced a condom, but when he tried to put it on, recalling recent guidance class demonstrations with a cucumber, his hands shook, he failed, and he lost his erection. Not to return.

What do you say, Gordon? What's the wisdom here? I knew that Taylor had found his wisdom already by confiding in me. How many fifteen-year-olds would have the maturity to share this news with anybody? He had taken control with this ride to our lake, a move to shape the moment, provide a structure that could recover some of his vanished dignity. He had forced each word up his throat and out past his humiliation so that I could help him. It was the hard stuff of real friendship.

After having been so far ahead of me, he had fallen back, but I felt no gratification. I just needed to think of a way to help. Perhaps I've never been wiser. I found the enlightened answer there and then, anguished still by my forever-delayed puberty, anguished more by my friend's trauma.

"You should talk to my dad," I said, the words strange in my mouth, my throat catching.

Taylor looked at me—Yes! That's right, yes. Fear still, but relief. His own parents—smart, loving, understanding, and gently sorrowing over Taylor's recent distancing from the Church: not available. Me: not able. Mr. B.: clearly the man.

The conversation with my father took place that afternoon, in Dad's study. It lasted more than an hour. I waited in my room, thinking about Taylor, hoping, but not really focused. Turning inward to my own worries, concentration intensifying ... I had no patience left, nothing could be so important. I can close my eyes now and still get close to the ferocity in me, all my being, willing change.

That intensity spilled out—can you guess how? Mum was off somewhere, Dad and Taylor *in camera* one floor down: nobody would hear me. I sang. I went at it with real focus and volume: pop songs, Christmas carols, whatever. "Joy to the World" did the trick, and let me tell you, I felt the joy. A few times over, when I realized that it began with a descending scale—just what I wanted, all those notes—and there, yes! And again! A wacky, comical scrape and crack in my voice. Yes, oh yes, that very day. I'd felt it, not heard but felt the tickling potential, right at the moment, Beaver Lake, when I took the mature step, recognized my responsibility to acknowledge what I didn't know and what I did, and told Taylor to go to my father. Now, mere potential no more, as though the physical change had stalled, waiting for moral preparation, and I'd finally taken care of it.

I inspected and discovered no more evidence, no previously unnoticed hair to brag about. I sang again, running through the scale: "the Lord has come." Crack. Hair, the rest of it, would follow, I knew—mature life.

After, saying goodbye in my backyard, Taylor looking wiped but relieved, he said, "We'll always be friends."

THE CAB DROPPED ME BY THE PARK ENTRANCE AND I WALKED to Beaver Lake. The cold bit shrewdly. At least it had stopped raining, though the forest still dripped. No ducks showed themselves.

The wave of pain that had gathered all morning, broken over me while I waited at the SeaBus station—it had retreated somewhere, a melancholy long withdrawal. I missed Trudy, felt her there beside me in remembered summer warmth. From one moment to the next I told myself that I was about to leave and head for the hospital, but I remained. I trudged around—twittering of a few birds staying on for the winter, the trickling water that drove the beaver crazy with the need to dam up the stream. The wind in the underbrush. Or maybe that was the sound of the lake's abrading edges, of its dying. I wanted to cry but it wouldn't happen. All my changes were there, at Beaver Lake? Well, sure: your father dies, your mother is stolen from you. Changes, I'd say. Look up. Big birds flying across the sky.

I walked on, out of the park, toward the West End, where Taylor and Yvonne lived.

34

He had, after all, spoken to me at the funeral. Going over that exchange later, I'd noted that he hadn't addressed me. But he'd spoken.

I could make an argument that the time was right; it's a cliché that death brings perspective, but it does; it's bigger than a friend's big mistake, a dumb review that nobody remembered by then.

He could have moved, but I doubted it. Years ago he and Yvonne had found a West-of-Denman place in an old co-op, a couple of blocks from Lost Lagoon, where the city becomes Stanley Park. Not the sort of place to leave.

It was raining again. I wove my way along the trails, took the underpass to the other side of the causeway and crossed the road into the city.

West-of-Denman is a little neighbourhood, about a square kilometre, which strives for a village feel: apartment buildings from the forties and fifties, some newer high-rises in there but also some good art deco and even one or two houses still standing. The vibe is a bit self-satisfied for me, but I'd be self-satisfied too if I lived a five-minute walk from Lost Lagoon, the forest, and the sea wall.

Five minutes, and I stood outside Taylor and Yvonne's building, getting wet.

They might not be in. They might be in but refuse to see me. See me but refuse to allow me past the door. Taylor could flip out. Yvonne could.

The catastrophe hinted at in Yvonne's note of years ago, could it be looming still?

Catching them off guard, on the other hand, could be good.

It could also destroy a real last chance.

It could be ideal; they'd be unprepared, defences not ready.

There's a Hollywood trope that features a character standing in the rain, inadequately dressed for the weather. Or running in the rain. Standing or running, never walking, but getting soaked. The character's indifference to the weather signals emotional intensity. Despair/desire/joy registers with such power that the downpour goes unnoticed.

Life didn't measure up to art, my competing impulses failed to meet the Hollywood standard, and I grew cold and miserable as the rain intensified. Pathetic, that's the word. Back in our undergrad days Taylor had explained the "pathetic fallacy" to me, the fallacious attribution of personal intent to weather: angry hail, indignant clouds. Vancouverites who are fallaciously tempted to take the rain personally aren't meant for the city. I resisted such an indulgence, but boy, I was pathetic, no question, and what if Taylor came out on some village errand and saw me there, drowning and too stupid to do anything about it? Or Yvonne?

Cold, wet, and thinking as much about bad Hollywood movies and old literary fallacies as I was about could-make-things-worse, could-make-things-better: not the moment for an attempt at life alteration.

I chickened out, slouched off to Denman and took the long, slow bus ride through the downtown and the rain to Douglas Park. I could come back another time, if I decided an ambush was the thing.

Home, I made another attempt: several paragraphs, no narrative, entirely descriptive—a house in a desert. I know nothing about deserts, but I made up an ecology, a landscape, and an architecture. Writers have done this, created worlds out of their imaginations, so detailed and committed that they've convinced many of a reality that's entirely false. Other writers, but not me. Select All. Delete.

DAY AFTER DAY, MUM LAY UNMOVING. THE PARAMEDICS I'D met had performed an emergency tracheotomy at the accident scene, and Mum breathed through the hole that remained in her throat. A tube delivered fluid to veins. The doctors said she could do without food for a while, and that feeding her through a tube to the stomach would be more trouble than it was worth, for now.

The winter break had ended and the boys returned to school. Jessica—back at work. I spent my days at the hospital, sitting beside Mum, reading, sometimes talking to her, telling her about Gavin and Leo, or things I'd done in New York. I took notes. Damned right. Never stop.

Taylor? Perhaps it was the right time, sure, but as I considered my approach, one thing struck me. I couldn't just say let's forget about it. I'd need to offer an account. If that account ... if I faked it, if I lied, Taylor would know. If I admitted that I still didn't really understand what had been going on, well, I couldn't feature the narrative starting there and leading to the upbeat dénouement.

I thought about it all the time. I had theories, none of them resonating truth.

Trudy called me every evening. Some nights I didn't know if I could bear any more, but I always felt better after we spoke.

Joseph continued to avoid me, except when he'd appear at my exits, affection-starved, longing for a rub, always too late, not because Mum would notice if I arrived later, but just because ... I had begun to leave, I had to follow through. I asked Jessica and the boys if they were interested, and they were. So Joseph moved into the Kitchener place.

Jessica found me a probate lawyer and I got stuff moving with Dad's will. I went through his things.

One of Dad's drawers contained cufflinks, tie-clips, and some of my reviews. I put the cufflinks and clips aside to pass on to Leo and Gavin. I picked up the reviews and sifted through them.

What stage of grief was I in? Do they give a name to the stage at which you hate yourself for all the ways you failed the one you've lost?

Mum and I made so little room for him. He was a talented man. Lots of those at the funeral who showed up from work were people he'd managed, and they told me they loved him. They loved their boss, Michael Bridge. His own boss sobbed painfully through the service.

How often did Mum and I interrupt our arguments or our pontificating to turn to him and ask how things at the office were going, what projects he had underway, what was challenging him, or causing difficulty, or anything? Never, Gordon. The answer is fucking never. "Gordon, I'm so proud of you." Now, your line, Gordon: "I'm proud of you, Dad." That was your line, and you missed it every time.

A nurse took the splint off Mum's arm and unwrapped her leg. The bruising left her face, and her oxygen levels continued to improve.

Mum's GP, early one morning: "Dr. Abriz, the neurologist, is recommending we ease off the medication, so she'll come out of the coma."

"Oh."

"The change will be made tonight. Then we'll see. If you're here tomorrow morning, that'll be early enough. It'll take that long for her system to start to clear."

"Okay."

"If she's able to talk, it'll be a whisper. No air gets past the tracheotomy, so the vocal chords, you see …"

"I understand."

"I really hope, Gordon, that your mother recovers. I really hope."

"Thanks, Liang. Me too."

One month had passed since the accident. At times I'd felt pointless. Now there would be a point.

I could help her. She'd need encouragement. If Mum awoke lucid, alert but physically helpless and dependent, would it shift us together? I could imagine a talk, unprecedented: "Mum, I need your help understanding something. I know you don't like to discuss these things, but I could really use your help here. You remember that review I wrote ... the review ... when I reviewed *The Stendhal Effect* ..."

35

Mum lay still, eyes closed, on through the day, the drawn-out tale she was telling keeping me in suspense.

Liang came by late in the afternoon. She took Mum's pulse. She shone a light in her eyes again.

"We'll know something soon, Gordon, one way or another."

Evening, night, other visitors leaving, patients sleeping, the ward growing quiet: vigilant by the bed, *tableau* barely *vivant*, I look right at Mum, and her eyes open. Several seconds. Then, whisper, "Gordon."

"Hi, Mum."

She tried to lift her head from the pillow, but she found that she lacked the strength. Her face had been expressionless for so long. A shock now—eyebrows up, eyeballs rolling, twisted mouth.

"I'm here, Mum. It's okay. Mum! You're in the hospital. Oh, Mum. You've been in a terrible accident. But it's all right. It's going to be all right."

"Oh."

I pressed the call button. Mum closed her eyes.

A nurse, Lucy, appeared right away.

"She's conscious," I said. "She recognized me and said my name."

"Mrs. Bridge?" said Lucy. "Mrs. Bridge? Can you hear me?"

Mum opened her eyes once more, now transformed, calling upon her dignity. So impressive, to reject all that confusion and hurt, to command again. "Who are you?" she said.

"That's the nurse, Mum. You're in the hospital."

"Oh."

"I'll call Doctor Philips," said Lucy, and she left the room.

"How do you feel?"

"Tired."

I stroked her forehead. "I love you, Mum."

"Where am I?"

"You're in Lions Gate Hospital. You were in a bad accident."

"Oh."

Bam, bam, bam went my heart.

Lucy returned and showed me how to raise the bed. Mum looked at me as she came to a half-sitting recline.

Philips entered and leaned over the bed. "Hello, Linda. I'm Doctor Philips. How do you feel?"

"Tired."

"Well, that makes sense. You've been on some powerful medication, but that's stopped now. You'll feel more lively after a while."

"I'm thirsty."

"Oh, I know. I know. I wish I could give you something to drink, but you can't swallow anything right now. I'll get one of the nurses to swab your mouth. That'll help. I'll be right back."

She returned quickly with Lucy, who eased up beside the bed, chirping sympathetic noises and leaning in with her swab in hand, a little stick with a chunk of pink foam on the end, offering it up, lollipop to a child. Philips gestured to me to follow her outside of the room.

"It's too early to do any kind of assessment. The drugs will take a while to wear off, and she'll need to sleep. I'll see that she's watched carefully overnight, and I'll leave notes for Dr. Abriz."

"I'm staying the night."

"I'll see that you get a cot."

THE NURSES CHANGED SHIFT, AND, AS USUAL, ONE CAME IN to move and clean Mum. I stayed just outside the room.

"I'm going to move you a bit so I can clean you up, Mrs. Bridge. Let me know if anything hurts. Can you lift this arm? Oh, good. Now, I'm just going to take this off you, so I'm going to roll you onto your side. Let me know if anything hurts. One, two, three. Good. There, it's off."

Oh, useful vague pronouns: "this," "it," not "diaper."

A nurse entered early in the morning, my mother woke, and I stepped out. When I returned:

"Where am I?"

"You're in Lions Gate Hospital, Mum. You were in a really bad accident, coming home from a New Year's party."

"Oh."

"How do you feel?"

She didn't look at me. She stared at the ceiling.

"Would you like me to raise the bed, so you're sitting up a bit?"

"Yes."

"How do you feel?"

"What happened?"

"You were in a car accident. You were injured very badly, but you're going to be okay. It was after a New Year's party. You're in Lions Gate Hospital."

An IV needle punctured her skinny left wrist. Straps held the wrist to the rail on the side of the bed. She raised her other hand to her face. "My God," she said.

"You're going to be okay, Mum."

"Where's Michael?"

36

"**M**um," I said.
She looked at me, confused and fearing, but still some of that expectation, the key clause of the old contract between us: no bullshit allowed.

"Dad's dead. He was killed in the accident."

"What accident?"

"You were both in a car accident. It was on New Year's Eve, after the party you went to. You were very badly hurt. You've been here in Lions Gate Hospital for a month."

She looked at the ceiling. I waited. She brought her free hand to her face and she began to cry. The crying continued, then it stopped, and Mum looked at me again, already confused once more.

"How do you feel? Are you comfortable?"

"I'm thirsty."

I got one of the pink lollipop-swabs from the nursing station and soaked it in cold water. I ran it around the inside of her mouth, and then over her teeth and gums.

"Is that better?"

"Why can't I have a drink?"

"You've had a tracheotomy. That's why you're whispering. You can't have liquid or food right now."

"Oh."

"Would you like me to read the paper to you?"

"Yes."

I read the front page of *The Globe*. She fell asleep, my cue for a bathroom break and a muffin from the cafeteria. She slept on when I returned, but she woke soon after.

"Gordon."

"Hi, Mum."

"What's happening?"

"Do you know where you are?"

"No."

"You're in Lions Gate Hospital. You were in a bad accident after you went to a New Year's Eve party."

"My God."

She looked at me, the fear I'd seen before in her eyes now come back, worse. Lips starting to quiver.

"Where's Michael?"

A surprise. A rush of temptation. The urge in me, so sudden and strong, disgusting. It's horrible to admit it even now. I trembled with it.

I knew what she was afraid of. When she asked about Dad, I could see dread, fear in there, pulse of the pupil—she expected the answer. The memory of what I'd told her earlier had lapsed, but something less than memory remained, a weight in her that still pulled, hinted that he was gone, and worse, she should know it.

Other words, terrifying, would I say them? Nothing more insulting: "I already told you."

I could feel my mouth forming the words, anticipate the subtle sneer in my tone: "Can't you remember, Mum? I just told you. I told you about the New Year's party a bunch of times, and I told you about Dad. Can't you remember that your husband is dead? You drove the car. You had the accident. He's dead, and you're lying in a bed in Lions Gate Hospital, which I've also told you, about a hundred times."

Do we make important decisions without being aware that we're doing so? Surely. It happens all the time. That is, *all* the time. To be aware, even for an instant, is sickening. Okay, nauseating. If I think about it too much, right this instant, I'll be wanting someone's comforting hand on the small of my back as I lean over to vomit, existentially.

If I'd referred to that contract of ours, written together in invisible ink over the years as only child grew ambitiously up and mother grew disappointingly old, I could have found my justification: to decline to say "I already told you" would be to condescend, and to condescend, clearly—it says so right here in sub-clause two, your honour—to condescend, *ipso facto*, is, *prima facie*, bullshit.

On the other hand, we have the spirit of the contract. Was that spirit mean? Recognize how long the temptation has been there, crouched, waiting only for the right desirable object to appear in order to leap into expression. Recognize, and then decide no longer to feel that desire to punish, amusing in a child wagging a finger—"you'll know how it feels"— not comic, no, not in a grown-up, mature, famous novelist.

"Mum, I'm so sorry. He was killed in the accident. Dad's dead. Oh, Mum." I took her hand. She started to cry, but her eyes had lost their wide terror.

My choice: whatever happens today, and tomorrow, and for however many days on, never will I say to my mother "I already told you."

About an hour later Mum and I played the "Where's Michael" scene yet again, shifts in nuance, good actors we, not repeating ourselves. Then Dr. Abriz arrived and the performers moved on in the script. Dr. Abriz: neurologist, gleaming, confident professional, not tall but nevertheless commanding. She conveyed the impression of being in a hurry and doing one a favour with this bit of time she offered, dressed so well and conservatively in black, matching long black hair, and sporting what could only be called a rock, a honking big one, a bigger wedding ring than any of the rings on any of the ring fingers of the women who administer Lions Gate Hospital, lead its medical units, and head its nursing departments. That's saying something, because in this micro-culture, I couldn't help but notice, they drive big rings.

"I'm Dr. Abriz."

"I'm Gordon, Linda's son."

"How's your mother doing?"

"You can ask her."

"I'm Dr. Abriz, Linda. I'm the resident neurologist. How are you feeling?"

Mum looked at me, hoping for a clue. I reached out and rested my hand on the blanket where it covered her thin ankle.

"Fine," Mum said to Abriz, challenging her to contradict.

"That's good. Linda, can you tell me what season it is?"

"Summer."

"Where are you right now?"

Mum turned her head and glanced around. "In this room."

"Well, undoubtedly. And where is the room?"

Steady gaze. Unashamed. "I don't know."

"I'd like you to do something for me, Linda." Abriz withdrew a clipboard she had tucked under her arm. "I'd like you to draw the face of a clock."

Mum took the offered pencil and began to draw. She managed a rough circle. Then, concentrating, a series of dots, arranged outside the circle, and numbers, perhaps, maybe private hieroglyphics, scattering off toward the edge of the page.

"There," said Mum.

"Thank you," said Abriz. Then she gestured to me.

"I'm going to step outside to talk to Dr. Abriz for a few minutes, Mum."

"Okay."

We sidled along the curving corridor to the nurses' station. Abriz gave me a no-nonsense look. Should I say "give it to me straight, Doc"?

"This is very preliminary, of course. She's only just regained consciousness. We'll run a full set of tests. But, Gordon, my gut tells me this is not good. I may be wrong. But my gut tells me it's unlikely your mother will recover from this injury. Her brain function is impaired."

"Well, I appreciate your being frank," I said, unable to squeeze my tone into something one could call appreciative.

37

■ ■

A month of bed rest—an assault. Mum turned her head, lifted a hand—hell, lifted her gaze—so slowly. She was asleep again when I returned to the room. She slept still when Leo and Gavin arrived.

I met them out in the hall, gave them an idea of what to expect.

We waited by the bed. Leo, taller than I now by several inches, put a gentle arm around my shoulders, alert for resistance. I gave none. You know what, Leo? Any time. You're afraid and despite your fear you still want to include Dad in your protective reach? Any time. We've got some years left to protect each other, and then happily I'll hand the entire package over to you, the more able, the far better qualified.

And then, open eyes, smile. "Leo! Gavin!"

Smiles back. "Grandma."

What they had was a conversation, so exhilarating, coherent, all about what Gavin and Leo were up to—school details, update on Joseph, announcement from Gavin: "Leo has a girlfriend," and then laughter and love about that— Elizabeth, a "Spock," according to Leo, beautiful, according to Gavin. My medically uneducated gut contradicted Abriz's.

The boys stayed while I broke for a dinner over on Lonsdale, the best I'd tasted in weeks. When I returned, Mum was asleep again, her body almost imperceptible under the blanket. Gavin and Leo had pulled chairs to the bedside, and they looked up at me, wanting to see their optimism shared.

I could have wept again, but I was prepared with familiar drawers in which to file the expected feelings. I had one for that old fear of paternal failure. Near it, a great big one for guilt, crammed with little scraps and reminders that got shoved to the back when I let Taylor down, then farther back still when I entered the huge report on the screw-up that led to my leaving the boys, and then the latest denunciation: I didn't do my filial duty, my father dead by my negligence, my mother here in this room. Yet the most important one, a deep drawer for joy—my boys, sons of mine! All affect in its place, to be sifted through calmly, sometime later, dry-eyed.

Once more after Gavin and Leo had gone I let Mum know: New Year's Eve party, car accident, Michael dead. It was such a falling back to end the night, Mum drifting to sleep just after raising her hand to her face, saying "Oh God," crying again.

Heading home, I began to feel an energy in me, so strange, after such a day. Could I do it now? Mum's return to consciousness, however troubled—would it free me, not for some bizarre outpouring, inspiration, but a start, some will to at least experiment, to write a bit, begin a rescue operation?

Into the empty house. I hung up my coat, made tea, forced myself into rational patience, and set up again before the empty screen. I opened the document, placed my fingers on the keyboard, and I had nothing. No will, no energy, just grief.

Brisk, that's how I'd characterize the day following Mum's awakening. Let's get moving. Move, first of all, to get that hole in the throat closed. She needs to begin eating. She'll have her voice back.

I marched alongside the gurney as they rolled the corridors to surgery. I held her hand.

"What's happening?"

"It's a minor procedure, Mum. They're going to close up the hole in your throat—the tracheotomy. You'll be anaesthetized for a bit, but the whole thing won't take long."

"Oh."

A long afternoon, aimless on Lonsdale, coffee shop to diner to library to coffee shop, and back to the hospital. Mum was pale, stricken. I'd been gone for three hours. She woke up an hour later.

"Gordon."

"Hi, Mum. How do you feel?"

"Tired."

Her voice wasn't any different.

" … Lions Gate Hospital …" "… accident …" "… New Year's Eve …"

"… injury …" "… dead …"

"Oh." Tears.

The next day came the swallow test, an ice chip, small and smooth.

Coughing, spluttering, red in the face, fear.

Another day, and again, between the orderlies, beside the gurney, holding Mum's hand. I could not deny that I felt not that hot, not good at all, a weakening in the ankles, a dryness in the mouth, headache, looming despair.

"What's happening?"

"You're having a minor procedure done."

"Oh."

Avoidance. I'm unable to live up to my obligations and say, "They're going to put a tube into your stomach so they can feed you."

38

One day, returned from the hospital, I was looking for anything now, anything at all. I'd write about me and Taylor. I'd be a reporter, note the facts, dull chronology. Ideas would come, or not, but at least I'd be putting together words and sentences. I opened a document and looked at the white screen. For how long did I sit, wanting to refuse something, to defeat something?

I wrote: "Here's the traitor Gordon Bridge buckling his youngest son in his car seat." I looked at it. Such shame, an agony of it, it's affecting my vision, the screen pulsing, and a silence, I'm entirely deaf, no ambient sound at all, I cannot bear it. Who is the audience for that sentence? Is that an embarrassing question?

I was leading a writing workshop, back in the early-in-the-career days, a teaching gig tied up with a festival appearance.

"I'm really just writing for myself"—one from the top of what I'd learned was a list of predictable responses to my criticisms, or even suggestions. The woman made her claim quietly, looking down at her manuscript. Maybe I'd had a lousy day, or maybe I'd just had enough of this evasion.

"It's a very good reason to write," I said. "Writing can be an important therapeutic technique. I'm not really qualified to give advice about effective therapy writing, but you can find workshops in it. Here, what we're doing is writing for an audience of strangers, and the idea is to capture the attention of that audience. But if you're only writing for yourself, we can move on …"

The young man sitting beside her grinned *schadenfreude*. The woman looked up at me, shocked and angry. So, learn something here. Think about where your defences lead you.

She didn't return after the break. The young man's glee persisted till I told him that the opening chapter of his hard sci-fi tetralogy could use a main character.

"You don't understand the genre," he said. It's another response off that list.

"Maybe not," I said. I named some examples that I've enjoyed—Haldeman, Lem, Liu, Reynolds—and I said something about the challenges their protagonists face, every one of them. He folded his arms and glowered.

This inevitable young man writing hard sci-fi is always furious. He is offended by any hint that the imagined world in which he acts out his killer frustrations with this real one is not interesting enough, one massive volume after another, for anyone but him. What he needs, urgently, is some therapy writing.

BUT MY SENTENCE, "HERE'S THE TRAITOR GORDON BRIDGE ..." I reread it. And along came another: "Here's the hypocrite Gordon Bridge imitating a good person taking his parents to the symphony."

Maybe I hoped that this process would get me somewhere with Taylor. Okay, I hoped mightily. The single reason, the true explanation for my inexplicable act, would come to me as I wrote and remembered. Was I treating myself as I mourned my father, tried to recover my friendship, and cared for my demented mother, or was I working, writing a memoir that would be interesting to strangers? You've read it all, from those beginning words, up to right here, this sentence. You judge.

39

The doctors pronounced my mother "medically stable," meaning they had given up.

She could walk, sort of, lurching along with the walker while supported from behind by the encouraging physio, but she'd never manage on her own. She'd never know where she was or remember what happened. Never be able to swallow, not even a tiny, smooth ice chip, without risking water in the lungs and then pneumonia.

Never manage a serious discussion about the past with her anxious son.

But stable. Get out of the hospital.

Out the door, down the block, in another door, an easy journey to this new place, named with cruel irony for the forever-young forest just a few blocks back up the hill: "Evergreen." A shared room. Mum, oblivious, so the loss of privacy is no loss, really.

Rush of harassed care aides. Lone nurse for Mum's unit—a tall, lean woman, early fifties, Adrie, with a just-detectable Euro accent. She wears runners, and she jogs. She *jogs* up and down the hallways, choppy-efficient social democratic stride, trying to help as many as she can.

Private care aides couldn't be employed at Evergreen—union regulations—but through chats with other visitors I learned that there were a few women companions who worked the place, offering solace, conversation, and calls to a nurse when needed.

Jittery, every morning, I opened the document. Would I still be able? I would. I wrote. I recalled and rambled. Early afternoon, the familiar journey.

I'd arrive and, always, the same subtle aroma, hovering under lemon detergent, ammonia-antiseptic: shit. Then Mum, parked in a wheelchair, some spot with sun shining through a window, yellow smoothie suspended over her in clear plastic, the tube leading down, the companion beside. Cheerful volunteer Kevin, with his dutiful black therapy Lab, Charles, might be having a visit.

"She's had a good morning, Mr. Bridge. She had a shower, and we've been talking about our families."

"Thanks, Veronica."

I wrote quickly. When I rambled, I told myself that'd be interesting, for a reader who wanted to learn about Gordon Bridge. I hoped I'd discover what motivated my literary assassination, but, as you've no doubt noticed, I came to see that I couldn't begin to understand what I'd done to Taylor without taking on much more—taking on my mother, that thing we had, and what we were leading up to. And I knew that unlike Tristram Shandy I'd catch up, the narrative would catch up to her and me.

It has done so. I've caught up now, and ... and, what? Have my digressions seemed pointless to you, or have you felt in them my striving, my sincere effort to face myself? Have they been pointless for me? Well, I don't feel ready for that journey to the West End. So, Select All and Delete? Maybe, if I had the guts.

40

■ ■

"She's coughing an awful lot, Adrie. Does she have a cold? Is it a concern?"

"She doesn't have a cold."

"And?"

"It's a concern."

I commandeered Charles, the therapeutic Lab. Charles flopped his head in Mum's lap and looked up at her as though expecting her to rise from the wheelchair, become under the influence of his drooling affection a healed woman.

"Doggy, doggy, doggy," Mum said, a word I'd never heard her use before, disturbingly juvenile, but better than violent coughing.

Gavin and Leo arrived at Evergreen that Friday afternoon as usual, a few minutes before I would leave, so welcome, because as Mum slept and coughed and stared, vacant, I'd been trying to stop myself from thinking about my memoir and about Mum in ways that I didn't like, and I hadn't been succeeding.

Gavin reached into his backpack and pulled out a paper bag, and from that he removed a flat, oval piece of pine, carefully sanded and varnished, and then he dug into a pocket and took out a steel marble. He presented the wood and the marble to me.

"I found this in your office ... in your old office. I thought maybe—you don't have to take them ..."

"Oh, man, thank you."

"You're sure you want it? Because ..."

"I wasn't thinking straight when I left it behind."

"WATCH THIS," GAVIN SAID TO ME AFTER SCHOOL ONE DAY. He'd cleared off the breakfast nook table. He placed a large piece of corrugated cardboard on the table and into it he pushed two tacks, about six inches apart. He tied the ends of a length of string together, looped the string around the tacks, and drew the loop taut using a pencil. With the point of the pencil on the cardboard, and maintaining the tension in the string, he traced a shape around the tacks.

"That's an ellipse. Where the tacks are, those are the foci of the ellipse. 'Foci' is plural for focus."

"I see."

"Now watch."

He moved one of the tacks so that the two were now farther apart. He repeated the operation, producing another oval, flattened.

"That's still an ellipse. Only it has a different eccentricity."

"Eccentricity."

"That's the shape of the ellipse. There's a mathematical formula for it."

"Got it."

"I'll show you something really cool."

He had me pick a spot on the perimeter of the first ellipse, measure the distance from that point to each focus, and come up with a total. Then again, with a different point. Same total. And a third time, with the flatter ellipse.

"That is cool."

A couple of weeks later, one night before dinner, Gavin emerged from the basement as promised. We gathered for his demonstration.

He dubbed it his "arena ellipse," cut from a piece of plywood, and encircled—enellipsed—by a raised metal lip, with a strip of bouncy rubber glued to it. A dot of blue paint marked each focus.

"Take this marble, Mum."

"Yes."

"Place it on one of the foci, one of those dots."

"There."

"Shoot it."

"Where?"

"Anywhere."

She shot it hard, and the marble rebounded off at an angle, passing over the other focus.

"Now Dad."

It didn't matter in which direction we shot the marble. It always rebounded directly to the other focus.

We kept the arena ellipse on the living room coffee table for a while. Weeks. Gavin thought I was flattering him, or kidding him, when he came home from school day after day and found me hunched over the thing, calm but also intense, watching the marble on its inevitable routes from one focus to the other.

"Is it okay if we put this away?" said Jess.

"I'd like it to stay a while longer," I said.

A few days later: "Are you done with it?"

"Not yet. Gavin worked hard on this. I'd like to show it off some more. Okay?"

My "okay" conveyed nothing but bright enthusiasm. Her expression showed no skepticism. If someone had asked, we'd have said nothing was going on. Nothing, as in no, not my failure to write and not Jessica minding.

For a few years Gavin's Christmas and birthday presents to me had been projects from school, objects I of course treasured. That Christmas, the arena ellipse finally in storage, I unwrapped a small box to reveal the same in miniature, beautifully done, sanded pine, stained, and a steel marble. I had to make an effort not to leave the room. Down the seasons Gavin continued the craft gift tradition, but nothing topped the ellipse, love on my desktop, not for years.

THE MINI-ELLIPSE, RECOVERED FROM MY OLD OFFICE, TOOK my attention again, just like old times. I flicked the marble from one focus and watched it rebound off the lip and head back to the other. Entrancing. But not so much as to prevent another idea from coming along.

No. It can't be so simple, and so humiliating, humiliation yet again. Is this another cheat, Gordon, another evasion? Are you seeing the truth, finally? You're not letting yourself off, are you? No, I'm not letting myself off, because if this is an excuse it's also a condemnation.

I'd been doing her bidding.

The pleasure I'd felt, writing the review, subtly panning Taylor's triumph—undeniable, sickening, I did it for Mum. Picture a hockey mum, screaming from the upper reaches of an arena at her son on the ice below: "Hit him! Hit him!" Picture the boy doing as he's told; see me at my computer, reviewing. "She was afraid you'd be better," I'd said to Taylor, and he'd agreed.

I'd wait for a lucid moment, and I'd confront her. Maybe she'd respond. Maybe, just telling her, I'd know for sure. After, I'd head to Taylor and Yvonne's. Taylor would hear me out. It wouldn't be an excuse, not a denial of responsibility, but, as I'd said, quite the opposite, for what more condemning, to be guilty of such immaturity, grown man obedient to a jealous maternal command from the childhood past? Taylor would see the truth in it.

You can't step into the same river twice. I know that. But friendship can be recovered. I know that too.

41

"Your mother has a slight fever, Gordon."

"Adrie?"

"It came on this morning. I gave her some aspirin, which took it down. It's up again now."

"I see."

"You can take some time, but not too much. A couple of hours. Then you'll have to make the decision."

"Okay."

"Antibiotics, or ..."

"I know."

"If you have any questions, just track me down."

"Okay."

Mum slept. My hand on her forehead felt the heat.

Adrie came by again in an hour.

"We should call Liang," I said.

"I let her know first thing. She'll be expecting to hear."

I called Mum's GP, and then I left messages for the boys at school, then Jessica at work, finally Trudy.

"I love you, Mum." She didn't open her eyes. Nor when Liang appeared and examined with stethoscope, taps on the chest, pneumonia confirmed.

The boys arrived in the afternoon, and on Mum slept.

Out into the hall, then into the street, Gavin, Leo and I walked, silent. We stopped at a corner.

"She's not going to wake up again, boys."

Gavin began to cry. No sobs, just tears running. Leo set to hammering the sidewalk with his heel.

"We should say goodbye," said Leo.

"That's just what I was going to suggest. And let me ... tell you what, you should know, when you speak to her, y'know, being your grandmother, that was the best thing ever, for her. She'd probably say that to you. How she loved you."

Still, no sobbing. Leo put his hands to his face, and Gavin looked at me, pale.

They took twenty minutes on their own. I waited in the hall. Jessica arrived. The boys emerged.

We hung on to each other, while Jessica took her turn. Then the four of us, in the hallway there. Jess and I had talked this over before, but you can't know if it's going to be the way you said it would. We took a moment just looking at each other, allowing for whatever might arise.

"Dad is going to stay. But we've said our goodbye. He'll call us."

Leo, tears streaming now, unashamed, drew himself up taller at that, prepared to speak, coped for a moment with something inside that urged him to object—to take on more. He looked at Gavin, who took deep breaths, gasping as he looked back at his big brother, waiting for his lead.

"Okay. That'll be ... that's right," Leo said. "Call us."

For ten hours Mum lay unmoving, eyes closed, breathing gradually accelerating. I tried the words out, said them out loud, not in anger, but gently: "Mum, I did it for you. I thought I had to, for you."

Speaking those words accomplished nothing. My conviction had thinned out into more uncertainty.

Mum heated up with her untreated fever, crusting lips open, breathing now fast and terrible, not hearing my banal goodbye, surely not hearing, just sailing off into the artifice of eternity.

42

My progress with the post-death bureaucracy clicked along through a predictable funk, thanks to my recent rehearsal with Dad. Such a dull, protracted anticlimax reminded me of the review of *Volley through Eternity* I liked best, the smartest, written by a University of Texas prof with a book blog. The big outlets had all thrilled to my New York novel, loving the vivid Manhattan scenes, but my man from Texas pointed out that *Volley* isn't an American book at all:

> Its conflicts never resolve. Bridge does not allow matters to erupt in violence or concretely dramatize something structurally final. Disputes, internal or otherwise, are always displaced, never to end. They are covered up, barely controlled, and left to simmer and threaten. Ultimately, it's a more mature depiction of the condition than what's implied by the "closure" fantasy so prevalent in our literature. We demand that the great whale die, the car crash be fatal, the community exorcise the ghost. Do we really think that means it's over? The slave is freed. Is evil defeated? Perhaps it is evil itself to think of the source of our

troubles as other, to succumb to our misunderstood Puritan legacy and think we can bracket off a devilish scapegoat who has nothing to do with us.

I had wanted to put the blame on Mum. I had waited for her death to end my memoir, like Capote waiting for Perry and Dick to swing from the gallows so he could conclude *In Cold Blood* and get on with his decades of dissolution. What more concrete? Yet nothing had resolved. At night, some devilish other lurked in the shadows. Through clenched teeth it promised to hurt me, bad. How Canadian of me, despite my betrayal in absconding south, to recognize that evil as a part of me.

How do I resist such evil? In reviewing *The Stendhal Effect*, had I succumbed? I'd been amusing myself. Seeking amusement, one becomes blind; I was blind to what mattered, just entertaining myself. Is that it?

My commitment, that's how I resist. I wrote the death scene of the previous chapter, still in the Douglas Park house. Committed to writing. The movers collected the furniture, the clothing, and the dishes, and I wrote. I wouldn't be stopped. Jess and the boys came over. I urged Dad's complete set of Joni Mitchell CDs on the boys, and Jessica took one necklace. I wrote.

The memorial at the cemetery—the attendance sparse, no Taylor—the dry ceremony lifted nothing; no insight slid into consciousness while the casket slid into the fire.

I needed an ending. That's not callous. It's not. It's committed. I'd hit 60,000 words, not long, but enough for a memoir by famous, still-sort-of-young Gordon Bridge. I'd hoped to have something to say to Taylor. I'd thought that Mum's death, whenever it came, would dramatize or reveal something. I can grieve for you, Mum, I can feel guilty about you, about Taylor, and still, I need this, to finish.

I sold the house and prepared to leave. Trudy said she thought maybe she'd go back to Trinidad for a visit; she'd be home in time for my arrival. She suggested that when I returned, maybe I should see somebody. I asked if she could find me somebody to see. I'd need help to get that threatening voice to lighten up a little.

I ventured out into the back yard and stood by the birdbath. I put my hands in my pockets. No, no, that would be a sappy ending, contrived as hell.

I set out to walk the sea wall around Stanley Park, but that gesture too seemed just plain too gestural. I stopped at Third Beach, nothing new in my notebook. An ending. Come on.

It was late, I was tired, and finally I just wanted to go home and sleep, but I took a few minutes—the forest behind me, the sea before, sun down and the air cooling.

Most of the North Shore people had shut down for the night and there were hardly any lights except the misty beams from a couple of freighters across the inlet. As the clouds shifted past the moon the developments that scarred the mountains receded, until slowly I began to think about the peninsula that flourished here once for native eyes. Its teeming forest, the salmon streams that had made way for the houses—the Douglas Park house, Kitchener Street—had once nourished the first and greatest of human dreams. For a long, graced moment people must have breathed free on this continent's edge, eased into an understanding, *involved* for a rare time in a unified world. Now a few gulls flew over the inlet; a worn-out surf spent its last energies against the sea wall, the exhausted, ragged edges of the great ocean that rolled on now as it had for years beyond imagining.

V

MISS GEORGE

43

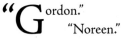

"Gordon."

"Noreen."

"It's wonderful."

"I'm so glad you think so."

"Meandering, but wonderful."

I'd emailed Noreen the memoir only three days before. She's prompt. With star Gordon Bridge, very.

"I have a few questions, little things mainly."

"Sure."

"First of all, Gordon, a very little thing. I never swear. You fucking know that, and in your version of our conversation you have me swear."

"You do swear, Noreen."

"Never, damn it. Never."

"Okay, look, Noreen, you just swore a couple of times."

"What is this?"

"You swear with your tone. You may not say the word 'fucking,' but you convey it. You're wonderful, such fine control. You say 'you know that,' for example, but if I'm to get the tone, in print it's just got to be 'you fucking know that.' It would be inaccurate otherwise. It'd do you a disservice."

"Screw the disservice. You can't have me use those words."

"What else?"

"The section titles are going to be a difficulty."

"They're supposed to be funny."

"They are. I chuckled. But you know what they'll say. Allusions to those writers? Talk about … what's the word?"

"'Arrogance.' The section titles stay."

"Well, good. They're funny. Just be ready."

"Right."

"Another little thing. You'll recall the episode in Portugal, at the palace."

"I recall everything."

"There's too much vomiting. It goes on too long. You need to cut one of the puking scenes."

"Tell me."

"Jessica. Her nausea when she's pregnant with Leo."

"It's a good scene."

"It's very good, but there's too much. Gordon—"

"Okay. Maybe you're right. Of course. It's gone."

"Good."

"So, next little thing."

"Trudy is from Trinidad, right?"

"Obviously."

"She grew up there, and then she moved to New York."

"Yes."

"How does she know Lotta Hitschmanova?"

"Come again?"

"Those commercials were Canadian. Lotta Hitschmanova worked for the Unitarian Service Committee of *Canada*."

"Interesting. I'll ask her."

"Those are the little things. I've also got news. Gordon Bridge has another publishing success on the way. You're going to edit a story anthology."

"Oh, joy."

"It will be a joy. I promise you joy, Gordon."

"Convince me."

"You never told me your tale about Mavis Gallant. I found that story you published. It's online, you know."

"Yes."

"I emailed a colleague in New York."

"Okay."

"She called me right away. We're going to do an anthology of rewrites, including yours, of course. It's going to be wonderful."

"Noreen, it's not a bad idea, but I doubt you'll find many takers. It's hard work, y'know, following another writer word-for-word that way. A little humbling."

"My colleague had a client with her when she called. You've heard of her. Louise Erdrich."

"Noreen?"

"Louise fucking Erdrich is going to rewrite 'Hills Like White Elephants.' I doubt we'll have difficulty finding takers to be included with you and Louise Erdrich."

"You knew how I feel about her work? Have we talked about that?"

"You've mentioned it."

"I love her stuff. She's—"

"I knew, Gordon, and we got lucky."

"This is going to be great."

"Joy, I'd say, coming your way."

"You're terrific."

"You need to say that more often. Shall we do the big thing now?"

"You never disappoint me."

"It's not finished."

"All right, Noreen, this doesn't make sense. It's short, sure, but I'm not nobody. Sixty thousand Gordon Bridge words. Not just words. My words."

"I didn't say it was too short."

"All right, all right, what? It goes right up to now, the present."

"You had trouble with the ending. That's because you thought there'd be a resolution with your mother's death. And I would've come to the memorial, by the way. You should've told me."

"I know you would have. I knew I could've counted on you."

"I liked the ending. I'd have said it was the best writing you've done, but my assistant pointed out that you stole it from the ending of *The Great Gatsby*."

"You didn't recognize it?"

"Just how many times have you read that novel, Gordon?"

"I've lost count."

"Exactly. I read it once. Forty years ago. Who do you think your typical reader will more closely resemble, you or me?"

"Okay, point taken."

"It's fine. It works. Maybe we'll even get lucky and you'll be accused of plagiarism. I might even arrange it. But the reason you had trouble, and that it's still not an ending—it's not—is you're wrong about the central relationship."

"Noreen?"

"You're going to have to face it. I'm sorry, Gordon, but you just have to. You see him. Then you write about it. Then you're finished."

44

■ ■

All the way home to Brooklyn, I fretted: sleepless flight, pacing around baggage claim, stuttered answers at customs, cab ride, up the brownstone steps, key-fumble into the foyer. Only as the door closed behind me did I begin to know that the source of my anxious sweats, stage-by-stage of the journey, was not what I'd thought. How is that possible, to be wrong about such a thing?

I'd thought I was worried about Taylor, what tracking him down and getting in touch would mean, how he'd respond. Then I dropped the bags, moved to hang my jacket on the rack, and saw my fate.

Trudy had not returned from Trinidad. I'd been freaked out all along about just that, and Taylor had been a distraction from what could not be contemplated.

Gone. Not coming back.

She'd warned me that she wouldn't have ready access to email, nor to a phone. Not a concern. Good for us, we agreed, after our months of nightly conversations, to pause before the reunion. She would've returned the day before. But she hadn't. I knew immediately, without calling out.

Noreen's innocuous question had started me; back there, out of consciousness, my busy little shadow had been at work and now it busted huge and ugly through the door, into the conscious light, and shoved its gruesome truth in my face. How had Trudy heard of Lotta Hitschmanova? Well, she'd lied about her background. I could imagine other explanations, all far-fetched, none with the compelling simplicity of the lie.

What would I do?

I'd confirm, first, that my certainty of her absence was not a delusion. Go through the apartment. Find the place empty and all her things gone.

Online, see the account I'd set up for her now drained.

Then? After a sleepless night, call our friends. "I haven't heard from her for a while, Gordon. It's been weeks, actually. What's going on? Is she okay? She didn't return my calls."

Her studio. Occupied now by someone else, conventional massage therapist, knows nothing about the previous occupant.

A clue, receipt at the back of a drawer, yes, she has indeed returned to Trinidad. I'd grown uncertain about even this part of her story. She can do accents, and I've no ability to judge subtleties, identify authenticity there.

Newark Airport once more.

I sit in a crowded vinyl departure lounge with arms resting on carry-on resting on my lap, sucking on stale airport air. I can find her. Half the population of Brooklyn, Trinidad is. I've got money and people will tell me things and I'll find her.

It'll be a full plane. Every seat in departure is taken. Lots of children. Families. The first rows are called.

Two little boys are playing with a truck, pushing it along between the feet of their mother, under the chairs. Their mother tells them to stop, they're going soon, stop. The brothers, grubby the pair of them, airport food messes on their faces, don't listen.

Another set of rows called. One of the boys shoves his brother. Wants the truck for himself. The other, smaller, makes a grab for the toy and is pushed aside. He flings himself back and grabs again for the truck, and they're both tugging at it, still ignoring the mother's commands. Then threats. They won't be allowed on the plane. She'll tell their father.

The smaller boy yells, "Let it go! Let it go!"

My row is called.

"Let it go!"

Leave, back out, back to wrap up my New York life. She's lied to me, lied and left, and it's done. Our life done, let it go, Gordon, and I sit on the oak bench in the foyer, and Trudy calls to me, "Gordon! You're home," and she runs down the hallway. "Gordon, what's wrong? Gordon?"

WHEN LEO WAS A LITTLE BOY, ABOUT SIX YEARS OLD, HE'D accumulated a substantial collection of stuffed animals. We piled them up in a stretch of netting suspended from the ceiling in a corner of his room.

He gave them all quirky names that showed his humour. Bedtime, he'd ask me to get one down for him, his company for the night.

What was I thinking? One evening, "Daddy, could you get Dilly for me?"

I plucked Dilly the bear from the net, along with Miss George, camel.

I handed Dilly over. I held Miss George up in one hand, beside my face, made a wounded plush camel voice—high, plaintive. "Why don't you want *me*? You never ask for *me*, and I get lonely up there."

Leo looked at me, puzzled. Then at Miss George. "I do ask for you."

"It's been a really long time. It makes me so sad, being left up in the net all the time."

"I do ask for you. I do!"

"It feels like a very long time."

Looking at me—"Daddy, stop that!" At Miss George—"I do ask for you!"

"But I get so lonely."

"I do ask for you!—Daddy, stop that!—I do!"

"Don't you love me like you love the other animals?"

"I do love you, Miss George! I do!—Daddy, stop!"

He looked back and forth from me to Miss George, addressing us in turn. I'm no ventriloquist, made no attempt, but it didn't matter. Now I'd gone too far. Leo crying.

"Oh, I'm sorry, Leo. Miss George knows you love her. 'He does love me. I love him too.'"

"I do love her."

We all had a love cuddle there—me, Leo, Dilly, and Miss George.

I suppose Leo recovered. He also remembered. I asked him when he was fourteen.

"Yeah, I remember. You tortured me."

"I went too far. I've always been sorry."

"You should be. You owe me one."

The fantasy/reality membrane is so permeable in children. But in adults too. Fiction wouldn't succeed otherwise. Some respect is called for here, the respect I neglected to pay Leo. Writers disrespect when we withhold information in bad faith. If my banal fantasy of Trudy's abandonment had gone on for chapters, if it hadn't announced its status from the get-go with a careful use of the conditional, that would have been bad faith. Even as it stands, it's a risk, takes advantage of your reflex to care.

Am I in bad faith for withholding the conversation with Trudy that followed a couple of hours farther along the anxiety pathway? First came our time in the foyer, me slumped there, Trudy hustling for a glass of water, return, kiss of forehead, hand through soaked hair, both hands on shoulders. Then, head held to chest. Next, once more the quick round trip, this time for a paper bag to treat accelerating hyperventilation.

When walking felt less impossible I got myself inside. I showered off the sour scum of my long panic while Trudy sat on the toilet seat, telling me about her holiday in Trinidad, watching to see that I didn't pass out, crack my head on the tub.

"How do you know who Lotta Hitschmanova is?" In my robe now, on the couch, herbal tea, crisis passed and aftermath of shame settling in.

Trudy, unfazed: "Remember my telling you about the family's trip to Montreal that summer? I was twelve. I'd barely seen television, it was a novelty, and then I got sick and could indulge. All those afternoons watching TV. How could I forget? She was compelling, wasn't she, with that Czech accent?"

"She was." And Trudy had indeed told me of Montreal, and I'd forgotten somehow. I made a mental note to go back and revise the manuscript, insert that story of Trudy's, make things true and fair. She looked at me, waiting to hear what my weird question was all about.

I could have included this information earlier, and you would have known, as you read my account of how my idiotic, cliché-drenched reverie of abandonment overtook me, known how, like Leo, I passed so easily through that special membrane. You'd have known that the fear was groundless; Trudy never lied. But I wasn't aware at the time of my crisis, so if I'd included the information earlier that too would have falsified the narrative.

"You're not well."

"I guess not."

"Let's go to bed."

I lay on my side, feeling Trudy's wise hand on my hip, guiding me toward sleep.

45

▪ ▪

"I booked appointments today. I should've thought, but, y'know, people … when I've been away … but I can cancel."

"I'll be fine."

"Don't do anything."

"That's my plan exactly."

We embraced in the foyer, scene of my flip-out the night before.

I didn't feel that bad. Worn out. It always helps to have a diagnosis, and mine was obvious: Dad, Mum, death—worn out.

It should've been good to be home, but all morning I couldn't settle down. I moved from room to room, tried to read but couldn't, tried to relax with some music but couldn't. I didn't belong there. My own place, and something was driving me away. My skin was … well it wasn't exactly crawling, but wrong—not itchy, but I wanted to scratch it. I called Trudy, and I hung up when I got the voice mail. With a client. I called again and left a message to let her know where I'd be.

She had neatly stacked the many fortnights of *LRB*s. I pulled the three oldest from the bottom of the tower and headed out—a walk down Flatbush to the new Gorilla Coffee on Bergen. Not doing anything, just going to a café to hang out. Being outside killed some of the edginess—good decision.

It took some fancy dancing to grab a table in the afternoon crowd—foxtrot in there just as someone stands—slow, slow, quick-quick, plop down the *LRB*s. Then my jacket on the chair, then up to the counter to order, slide back to my staked claim by the window, carrying a decaf on account of my recent troubles. No chance I'm doing any kind of drugs now. Open an *LRB*—I'm surrounded by laptops, the only print-oriented bastard in the place. Okay, Gordon, relax into this day. Don't try to solve anything. Don't begin to plan the fulfillment of Noreen's expectations for your memoir. I said don't.

The first *LRB* was a dud, nothing to take my attention, and the second the same—not the content of the review, I guessed, but a new symptom here, probably temporary: boredom with the *LRB*. I finished the Americano. A man stood with his back to the counter, coffee in hand, looking at my table, coveting.

En route to the toilet I passed by the counter. "You can share my table, if you promise not to talk." He frowned. When I returned he'd gone.

I people-watched, taking time over my second decaf. Lots of Mum and Dad images came to me and I tried not to wish or regret, but just to see them some more, because I missed them. Mum's at her typewriter and I just notice as I pass her room. Or she's playing with the boys. At the dinner table, Dad's looking from me to her and back, saying nothing, but enjoying his wine and our talk, getting a glow on. It was progress, to see them and long for them without succumbing to anger and guilt, to know that I could cry if I wanted, choosing not to.

Out on the sidewalk two guys rode by on a longboard, the taller in front, doing the kicking; behind, the shorter, cruising easy with a little retro boom box propped on his shoulder—snatch of Neko Case, maybe, beneath the soft roar of polyurethane on concrete, or maybe just my imagination skipping in the direction of one of Gavin's favourites: "I leave the party at 3 a.m., alone thank

God." The pair of them were a bit too old for their pose, trying too hard for carefree, kickin' down the cobblestones.

Everybody, it came to me, everybody in the café, or strolling the broad Bergen sidewalk, all the people providing my entertainment, looked damaged. As I realized what I was seeing, the impression intensified. Masking desperation, these people. The sadness! Even the apparently cheerful few, smiling into their computer screens or swinging toward Flatbush ... reconstructed, so terribly damaged, smiles teetering on failure.

Was it Madrid again, and London—my imagination sprinkling Brooklyn with the persisting residue of trauma? No. That's not it. It's the more recent, more personal loss, because those faces, they looked so stricken, abandoned, so clearly ... orphans.

The very word is like a bell, and I'm back to Taylor again. Oh, Taylor.

THE FINAL UNIVERSITY YEAR HAD COME ALONG, TAYLOR wrapping up the English BA, me PoliSci, and we'd faced down our worries about possible competitiveness, awkwardness, and taken a Creative Writing elective together. I produced more commentary than Taylor when we were dealing with our classmates' offerings, a bit of a surprise. But Taylor held back deliberately, knowing that if he weren't careful he could dominate in a way that wouldn't be appreciated.

Talk turned regularly to novels, each student expected to submit an excerpt and outline. But the discussion began not to please our serious instructor, encouragement to fade week-by-week, gravitas shifting toward grumpy frustration.

"What's a novel?" he asked-demanded at the beginning of a class. The question insisted that we were wrongheaded in everything we thought might be the answer.

Not only did we not know, but we *should* know. Our ignorance was a moral and intellectual failure. "It's a simple question. You're planning to write one. What's a novel?"

Another student offered herself up so that we could continue: "It tells a story. It's a long story in prose." Mumbled, but audible.

Our professor put down his pen and took a breath, but before he could speak, another brave one, Taylor: "That is useful; it's Forster's answer. But Forster would acknowledge, we all would, that it's a starting point only. The issue here is novelty. Novels. What's novel about them?"

"Shall you tell us?" said our instructor, amused.

"The big mistake," said Taylor, "is to think of the novel as outside history, to take novels for granted as somehow above or before genre, the thing we all know."

"I'd like you to cut through. What is a novel?"

"Well, then," said Taylor. And he looked at us, fifteen students, one professor, assessing whether we were ready for him.

"A novel is a story about an orphan who dies."

I laughed, Taylor grinned, the rest waited for a more authoritative cue.

"Is it? Really?"

Nobody wanted to jump on Taylor, whose intervention had shifted the ugly mood, but eventually, comment after tentative comment, it emerged that his definition wouldn't do. The class identified some novelistic orphans. But many protagonists don't die and lots have parents.

I said nothing, not till the consensus grew undeniable. Then I put in with "Don Quixote. He's an orphan. He dies."

"He's middle-aged when the book starts," said another.

"Certainly," I said. "Middle-aged, without parents, an orphan, the first novel and the first novel's protagonist." Yeah, yeah, I sounded arrogant. But I had to say something. Taylor didn't need my help, but I needed, intensely, to show that I could participate. I was about to be left behind, once again.

"I can explain," said Taylor.

"The novel proper is about a modern, unguided, *homeless* individual, whose state is represented most concretely, efficiently, by orphanhood. This modern character struggles to find a way back home, a route to traditional belonging, yet struggles at the same time to sustain individuality. It *cannot* be done. That impossibility is represented most concretely, efficiently, by death.

"When the protagonist is neither orphaned nor finally dead, literally or figuratively, we have the persistent traces in the new, *novel*, form of earlier genres: quest romance, confession, allegory, and so on. We have nostalgia for those genres' worlds: class stability, spiritual progress, immanence, community."

He was so confident. He cowed us all. I had a novel planned, and its protagonist certainly wasn't an orphan, and I had no design to kill him off. Was I on the wrong track? I wanted to challenge, but I didn't know how.

Another classmate asked for me: "So you're saying my novel's no good unless I kill off my protagonist's parents and then kill her off too?"

"I'm saying your novel stands a chance to be better, if … well … if you keep them alive, then your novel will be better if you think about what you're longing for."

It hadn't occurred to me that I longed for anything at all, but at once I knew it was so. A submerged pain was surfacing, an uncomfortable surprise. I could see that some in the class were responding the same way: not just seeing their projects in a different light, but acknowledging something in themselves that had been denied. Trying to locate the object of a longing so deep and longstanding they'd never even noticed it.

I TRIED ANOTHER *LRB*. AND HA HA HA—EVERY SINGLE STORY was about orphans: a review of a book on the history of child refugees; another review of a bio of an obscure Bloomsbury figure, abandoned by his parents at a famously sadistic public school; a "Diary" entry by a woman recently diagnosed with the same kind of cancer that killed her mother. I felt like one of those grad students who see everything in their world through the lenses of their dissertations. Here's a review of a new history of the interwar period in England, and, wouldn't you know, the most interesting part is about the children of shell-shocked soldiers and their traumatized-at-one-remove wives. It gives England an entire generation of psychological, yes, orphans. That's the word the book uses.

I put the paper aside. But now I see a boy. He's in elementary school. It's such a surprise and yet so logical, to see him again at this moment, after so many decades. He's trudging around the school grounds at lunch time, picking up garbage with a pair of tongs, punishment for who-knows-what. I must help him, somehow. I must do something to allay his obvious misery, and instead I turn away. Consciously, aggressively, I refuse to think about him.

His name was Donald Barclay, and he was an orphan. He was a year ahead of me, and always in trouble. Everyone knew he was in foster care. He had no friends. He got into fights.

I was glad that Orphan Donald wasn't in my grade. It would have fallen to me to do something for him. But, separated by a crucial year, I had no obligation to include him—invite him to a birthday party, or even speak to him. I felt guilty, but not so much as to take action. My odd feeling of responsibility persisted, buried under lots of distractions but always there. Why would he so often glance up from his punishment and look at me, me alone, among all my schoolmates, singling me out for his plea to be rescued?

Relief from this moral irritation came when Donald moved on to high school. I still heard tales of his shocking transgressions, but at least I was spared the sight of him.

Then, the first day of grade eight, there he was at the back of homeroom. They'd made him repeat the year, evidently, and my reprieve was over.

He lounged at his desk, baseball cap classically backward, and he caught my eye as I took an evasive seat at the front, knowing, at the same time, heart sinking, that the effort was pointless. I was meeting my fate.

Roll call. Off the top: "Donald Barclay."

No response.

"Donald Barclay."

Louder, yet once more. "Donald Barclay."

I glanced back and saw him, a hand cupped around one ear, grinning right at me: "Did you say my name? What? Speak up! Cunt hear you. Must have an ear infucktion. Bare ass me again."

So out he marched, jaunty, to the principal's office—out of our lives. I was again relieved, the only emotional complication a bit of admiration for the final and best of the three puns. Clever, Joycean even, in a grade-eight way.

"Gordon Bridge?"

"Present."

For a while, speculation circulated: reform school, whatever the hell that is, or prison. Soon I put the incident out of mind. A few weeks passed, and then Taylor told me about his rock collection, I him about pennants/penance, and my fate shifted. Maybe my animus to Taylor had its roots there, my guilty conscience; I'd escaped the true doppelgänger, Donald, and substituted the false double, Taylor.

"Donald? Where are you? Prison? Homeless? Did you find somebody to act as parent, a point of leverage to yard on and lift yourself up? Donald, I want to know … I'm sorry to ask but I want to know … have you ever forgiven me?"

"GORDON? GORDON, YOU'RE TALKING TO YOURSELF."

"What? Oh, shit. Hi."

"Have you been here all this time?"

"What? What time is it?"

"Five-ten."

"Already?"

"You've been here all afternoon."

"I guess. Yes."

"Who were you talking to?"

"An orphan."

"I'm taking you home."

46

■ ■

I postponed the next step, because I feared the step to follow. But Trudy pushed me along in her gentle way, a serious smile in the morning, extra silence at night, and several months on I saw someone.

Trudy had lined him up as promised, Jürgen, wise fellow, happy pluralist, moving untroubled from Freud, when Freud was handy, to Adler, all the crazy way to cognitive behaviourism, if truly called for. Good humour always, sitting behind his desk, behind him a wall of books with a comforting amount of excellent fiction, a sign that Trudy had indeed chosen well. Jürgen didn't have much advice, just fine, challenging questions, or a hard-to-resist tug with his interrogative "mmmhmmm?"

Not much advice, except, somewhere about session ten: "Well, I haven't read it, obviously, and I'm no editor, but, just by your tone, and what you've said about it, she does have a point. Or, we could say, editorial concerns aside …"

"I need to see him."

"Mmmhmmm." No question mark.

"Do you think I'm ready?"

"Gordon, you're grieving, and your issues are complex, you know that, but such complexity isn't unusual. You'll be working on it for decades. In the meantime, life isn't postponed."

"No. Of course. You're right. I just need to figure this out, how to approach it."

"Mmmmhmmm?"

I SAT BEFORE MY COMPUTER AND TRIED TO IGNORE MY symptoms: clenched stomach edging toward nausea; damp palms; hands unsteady—foretaste of intentional shakes if I inherit from Dad—a full assortment of deep apprehension clichés.

I could email, phone, or write a letter. Taylor might have moved. I might have been standing outside a building he'd long left behind, that rainy Vancouver afternoon of embarrassing pathos. It wouldn't be hard to find out.

I delayed with a glass of water, some pacing, and the CBC *World Report* online. Then from my shambling I spotted an answer. I found her email easily—college instructors are easy to find. I wrote:

> Dear Yvonne,
>
> I'm going to be in Vancouver for four weeks, beginning on the fifteenth. I have a favour to ask, which is that you meet with me, even if only for a few minutes, though if you have more time I will gladly take it.
>
> I can see you anyplace that's convenient for you.
>
> I know that you will use your good judgment as to whether it's best to tell Taylor of my request.
>
> Gordon

I hit "Send," just as Trudy walked into the study.

"You know, it's been quite a while since you saw the boys. You haven't called them as often as you should. They won't ask now. They'll feel they're too old."

"I know. I was thinking the same thing. I'll book a flight. I was going to do that."

"Whatever you do in Vancouver, the trip is a success if you see them."

"You're right. Absolutely. You're … absolutely."

"When they say, 'everybody makes mistakes,' what they should say is 'big mistakes.' Everybody makes big mistakes."

I nodded.

"Everybody needs forgiveness."

"I forgive you."

"I know you do. I knew it when I read your novels."

"You did."

"Oh, yes. Don't tell me that you're unaware of what you do, Gordon Bridge, with those nasty characters of yours whom you understand so well and manage to leave with their dignity anyway."

"I'd never contradict you."

"Wise man."

I booked the flight, waited for Yvonne's reply.

I packed, I pondered, I thought about telling Noreen what I was up to and decided not to; she'd learn when she got the manuscript. The eve of my departure: still no word. I'd said I was coming out regardless, and she could think that there was no hurry. She'd have time to reflect or talk to Taylor and get back to me after my arrival.

I was tired, but too wired for sleep. Anxiety building, I paced the flat.

"Gordon."

"Yes?"

"Let me tell you a story."

258

47

∎ ▪

"It happened when I was fourteen. I've told you about my older sister, Helen. She was sixteen then.

"I'm going to interrupt myself already. It's rather a long story. Let's have some tea."

In the kitchen, waiting for the kettle, I watched Trudy. She sat in the easy chair, leaning forward with her hands on her thighs, looking at the floor. Intense pose. Important narrative incoming. This story would be for me, to help me as I faced my crisis.

"Helen was the family star, the centre of attention without trying. When she was around, always so funny, so enthusiastic, you felt like there was no place better to be. She was a fine athlete, and she played guitar in a band. A girl leading a band, Gordon, in Trinidad.

"Her band was returning home from a concert at a school. A truck crashed into them, and Helen's leg was broken.

"She wore a cast, and as the months passed, she changed. She became anxious, and then needy, and angry. It affected everyone, my mother most of all. Helen had always been sweet to her. She was that kind of daughter, doting on her mother, but she grew mean and belittling. My mother has almost no education, unlike her two older sisters. Helen brought it up in conversation, needling her.

259

"All we could do was wait. Everything depended on Helen, on the cast coming off. It would make everything better, back to the way it was.

"When the doctor said it was time, everyone was relieved, but you can imagine, Gordon, how anxious we were. What if Helen didn't return to her old self? My mother sat at the table in the morning, drinking her tea, head down, while Helen got ready to go to the clinic. Helen kept saying 'don't anyone help me.' I can still hear her sarcastic voice, as though we'd all refuse to help if she asked. So unfair."

Trudy sipped her tea, watching me. I watched back. A broken leg. An angry young woman. Work hard enough, and you can connect any story with any other, but I wasn't seeing it yet.

"After they took the cast off, Helen couldn't bend her leg. But she improved as she hobbled all over the place, getting stronger. The anger began to leave her, and we started to relax.

"Then, Gordon, it stopped. She stopped healing."

Trudy smiled at me, but she wasn't inviting me to speak, and it wasn't a cheerful spot in the story. A smile of support, that's what she offered, an interesting moment for it, that point when someone fails to heal. Was this it? Parallel failures?

"They took X-rays and found nothing. Helen just had to be patient.

"A few months later she still had a terrible limp. She pretended not to worry, but she ... oh, it was awful. She stopped seeing her friends, she lost ... she just got lost. It was even worse than before.

"My parents didn't know what to do. They gave up. The resignation that came upon everyone ... my, I can feel it still.

"My sister began to be someone else. She thought of herself as the girl who limped. What an identity, no?"

So, a story about healing and identity. Is this where the story becomes about me? Gordon limping along, year upon year—the man who limps. Would Trudy draw the moral for me? Did she think this would help?

"Gordon? Gordon, please. I do need forgiveness. I blamed Helen for her failure to recover, and I blamed my parents for not pressuring her to do things to make her leg better. Most of all I blamed them because I stopped mattering. Good things could happen to me. I could do well in school. None of that mattered. The only thing that counted was the change in Helen."

Okay. Selfishness. Sure, I've been selfish. Let me count the ways. Why not just say it?

"On a Sunday afternoon, as usual, Auntie Agnes and Uncle Suraj came to visit. My mother looked up to Agnes, because she had the education, and she worked in a government office. I've always thought that she paid for much of our trip to Montreal.

"Uncle Suraj sat, smiled at his wife, and smoked his smelly cigarettes. He'd fold his hands over his pot belly like it was something to be proud of, and he'd scratch his skinny legs. When I was little I didn't like him because he didn't notice me. When I was older I liked him even less because of the way he did notice me. He'd sit on his own, not joining the conversation, and he'd catch my eye, smirk, and scratch his leg.

"That afternoon I said hello to my aunt and uncle, but I withdrew to my room as soon as I could without being rude, though I wanted to be rude, and I wanted them to notice me.

"Later, someone knocked at my door. Who would bother? Auntie Agnes, demanding I come out? My mother, finally worried about me?

"Uncle Suraj. He smiled and stepped toward me. I retreated. He closed the door behind him.

"I could hear Auntie Agnes talking away. I knew that I could cry out if I needed too, but still, I was afraid.

"'Got something for you,' said Uncle Suraj. He had one hand behind his back.

"He showed me what he'd been hiding—a paperback book. He held it out, but I wouldn't take it.

"He put the book on the floor. I'd backed up against the opposite wall. 'For my niece,' he said, and he sneered-smiled, and then he left.

"That year I'd discovered romance novels. I thought he'd probably noticed, and he was passing on one he'd found somewhere. Maybe Auntie Agnes had read it and didn't want it anymore. The cover didn't look promising, and I didn't know how to pronounce the title. I didn't want to read the book and be expected to thank him for it.

"The back cover said it was a classic, one of the greatest novels, which made me curious, but only a bit. I couldn't imagine Uncle Suraj giving me something good, and 'classic' sounded boring. That evening, however, I had an excuse to avoid everyone. 'I need to read a book that Uncle Suraj gave me.'

"*Wuthering Heights*. The long, tortuous sentences frustrated me, and the characters were weird. I especially hated Heathcliff because he was so mean. I gave up. I sat in my room, lonely and sorry for myself."

I was feeling sorry for myself too, and lost, because Trudy's meandering story made no sense. Maybe the tale wasn't so important, to me, that is. Did she just feel that now, with everything coming to a head for me, she needed to move me and my life out of the centre of the picture and take over? A little selfishness for Trudy?

"I sulked. You know that child, Gordon—happy to be unhappy, indulging deliberately, a good sulk.

"Then something happened. I like to think I grew up a bit in those minutes. I grew angry with myself. I saw how childish I was being. It's such a vivid memory for me. I was proud of myself for deciding that this sulk was stupid, and then I decided it was better not to be proud, to accept that something had simply been given to me. I grew determined. I can see my hands in front of me as I clenched my fists, urging myself to overcome my failure."

Okay, a story about failing to heal, about identity, about self-pity, overcoming it and growing up. Feeling pride and then rejecting it—that was familiar to me.

Wait. More than familiar. Trudy. Clenched fists. I could see her, but I could feel myself, the child me, taking the same position ... sometime, at some point in my past. Yes, I've even written of it. You've read it. Clenching fists, vowing to continue writing, little grade-nine Gordon trying to write a story. But ... I'm already on my way. Why do I need to hear this?

"I read into the evening, sitting on my bed, lying on the floor. I didn't understand a lot of it but I didn't care. Heathcliff, Catherine, all of them. Thank you, Miss Emily.

"It wasn't much later, but the house was quiet, and something happened to me, quite rare in Princes Town, Gordon. I grew cold. I got under my blanket, but a terrible chill came from within me. I kept reading, shivering away in the warm night and just enthralled, such darkness, you know. The love and hatred, the intensity, my God.

"Eventually I warmed up. How odd, to feel such cold and then for it to pass, without reason. I threw off the blanket. I realized that I was reading words and sentences—that sounds weird, but you know what I mean. The characters gripped me, but the book was not only made up of characters. I was reading words and phrases, they were something ... so strange, so compelling. I wanted those sentences in me. I wanted to be the words! I whispered them out loud, and I heated up, burning desire. Oh, Gordon, you must have had such reading experiences. I know you have."

Recognition again. I know this. A reading experience? No, a writing experience, my Mavis Gallant imitation. And yes, that first writing attempt, heat and cold, all mixed up here. So many echoes, rhymes, Trudy's story and my past.

"The heat abated, but then ... then something happened to my skin. It felt so dry, and as I noticed the sensation it got worse. My hands, their skin, tissue paper. It could tear with the slightest tug. What was this book doing to me?"

What? Yes, work hard enough, connect any story with any other. Create connections that aren't there. But this? The cold! The heat, dry skin, I was back in my child's room, writing the first story, thinking about Taylor, my robber passing a note to the teller, caught up in a fever of creation. I wasn't making it up. What did Trudy know? What?

"Somehow I fell asleep like that. I just grew so tired as the night advanced, and I fell asleep at the height of a terrifying storm on that hilltop, a storm of wind and anger and words.

"Before dawn I awoke. I got up, and the book fell to the floor. When I bent to retrieve it, I had to reach for the bed to steady myself. The room began to spin. I had a fever. *Wuthering Heights* had brought me to a joy fever."

I don't know now, don't know, as I recall Trudy's words, whether I've got it right. Even at the time, listening to her, I doubted. Was I taking what she said, and changing, rewriting my past, matching her reading story with my writing one? But it seemed true to me, preposterously true, the strange overlaps so fitting. Perhaps I was imagining, expressing my old desire for magic, resisting the prosaic Gordon/Trudy story that had replaced the first one, so badly told but still gripping for me, its romanticism. I wanted our connection to be more than convenience and compatibility.

"I went to the bathroom to get a cloth, to wet it with cold water and put it on my forehead. As I passed Helen's room I heard her snoring. I entered her room.

"I stood over her bed and watched her, and I ached. I sweated. I saw her face in the moonlight, her expression slack as she snored and snuffled. I bent over towards her. 'Helen, Helen,' I said, and she opened her eyes.

"She looked at me. I stepped away from the bed, and the swimming dizziness came upon me again. I put my hand out to stop from falling. I gripped her leg, the one that she'd broken.

"I'll tell you what I said then. I held her ankle, and I asked her, 'Who are you, Helen?' I moved my hand up to her calf and I said it again. I held her ankle with one hand and her thigh with the other. 'Who are you?'

"It felt like a long time, the room still turning, sweat stinging my eyes. I don't know why I placed my hands where I did or why I spoke those words. As I let go of her and stood to leave, Helen took one of my hands, and she said, 'my sister.'

"In the morning, Gordon … you know now what this story is about. You wanted me to tell you. In the morning Helen no longer limped. She returned to her old self.

"I've never really made sense of this story. Not really. Did reading *Wuthering Heights* have anything to do with what I was feeling? Perhaps I just had a fever. What I said to Helen, did it contribute to her healing? I've even thought, Gordon, that I was just talking to myself, that I've always been talking to myself. 'Let it go,' for instance. Certainly, there's much that I'm still struggling to let go of. And 'Who are you?' That's a project I'm still working on.

"It wasn't till years later, quite recently in fact, that I learned that the 'Caribbean' reading of *Wuthering Heights* was news to some people. I'd assumed that Heathcliff was from the Islands. It was so obvious, so strange that others hadn't noticed.

"I'd entirely misjudged poor Uncle Suraj, who supplied me with novels for some years, lots of Caribbean writers, but others too. His ugly smile was just nervousness.

"Gordon? Does it seem to you that I don't know who I am? When you come back, will you help me with my story?"

"I will."

"Swear by your sword, Gordon."

"I swear it."

Enthusiasm in that oath. Many readings of Trudy's healing narrative occurred to me, but surely one of them, the simplest, so perhaps most convincing, was that she wanted to ensure my return.

48

Oh, Jesus. I had indeed left it too long.

We went out for dinner the night of my arrival. Gavin was too happy to see me. Leo would not laugh at a joke, would flatly agree with anything I said and offer no opinion or contribution of his own. Yes, Leo, I now know how it feels. Wag your finger at me. Thanks for showing me.

When, at the meal's end, Gavin got up to use the toilet, Leo watched him walk around the corner, then, silently, he turned a narrow-eyed gaze on me. He was angry on behalf of Gavin, not an untruthful thing to be saying to himself, incomplete but not so much as most narratives about our selves.

"I'd like to tell you something," I said when Gavin had returned. "It's a story you don't know. It's about Taylor and me." Each sentence surprised me as I uttered it. I hadn't planned this move.

"Who's Taylor?" said Gavin.

"Taylor Shepherd."

"The writer?"

"Yes. He used to be a friend of mine."

I made the tale brief: I wrote a review; it was aggressive and dishonest, and I still don't fully understand why I did it. It ended the friendship. It still shames me.

"I knew, a while ago, that I had to try to see him again, and it would be on this trip. I'm afraid, and so I put things off. So, I let you both down. I'm sorry. He's important, and this problem is a very big deal in my life, but he's not as important as you are. I messed up. I've really messed up here. I know it."

"Will he see you?" said Gavin.

"I don't know."

"I'd like to read the review," said Leo. He wasn't going to let me off the hook. He'd inspect my crime and arrive at independent judgment.

"You can find it online."

"I've got an early class tomorrow."

We said our goodnights on the sidewalk outside the Kitchener house while I waited for the taxi. Gavin gave me a big hug. Leo passively accepted one from me.

"I'm staying at that hotel on Robson, The Landmark, the one with the revolving restaurant. I thought it'd be fun. We could have dinner, or just drinks in the lounge, take in the view."

"That's goofy," said Leo.

"Yeah, that's why I did it."

His anger hadn't gone, but at least he'd responded.

I got to my room at The Landmark and logged in to my email.

> Gordon,
>
> I assume you're in town now. I can see you 11:00 tomorrow morning, at the Art Gallery Café.
>
> Yvonne

I woke early, skipped breakfast, and walked around the downtown. Ten minutes to eleven, I got to the café. I scanned the offerings under the glass counter and ordered nothing. The place wasn't yet filling for lunch. Nobody would care if I didn't eat.

I saw Yvonne, coming in from the street entrance, at the same time she saw me. She hurried over, quick walk, good posture still, wearing jeans and a T-shirt. I stood and we shook hands. Civil, we, but clearly a time to refrain from embracing.

"I'm going to get a coffee. Want anything?"

I shook my head. She stepped over to the counter.

She'd put on some weight, not a lot. The beginning of bags under her eyes, nothing shocking in that. Under mine, too. I'd forgotten how short and how pretty she was.

Returned, she put down her coffee, sat opposite.

"I want to see him."

"What for?"

"The obvious reason."

"If it's obvious it should be easy to explain."

"I want to be friends with Taylor again. I want to rebuild our friendship."

"You don't have a friendship to rebuild."

"Fine. I want to build a new friendship."

"He knows you're in town. He knows I'm seeing you right now."

"What'd he say?"

"That's confidential."

"Fine."

"Gordon. This is not so straightforward."

"I didn't expect it to be."

"What do you want from me?"

"What you've already done, in part. You told him I'm here and that I contacted you. I won't be calling him—emailing, whatever, out of the blue. That'll make it easier."

"Don't do it."

"Why?"

She didn't answer.

"Last time, I just accepted it. 'Stop writing him,' you said, that note, you gouged the words into the paper. I stopped, obviously, for years."

"Don't do it." She was looking at her coffee, her hand holding the cup.

"Give me a reason. Something a little more detailed than 'it'll upset him.'"

"You're not having anything. Not even coffee. Did you have breakfast?"

"No. I don't have an appetite."

"That's what happened to him."

"What?"

"He lost his appetite. After the review, he didn't eat."

"He was upset, as you said."

"He didn't eat for seventeen days. I mean, he didn't eat. Not one goddamned bite. I forced him to drink water. Even that was hard. Then he started again, and then he stopped when he got your first letter, and so on. Every letter you sent, another fast, days and days."

"Jesus."

"Yes, Jesus. Don't try to contact him. It was hard, but he's moved on, long ago. Move on."

She rose as she spoke those words, conversation over; no questions or comments to be entertained, she left.

Move on. Call him after all this time, and maybe he'll starve himself to death. Move on.

The restaurant filled, people standing with food-laden trays, frustrated looks my way.

I texted Leo. I could be out at UBC in an hour. Did he have a break any time during the day? I wanted to hear about his courses.

Back at the hotel, I waited for a while to call Trudy, but then I phoned when I knew she'd still be at work. I left a longish message, summarizing what Yvonne had said. I told her I was going out. I went out so that wouldn't be a lie, and I walked around the downtown some more. Leo didn't text back.

No sympathetic eating disorder threatened. I was hungry after not having eaten all day, and I ate at a Thai place on Robson, and then I ascended the forty-two stories to Cloud 9.

Worn carpets, worn staff. Lively view, however—a rare clear Vancouver winter afternoon.

The North Shore mountains, then gradually the city, east all the way to distant Burnaby Mountain, a pale smudge of concrete on the mountain top—SFU.

I should have waited and spoken with Trudy.

A sip of my drink, then our Art Deco City Hall, the West Side eases into the frame. Lush Douglas Park, lusher Shaughnessy, Point Grey, then Burrard Inlet—some racing dinghies hoist spinnakers—and the mountains again.

One hour. No texts. What have I done to my boys?

Stanley Park, city east to SFU ... the winds are light and the race continues, and the sun is setting on the freighters ... greyhound, City Hall, Shaughnessy ...

I picture Yvonne, walking briskly toward me with her coffee, business to take care of, and what's that odd feeling? Gordon? She sits now, speaks, and I look at her hand on her coffee cup. An intention forms; I want to touch her hand? Tremor in my hand?

No texts. I should have stayed in my room and called Trudy. She'd have had something to say about Taylor and his fasts. I wouldn't be wasting time here, circling, mistaking the sensation of curried prawns uncomfortably mixing with Manhattans for a bizarre emergence of feeling, something buried or just overlooked long years ago.

FIRST THING IN THE MORNING, NOT MUCH OF A HANGOVER, I sent another message to Leo:

> I've got all sorts of time. I'd love to hear about the university life. Any openings today or tomorrow?

Then to Gavin:

> Want to do something after school?

And to Jessica:

> The boys are mad at me. I get it. I'm working on it.
> Apologies to you, too.

I took a chance, nothing else to do, and bussed out to the university, crammed in on the Broadway express, hissing along in the rain with a damp passel of ear-budded undergrads staring at their smartphones. If Leo were available, I'd be right there to take advantage.

I stepped off the bus and at that moment got Leo's text, read it with the students scattering past me at the UBC Loop.

> I didn't go in today. I'm home. Come by if you want.

I wanted, of course, and permission, no enthusiasm—good enough. Right back on board for the long ride east across the city, wondering why Leo had blown off a day of classes.

It had stopped being my place long ago. I knocked. Leo shouted, "Come in."

I found him on the couch, where Joseph, elderly, lay curled in his lap and blinked yellow eyes at me without raising his head. Beside Leo, a library copy of *The Stendhal Effect*.

"You've been reading."

"I finished a couple of hours ago."

"What'd you think?"

"It's really good."

"Yes."

"Maybe it's the best novel I've ever read."

"I think so too. Maybe the best."

"What were you thinking?"

I sat beside Leo on the couch. He moved away from me, just a bit, to give me more room.

"I don't know, Leo. I really ... still don't know. People do things, sometimes—we do things we don't understand."

"I was going to read your review, but I didn't."

"Thanks."

"I barely remember him."

"He liked you. He's a great guy."

"Was he tall? That's what I remember."

"He's six-four."

"Why'd you do it?"

"I wanted to hurt him. I must have wanted to hurt him."

"Why?"

"You know, Leo, I've got all sorts of answers that make sense, and yet none of them feel like the truth. I don't know why."

"Were you jealous?"

"That's one of the ones that make sense."

"He's six foot four."

"Sure. That one makes sense too."

"You were really good friends."

"Yes."

"I just don't get it."

"I'm hoping that I'll be able to figure it out by talking to him. He's extremely smart. He might be able to tell me."

"I hope so."

"Thanks."

"I miss Grandma and Grandpa."

"Me too."

"What were you so angry at Grandma for?"

"It was obvious?"

"Yeah. I know you loved her too."

"I was angry at her for leaving me."

"But not now."

I laughed. "Okay. I'm still angry, but not as much. How's that?"

Leo nodded. "Did you feel pressured by her?"

"Probably. That didn't make me angry. I don't think so, anyway."

He lifted Joseph and gently laid him down beside him on the couch. He stood, tall Leo, looking down at his dad. We weren't done. More to come, just not now.

"Gavin will be home in a minute."

"I texted him this morning, but I haven't heard back."

"He doesn't take his phone to school anymore."

"No?"

"It stops him from communicating with people face to face."

He hadn't blown me off. Leo went into the kitchen, so I didn't have to stop myself from grinning.

Gavin arrived and lightened the rest of the afternoon. Leo gave me the UBC scoop: French, Spanish, Arabic all in the mix, maybe a law degree coming up, and then something international, or maybe graduate studies and an academic career. All the details came without affect, till, "I'm taking physics, to get my science requirement out of the way. Gavin's helping me."

"I am not. You don't need any help."

To me: "He does help." To Gavin: "You do. You're better at it than I am and you know it." To me: "I run my stuff by him and he helps me figure out what I don't get."

"You always figure it out yourself."

"You always help me."

There's some genuine discomfort here, Gavin not liking this position, being smarter than Leo at something.

I said, "When I was in first year I took Biology, scored a C and ran with it."

"I've got something for you," said Gavin.

"It's your birthday present," he said when he'd returned from his room, handing me an object wrapped in red tissue paper, book-sized but much lighter.

"I'd forgotten about my birthday."

"Open it," said Leo, official.

It was a slipcase for a book.

"It's, uh, I got the idea from a website. I thought ... if you had a special book, you could put it in there. It's not very practical, but I thought ..."

It was a standard size for a hardcover book. Carefully done. Some sort of heavy cardboard, fashioned into a rigid box. But the paper, the exterior covered with paper, deeply textured ...

"Where'd you find this paper?"

"I made it."

"Made it."

"It's not hard."

"I've never seen something ... Shit, Gavin."

"You like it?"

"It's gorgeous," said Leo. Reverent.

"Happy birthday."

"Gavin, these flecks of colour, what are they?"

"I chopped up flowers, and some leaves."

"Well."

"I thought if you had a special book ..."

"It's really beautiful," said Leo.

"Thanks."

I got up. Gavin started to laugh. "Don't leave the room," he said. I sat.

"When are you going to see Taylor?" said Leo.

"I don't know. I have to contact him and see what he says."

I would do it. I would ignore Yvonne's order. I would risk ... he would want me to. Despite what Yvonne said. He would want it. I knew it right then, talking to Gavin and Leo.

"Get it over with," said Gavin. "Do it right away, and then you'll be able to relax with us. I mean, if you think that'll work."

"I will. You're right. I'm sorry I'm not more relaxed."

We said our goodbyes, and then as I headed down the front steps, along came Jessica.

Tired lawyer coming home from work, doesn't need more demands on her attention.

"I'm just on my way," I said.

"C'mon back in for a bit," she said, maybe not so tired, maybe not yet done work. "Or haven't you got a few minutes?"

49

The boys, still in the living room after my promise to see Taylor and my goodbye, looked up in surprise when I returned with Jessica. Something in her expression gave them the message to scatter upstairs. I followed Jess to the kitchen, where she got a glass of water for each of us. We sat in the nook.

"I hardly know what to say, Gordon."

"I haven't been doing so well. I explained it to them. They're still angry, but I think they understand."

"Sure."

"Y'know, I could have been in town and not been any more present. I haven't been present to anyone at all, not for a bit, anyway."

"For a bit, Gordon?"

"What's your point?"

"Yeah, my point. Let's see." Sip of water. "My point is who the hell are you? Really. I thought, okay, he's moved to Brooklyn. He's lined up a new partner in a matter of days. His parents have died, and we need to try to understand what a blow that is. Such a blow. So, clearly, he's been messed up for some time and still is. But he won't stop being a father. That's who he is. He won't abandon that, surely."

"That's something like what I said to Gavin and Leo."

"Yes. I'm sure you said something like that. Good for you for saying it. It's a fine thing to say."

My turn for water. "Okay. Look, I'm not going to argue with you. I've already apologized. I know that doesn't make it right. An apology doesn't make it right. But I'm also doing something. I'm taking care of things so that it doesn't happen again. If you'll forgive the trite language, I'm learning from my mistake. I've learned from my mistake, your honour."

"How about you demonstrate your sincerity by not being sarcastic."

"That was kind of directed at me, Jessica, not you. Can I do that, a bit of dark humour at my own expense, making fun of my plea for leniency in sentencing?"

"Let's not turn it into a trial, Gordon. That'd be a bit convenient, wouldn't it? I'm not trying to convict you of something. I'm trying to get through. What you're trying to do, is it going to make a difference?"

"I'm not making guarantees. I'm telling you I'm trying. I'm going to see Taylor. I'm going to try to put that behind me, after all this time. Maybe that seems selfish to you, maybe I should be able to just be a father to the boys and forget about old friends and old literary trivia. It's not that easy and uncomplicated.

"Let me suggest a way it's complicated. You say I should be a father to the boys. That's who I am. But what sort of father am I if I have no identity independent of that, of that role? We say, 'Gordon is a father.' Who is this Gordon? If he's nothing but a father then we've got some circularity, wouldn't you say? 'The father is the father.' That's empty. So I'm taking care of something that gives it some content. I'm a friend. I'm a writer. Those things create the 'I' that I'm talking about when I say 'I am a father.' And of course the other way. When I say 'I am a writer,' that 'I' means, most of all, father, as well as friend, failed friend, and failed husband. Without that, I couldn't be a writer. I'd have no identity out of which to write."

"Oh, for Christ's sake."

"Okay, it's a bit ... okay, look, all I'm saying is that I can't be a father and nothing else. That'd make me a bad father. And if the 'else' stuff fucks up, I need to try to fix it. You said the same thing once, with rather a lot of force, if you'll recall. The force of a threat."

"Really."

"Don't say you don't remember."

"I don't remember."

I gulped some water, finished the glass, got up and refilled, and sat down again. "C'mon, Jessica."

"You 'c'mon'. Stop playing games. What? What fucking threat?"

"You waited for me instead of going to work. I took Gavin to daycare and Leo to school, and you waited for me. 'You're a writer. You start writing. You have to.' Your words. Word for word."

"Well, you're right, Gordon. I do remember. Of course. Very clearly, in fact. I remember how worried I was. I was sick with worry for you, my husband, and I couldn't keep silent any longer. I went to the door to leave for work, and I just stopped, because nothing else mattered so much. So now, tell me, please, where is the threat?"

"What?"

"The threat! You said I threatened you! What is this, Gordon?"

"'You have to!' That's what you said!"

"So what was the goddamned threat?"

"Or else! 'You have to, or else I'll leave you!'"

"What? I didn't say that!"

"It's what you meant."

"You're not serious."

"It's what you meant."

"That is not what I meant."

"It is."

"Gordon."

"It is."

"You have to … you have to, or else you'll be so unhappy, or else you'll betray yourself, or else you'll just keep on like this, weakening so badly, punishing yourself more than you deserve to be punished. You have to because I love you so much and you know it."

"That's not what you meant."

"That's your story. It's not the story I'm telling. Your story, Gordon, and if you've been carrying it all this time, retelling it to yourself, well, that does explain some things. I guess I shouldn't be surprised, because you've always done it, haven't you? You make up stories. Some of them you write down, and some of them you just fit us into, don't you?"

"Like what?"

"Like the story of your beautiful, distant wife. I know that one, Gordon. You were telling that one from the beginning, and I let you because it was flattering to be thought of that way, and your story of our miraculous sons, Gavin so sensitive, Leo so mature and gifted. They never needed to be that to be miracles, you know. But I colluded there too. I was happy to be part of that story. You tell it so well that it becomes real and it's exciting to enter into it.

"No! Don't say anything. Yes, I know you'd say that *is* reality. I can hear you. I could create an entire Gordon Bridge speech if I had to—reality *is* narrative, narrative *creates* reality, blah blah blah. Blah blah fucking blah. I'm not impressed, okay? Take some responsibility. You're the author. They're *your* stories. Quit blaming other people when they don't turn out the way you want. Quit using them as excuses when you don't behave as you should. Be a better goddamned father."

"I will."

"Tell a better story."

"I'll try."

50

Let us compare mythologies, mine and Jessica's. I'm not sure I'm more of a storyteller than anybody else. I'm also not sure that being a novelist gives me more responsibility. We can't ever really see the stories we're telling, and that's as true for novelists as it is for anybody else. If we think we can see that stuff, all we've done is create a new story.

I know, that's exactly the kind of Gordon Bridge talk that Jessica said she could reproduce if she tried. I don't doubt her. But Jessica is as beautiful as I've said, Gavin as sensitive, Leo as bright. I'm sticking to my story. The threat? Let me ponder.

I BROKE MY PROMISE TO LEO AND GAVIN. RIGHT AWAY would have been … right away: that night, maybe the next morning at the latest. But I needed time, and I needed a way forward. What could I say to Taylor that would compel him, draw him along?

I spent a couple of afternoon hours revolving in the Cloud Nine lounge, with Gavin's slip case, beyond words beautiful, there on the table for my adoration.

Rainy downtown; herbal tea; creamy, jewelled slipcase; rainy Point Grey; other side of the slip case; trace the colours with my index finger; more tea; no more boozy cloud-forest nostalgia; 360 sober degrees of grey, rain, Vancouver.

The precipitating incident, the answer to the question of how to begin: I learned of it after descending to my room, when I turned on the CBC for the news. I followed up with online reports, the first obituaries.

I'm holding books in my hands, I'm reading stories, I'm discovering worlds ... of sentences, places. But she's gone.

His email address was on his author website. I intended my hands steady, wrote:

> Dear Taylor,
> I just now learned that Mavis Gallant has died.
> Please, see me. Name a time and place.
> Gordon

What then? He might not check email for hours, might not respond for days, or at all. What to do with my time? Email Leo and Gavin to let them know I've made the move? No, terrible idea, pathetic, to announce an inch of progress as if I deserved admiration for it. Same for telling Trudy. So ... what?

The right choice emerged, a relief. I'd like it if you could feel good for me here—I know that at this point in the narrative I'm not winning warm support. How to fill the time? What story do I tell now? Open it, Gordon.

Open the document.

I continued. You have the proof in your hands. I picked up right where I'd stopped many unproductive months ago. You remember— back when I left Vancouver, not long after Mum died. I launched the new section, following my theft from the end of *Gatsby*.

I wrote,

"Gordon."

"Noreen."

"It's wonderful."

"I'm so glad you think so."

And on. I pushed ahead, determined, not inspired, a way not to compose responses to Jessica in my head, a way not to fret about Taylor while awaiting his answer. Also, a way not to brood on Mavis Gallant dying poor in Paris. (What? Poverty? Mavis Gallant? Why didn't I know? I could have signed a cheque. I could have helped. I could have … really, I could have justified my life.)

The first chapter of the new section, this section, I got all of it done that afternoon-evening, uninterrupted, right up to Noreen again: "You're going to have to track him down. I'm sorry, Gordon, but you just have to. You have to see him. Then you write about it. Then you're finished."

CONFIDENT—THAT IS, NERVOUS BUT CONFIDENT, AS though science fiction-wise this chunk of past telling will generate the energy to charge some present result—I check my email, first time since I've begun. And, *voilà*: Taylor.

All right. Tomorrow. The Art Gallery again. 11:00.

Delay could have been good for memoir tension building, but I was happy to let that go. An evening and early morning wait was long enough. What to do till then?

Write on, the recollection of my conversation with Leo and his stuffed animals, Dilly and Miss George, no idea what place it takes in the memoir, then the journey back to Brooklyn and the panicked, juvenile, nightmare fantasy—"Trudy had not returned from Trinidad"—and then, recognize the obvious connection between the two episodes, flip the order and edit. Another chapter done. I'm a distance away still, but I'm coming up to it, not falling comically behind, but seriously catching up one more time to the present. To Taylor.

51

■ ■

Jittery, some kind of pressure on my eyeballs, I headed out, then I stopped at the elevator, returned, wrapped up Gavin's slipcase and put it in my backpack, and then off once more.

I arrived at the café in plenty of time, but Taylor had already commanded a seat at the back, facing out, tall, surveying, still, not haughty but a gaze that managed to be direct and withdrawn at the same time … withholding.

"Hi."

"Hi."

"Thanks for seeing me."

Nod.

He had a salad on a plate in front of him, close to finished. I looked at it, back at him, he nodded again, and he emphasized the point, eating a forkful, spinach and mushroom.

"I'm sorry, Taylor."

"Yes."

"I read a bio of Mordecai Richler a few years back. On his deathbed he got a note from Brian Moore. He wept. They'd been tight friends, intimates, and then they weren't. Something happened. Richler wept because they'd blown it. He'd blown it. Decades of friendship lost."

"I read it. What do you want from me?"

"Did you know that Mavis Gallant was poor? I learned about it yesterday."

"I didn't know. I'm not here to grieve for Mavis Gallant with you."

"Mind if I get a coffee?"

"Go ahead."

I had no plan. I got my decaf and returned to the table. Taylor had finished his salad.

Sorrow, regret, confusion, pain, confusion, guilt, guilt, heaps of it, and guilt's old partner—anger: take a sip of coffee.

"I just … let me show you."

I unwrapped it. "Gavin gave the slipcase to me, yesterday, for my birthday."

Taylor looked at it, dull eyes.

"He made the paper himself."

He put his hands to his head, face downward, then looked up at me. "Gordon," he said, frustrated. Okay. The object, sacred or not, would do nothing. Talk, then. Launch. I wrapped the parcel up and restored it to its place in the pack.

"I want to understand something. This could sound like an accusation, but it isn't one. I did a terrible thing. I apologized, many times. Why wasn't that enough, not to make things right, but to communicate, at least? Why wasn't it enough so we could try? I did a terrible thing. Lots have done worse and then made efforts. Yvonne told me. She told me—"

"I couldn't eat."

"Taylor …"

He held up one hand and glanced at the ceiling. At me. Then, gaze resting on his empty plate, hands on either side holding it by the rim, as though to steady it: "Not being able to eat embarrassed me. It felt theatrical. Histrionic. And it really worried Yvonne."

"No kidding."

He lifted a hand and waved it a bit before grabbing the plate again—spare him the understanding interruptions. He lifted the same hand once more, rubbed his forehead, yet again gripped the plate.

"It took me a bit to understand. I didn't have an upset stomach. When I tried to eat, the sensation simply …

"It's easier if I take this from a different angle. I read the review. It startled me. It took some time to realize what startled me. I didn't know you."

He shifted the plate, spun it slowly, a quarter turn, a dab of spinach near the rim moving from noon to three.

"You were not who I'd thought. You were my closest friend, obviously, by far, and you were not who I'd thought, and our friendship, in that case …

"Yvonne has a friend, a woman—you don't know her. Her husband came out. He left her for a man.

"She fell apart. Her husband wasn't the person she'd thought. Their marriage wasn't what she thought. Still, why fall apart?

"There's not much of a deduction left. Just another small step. You know how this goes, Gordon. Who are we? What happens when the relations in which we're enmeshed … when the relations that shape us and make us get overturned? What happens, in other words, when we discover that *we* are not who we are?

"Gordon Bridge. It turns out that Gordon Bridge is the writer of a dishonest, subtly vicious review. That's who he is. Not who I thought! No! Nothing like that! Our friendship … obviously, obviously it's not what I thought. It's not even … it's not friendship, is it? Is it?

"No. And so, and so, *I* am not who I thought. Which leaves me a little problem. A problem. Who the hell am I?

"I thought I was Gordon Bridge's friend. That's who I believed I was. The fundamental me. You were so much the stronger of us, the leader, even when I'd been the first to publish, God, how I'd relied on you.

"I'd take a bite of food, and the sensation—to call it disturbing would be a sickening understatement. I tried to talk myself out of it. I was overreacting. I tried. But I wasn't to be persuaded. I felt … occupied. Okay? I was one of the taken. Really. That's the best way to describe it. Tasting, chewing, swallowing, all of it … God. I was so alienated from my self. The sensations of eating … You have no idea. It felt as though they belonged to someone else. So, I couldn't eat. Rather fundamental, you know? Then it began to ease, and then, well, I'd get another of your letters. You timed them so exquisitely.

"I don't know what you want, Gordon. What do you want? A Gordon-Taylor reunion tour? It's not going to happen."

He shifted the plate, spinach on to nine. "Go ahead," he said.

I'd been ready, in a way. I'd expected him to be extreme. I had some things to say, not quite clear yet. Now I didn't want to say them, to apologize pointlessly again, much less to explain, less still to argue. I also didn't want to stop there. So, here we go:

"What did my father say to you?"

"What?"

I was thinking the same thing—What?

Taylor was turning the plate again, and I reached out and stopped it, pretty aggressive under the circumstances, and he looked at me.

"He's dead and I'm trying to get some things sorted out. You know what I'm talking about. What did he say?"

52

■ ■

Perhaps what's best now is another digression. Maybe try to charm things up with a resumption of the tale of my tortured puberty, left off, you might recall, in my bedroom, where I sang the joyous coming of the Lord and coaxed my voice to crack. It would force you to wait and ramp the tension a bit before you hear again from Taylor. No. Not up for charm any more, not sure now if I ever achieved it, trading however heavily on my sons, certainly not up for ramping.

I released my grip on the empty salad plate. Taylor fidgeted the spinach time on to ten. He clasped his hands in front of him and exhaled.

What did I ask that question for? What did it have to do with anything? But I wanted to know. Singing in my bedroom, celebrating the arrival of my excruciatingly postponed change, I'd been longing for knowledge of that discussion down below, exactly, word for word. But I never asked. Nothing volunteered, ever. Privacy respected and preserved. No longer.

"All right," said Taylor.

"Okay."

"You want to know that."

I waited.

"He told me it was very common. He reassured me. He said I should practice putting on a condom a few times by myself. I'd catch on, I'd be relaxed, and there'd be no more problems."

"Yes."

"He could tell I was worried. I didn't have to say about what. He told me there was no chance she would say anything. I was fifteen years old, and I feared that when I went back to school that Monday, everyone would know, my humiliation a lurid farce for lunchtime cafeteria entertainment. He guaranteed that she wouldn't tell anyone, not even her best friend. That's what he promised."

"You talked down there for more than an hour."

Taylor took a big breath and looked around the room, filled now with the early lunch crowd.

"I don't remember every word."

I reached across and shifted his plate counter-clockwise. "We haven't spoken in years. Maybe we won't speak again."

"He said that sex makes people vulnerable. We should take care of that. She was too young to take care of me, or I of her.

"It's all mixed up now, what he said. What I made of it. He said that things go wrong, and when they do, you have to be able to laugh about it. He didn't just mean sex. He said I should be prepared for big things between people to go off track, and that I shouldn't blame people, or myself."

"Off track."

"Later, not then, but a while later, I thought he was talking about his marriage."

"That would have been a big thing."

"You asked me … I told you I don't remember, but this is what I made of it."

"Taylor. Everything I did before I wrote the review, everything after, it was just as much me. Wasn't it? Is that who I am, one moment, one error, a failure, that big thing?"

"A carefully written review is rather a willed undertaking, wouldn't you say? More so than a lost erection, or a compromised marriage, for that matter."

"Maybe."

"Maybe."

"Sure, it's more willed. Of course. Or probably. Or maybe not. I thought at first that I'd been trying to show off our friendship. Maybe that's true. I thought I was trying to hurt you, I don't know why. I thought for a while that I was doing it to please my mum. What if it's just something that starts one way and then goes off track, doesn't even have anything to do with what it seems like it should?"

"It doesn't matter now."

"Do you know why?"

"It doesn't matter. Let it go."

Taylor took his napkin from his lap, crunched it up in his hands and dropped it on his plate. Our grand meeting, over so soon. He looked at me, waiting for me to leave. I didn't move.

I didn't move, and Taylor waited. I had nothing to say or ask, the conversation so deflating, but I needed to stay. He'd signalled the talk done; he could be the one to go, if he wanted.

He didn't get up. He shrugged impatience. He reached for his water glass but didn't take it.

Then, in a series of painful stages he rose. He placed his palms on the table to take some of his weight in his shoulders, leaned forward to shift his centre of gravity, grimaced fiercely, unfolded, pushing down agony, and rose. From behind him on the bench seat he fumbled out a wooden cane. He shuffled. One hand on the cane, the other on the table, he eased out, he hobbled; pain in his knees, hips, feet, he lurched to the exit.

53

I stayed in the café after Taylor's crippled leaving.
First, the boys:

> I saw him. Let's get together.

Then, what? I took some time, deep breaths. Just say it, Gordon.

Yvonne and Taylor:

> I just watched Taylor leave the café. Taylor, I'm sure, I know, I can make you well. I can. Call me at The Landmark. I'll explain.

Trudy:

> I need you here. Phone when you're done work.

What next? Back to the hotel—walk out of the restaurant, jog, run along Robson Street. Why the hurry? My room, my laptop, Cloud 9, and into it yet again: I was writing to deadline, racing to overtake the present, as though doing so would change it, that sci-fi business again.

Trudy called: "I'll post a notice saying I have a family emergency."

Yvonne called: "What the hell is this, Gordon?"

Several emails, then the phone again with Taylor, with Yvonne. My diagnosis grudgingly confirmed: the sedentary writing life wrought worse than Taylor's clumsy active youth, far worse: muscles pulled, not to heal, joints swelling and rebelling, back a catastrophe, and nothing worked. No treatment. By contrast, my neck ordeal a trifle.

What could they do but doubt? I re-emerge after years, clearly agenda-armed, and, nothing to go on beyond the sight of Taylor battling his affliction, I claim a special power, Trudy, she will do it. Not quite plausible.

I wrote another email and returned to the memoir while awaiting reply. Another refusal, again a plea, back to the memoir ... rejection, attempt once more, write some more. On.

The Taylor-Yvonne responses grew curt, diminishing toward silence, when, of course:

> Taylor, Yvonne,
> Just to be clear. I should have been more clear on this.
> There is no *quid pro quo*. I ask for nothing. I know we're done and over. Trudy is coming. She arrives tomorrow, and in one hour she will make a change, if you let her. I swear I'll ask for nothing.
> Gordon

Yvonne replied. Would I be present? I would not. Could she be there? Not in the room, but right by. Okay then. The next afternoon.

I called Gavin and Leo to let them know what was up, then, then ... opened the document and wrote.

"GORDON, I'VE NEVER SEEN YOU LIKE THIS. YOU'RE GOING TO make yourself sick."

"I don't know what to do."

"Stop pacing. I'll get dressed and we'll go out."

"Go out?"

"We have three hours, Gordon. Yes. Out."

We walked to Stanley Park, where Trudy checked the Aquarium hours while I looked at my watch and fretted. "We don't have time," I said.

"I'm not wanting to go in now. Perhaps afterward. I think it would be good for you to watch some fish."

"Trudy."

"All right; let's go back."

In the hotel room, I futzed, I got ready to leave, I asked Trudy, "should I wait till they get here, and then go, or should I go now?"

"You should stay and introduce us, and then leave."

"I should. All right."

They arrived on time, knocked. I'd been expecting them to call from the lobby, or something, but that made no sense. Trudy introduced herself, all business, I wasn't needed: "I'm on my way out."

"Don't come back till after I'm done," said Taylor.

"I won't."

I spoke no more. Yvonne too was silent, and clearly not wanting to leave with me, so I exited with my laptop.

54

"How'd it go?"

"He feels much better. He's going to see me every morning for a week. He's got severe problems."

"You look tired."

"It's just jet lag."

"A case like that, it doesn't take anything out of you?"

"No."

"You can't tell me what you said to him, can you?"

"I'd love to go to the Aquarium."

"No marine mammals."

"Just fish."

THEY SET THE ONE-HOUR APPOINTMENTS FOR TEN EACH morning, which suited me. I left fifteen minutes before and returned half an hour after, leaving no chance of an unwanted encounter. In between, at a café on Robson, I wrote, still focused, not urgent, but undistracted by thoughts of what was happening back at the hotel—strange, the concentration coming on like that.

On each return Trudy said something vague without my having to ask: "It went well," "He'll be fine," "He's getting much better." I appreciated not having to inquire and knew not to seek details.

Trudy headed into the city after the appointments, leaving me to write. Evenings we did the town. We saw Gavin and Leo. Toward the end we all had an early dinner, and then they carried on, to a play, and again I wrote, all week.

WAITING FOR ME, THE THREE OF THEM, WHEN I ARRIVED.

I sat my laptop on the dresser, opened the closet to hang up my coat, thinking about these movements—would I later write something, specify some simple, vivid detail in the gestures or objects in a way that would help place you, the careful reader, here with us in the hotel room?

I'd just completed the scene in which Yvonne told me the story of Taylor's terrifying response to my review. Coming up—me and Taylor. I could see a series of short installments following that episode. I'd write them alone in the hotel room or up at Cloud 9, with *Pegnitz* in Gavin's slipcase, to touch and revere when I wanted.

Those brief sections would take me along … up to here, now. I was standing in the room but also in the end of the memoir.

A few coat hangers hung in the closet, the hotel-room standard, only a knob on the end to fit into the hook, fixed to the chrome rod. Worthless to thieves. It took me two tries to slip the hanger holding my coat into place.

And now everybody's ready.

Yvonne got us started. "We just wanted to say goodbye. That's all."

Another of those times when Bridge is not called upon to speak.

"That's all," she said again, needing to convince someone. She looked at Taylor, and I thought, maybe she hoped.

Taylor was fully dressed, sitting on the massage table, and he vaulted off and strode toward me, free and lanky, extending a big hand. "Thanks."

I shook his hand.

"I don't know," he said. "I'm not sure I understand anymore."

"Taylor," said Yvonne. He looked at her. Was she trying to convince him to relent, or not to?

"Me neither," I said—in my throat, ready to burst, a violation of my promise not to ask for anything, a plea, for something—it droppeth from heaven, I've heard.

"If my father were alive," I said, with no idea how to continue. A plea to the Taylor I'd been writing of, all right, but this man? Was he worth it? Walking easy, taking Yvonne's hand, and strolling, strolling now out of the hotel room. Yvonne glanced back once, then turned, looked up, way up to Taylor and said something I didn't quite hear.

"What?" I said. "Yvonne, what did you say?"

"Nothing." She didn't turn this time. Out the door, the door closing. But she had said something. It probably wasn't important. A mystery bringing us to an end. The end of them. Days of awe.

The lake, the lake dies, or not, not, the water flows elsewhere, it does, I'm lost, I'm not, and so I turn elsewhere, there she is. I turn to Trudy.

I will never total it all. I've given up looking for the one big reason I panned Taylor's novel. Such explanations seldom exist. We can convince ourselves that there's a single source for the Nile, but the hope for one, pure origin was always wishful thinking, displaced Victorian hankering for one God. Everyone knew the truth, one way or another: the old simplification had abandoned them. I knew it, but I didn't allow myself to see.

You know, Taylor, you did change, but I think of our problem differently. I messed up, but that was nothing new. Your change went deeper. You did stop being Taylor. That Taylor, the one I knew, there was something he could do.

He could hold on to the idea of our complexity. He could always see how compromised and troubled we are and yet still how worthy. You, on the other hand, you want to reduce us, no more than betrayed and betrayer, two such thin creations we can slip past each other without really noticing. You're not him.

Oh, I know that I'm not now exactly the same person I was then. I'm not the same person I was when I began this memoir. I may catch a glimpse of gold lamé across a restaurant and find my cheeks are flushing hot. I might write a novel that reveals a longing for an idealized past and find that what's called to my mind is a lonely child's collection of faux-heraldic pennants. But I've changed. An ellipse has shifted eccentricity, if you like.

You too, reader, you've changed. One more time I give you the gift of direct address, reward for having come all this way on such a wandering journey. Let's forget about those who just looked ahead to the final pages, or the careless, who, unwilling to take any trip in which the ending isn't clear from the beginning, abandoned ship, dove into the dirty harbour and swam through the floating garbage back to shore. You've changed. That's not arrogant; it's simple truth. Wherefore read a book while knowing that when you finish it you'll be the same person who began? Wherefore?

Heraclitus says—oh, Heraclitus deserves the present tense if anyone does—he says that you can't step in the same river twice. So for all experience. Rivers alter course; people flow and change. Lakes shift; people, too, abrade. Selves fall into selves and alter. The careful nets we set come loose, and they trap at random, ghostly they sink, weighted by the arbitrary dead, settle on the ocean floor with our own selves wrapped and drowned. The unforgiving and the unforgiven, the victim and the victimizer, all changed, changed utterly. Let it go. Gordon. Let it go.

Revise carefully to ensure that I flatter no one. Open the email to Noreen. Attach this document. Short, weighted moment.

Send.

ABOUT THE AUTHOR

Paul Headrick's first novel, *That Tune Clutches My Heart*, was a finalist for the Ethel Wilson Prize—the BC Book Prize for Fiction. *The Doctrine of Affections*, a short story collection unified by the theme of music, was a finalist for an Alberta Book Award. Stories from that book appeared in *The Malahat Review*, *The Antigonish Review*, *Event*, and *The Journey Prize Anthology*.

Paul's literary studies took him to Montreal, Toronto, and London, England before he resettled in his home town of Vancouver. He taught English literature and creative writing at Langara College, as well as giving short story workshops at writers' festivals from Denman Island, BC, to San Miguel de Allende, Mexico. Paul currently teaches a graduate workshop on novel and memoir writing with Simon Fraser University's Writers' Studio.